THIEF
TAKERS

This is a Carlton Book

First published in Great Britain 1996
by Carlton Books,
20 St Anne's Court,
London W1V 3AW.

10 9 8 7 6 5 4 3 2 1

ISBN 0 7475 2521 8

Thief Takers is a Carlton UK Television production for ITV.

Also available from Carlton Books:

THIEF TAKERS
The Official Inside Story of the Blockbuster ITV Series
Illustrated in full colour with unique behind the scenes photographs

THIEF
TAKERS

Lee O'Keefe

CARLTON

ACKNOWLEDGMENTS

With special thanks to my agent,
Robert Kirby, and Lorraine Dickey
of Carlton Books.
Thanks also for information received, encouragement,
and general handholding to:
Mark Stedman of the Docklands Development
Corporation, Martin Weaver, Jay Knox-Crichton, Alex
Stewart, Molly Brown, Julia Quine, Sharon Springel,
Dave Fletcher, Averley James, Rob Silk, Andy Lane, Tina
Anghelatos, Ben Jeapes, Chris Amies, Gus Smith, Varney
Richard, Barbara Morris and everyone from
The Road Trip.

PART ONE

NO ONE LIKES
TO SEE THAT

CHAPTER 1

Dennis Worsley sauntered towards the mesh of the rear wall of the exercise yard. He was counting. He'd been counting ever since the screws let them out – it was the only way he could keep track of the time.

No-one bothered him. Not the screws and not the other inmates. His minders took care of that.

Being inside wasn't so bad. Not once you got a few things sorted – like, who was in charge, for instance, and where enough of life's little luxuries were coming from to make life bearable.

But it was still prison, and Dennis had unfinished business on the outside. He grinned, not pleasantly. Any minute now, the screws would call time. He slowed his pace. Mustn't seem anxious. Mustn't seem like he was expecting something. But he didn't want to get too close to the back wall, either.

He stopped to pick an imaginary bit of gravel out of the sole of his shoe. Out of the corner of his eye, he saw Carter move to intercept Big Mac, who was heading in his direction. The little Scotsman had a determined look on his face. The scar that traced down his right cheek from temple to jaw writhed as he argued with Carter. He probably thought someone had stiffed him on a deal for phone cards or fags, and wanted Dennis to sort it out. But Dennis had made it plain to Carter that he wasn't listening today.

Come on, he thought, come on. Somewhere in the back of his brain he was still counting down, and he knew he was running out of time.

In the corner of the yard, a small knot of screws had formed and was beginning to break apart. That meant time was nearly up. He'd have to start in if they called – that or find a way to buy more time. Just then, he heard the faint purr of an engine on the road outside. It stopped. He smiled. "Three," he muttered.

A car door slammed open. His smile widened. "Two. One," he finished.

There was a burst of light from beyond the wall, followed half a heartbeat later by a dull thump as the brickwork exploded inwards. Dennis got his arms up in front of his face just as bits of steel mesh and brick tore past him. Greasy smoke billowed across the exercise yard.

He wasted a second looking up. Then, as the sirens began to whoop, he pelted across the yard towards the hole.

Dennis shoved someone out of his way. Then someone else.

Carter said, "Boss?"

"Piss off," Dennis snarled. He barged past his former minder, picked Big Mac up bodily and dumped him to one side, then launched himself through the hole. A wave of heat hit him from the still burning car that had held the bomb.

Dennis wasn't the first out, but that was fine. He wouldn't be the last, and the more of the dregs that got out the better he liked it – let the screws waste their time with them.

Left of the prison – that had been the arrangement. God help Langley if he wasn't there, because sure as heaven he'd think the devil was after him when Dennis had finished with him.

Dennis's feet pounded on the pavement. Behind him, he could hear the screws trying to round the others up. They'd got the dogs out already. That was fine.

Still – better to be safe. He pushed himself a bit harder. He'd kept in shape while he was in the nick. Letting yourself get flabby was a mug's game – and anyway, he'd always known he'd get out a damn sight sooner than would give Her Majesty any pleasure.

The Merc purred up alongside him. He glanced back. The screws were onto it, but they were nowhere. One of them let a dog loose, and the beast came bounding towards him. Langley had the door open. He slid inside just as the dog leapt. One of the screws threw himself forward, but Dennis slammed the door in the scumbag's face.

Langley floored the accelerator. Dennis turned and looked out the rear window. A couple of screws were watching him, but the rest of them were still trying to grab hold of the other prisoners.

He turned back and slumped into the leather seat. He was barely breathing hard, though his pulse was thumping.

He smiled.

***

Mabel Gardner fished around in the sink and finally hooked a fork out of the soapy water. Behind her, her son-in-law Michael read his Daily Mirror while he gulped his tea. He hadn't spoken to her yet, but he was in a hurry. Then again, he probably wouldn't have spoken to her even if he weren't. Out of the corner of her eye she saw her three-year-old grandson, Darren, slap his spoon up and down in his cereal. But his heart wasn't in it. The poor lamb was running a temperature, and in Mabel's best opinion he was probably coming down with a cold.

She'd tried to tell Michael, but he'd touched Darren's forehead with the back of his hand and said he reckoned the lad was all right.

As if Mabel hadn't brought up three of her own... and her daughter Rosie wasn't much use. She just sided with Michael.

She sighed. I'm only trying to help, she thought. She picked up the tea towel and started to dry last night's dinner plates. She knew what the problem was. They were scared that Darren would turn to her, what with Rosie out all day. They'd rather pay out for a nursery place than let her take care of him.

It near broke her heart. But she didn't say anything. Of course she didn't.

Rosie came in, holding a stack of letters. She was frowning. One of them would be from the bank manager, Mabel thought, and there might be one from the credit card people. Money was something else she wasn't allowed to help them with, oh no.

She turned. Darren smiled up at her, a little blond angel with milk all round his mouth. It was all Mabel could do to stop herself from wiping his face. Look at his poor pale face, she thought. Next Michael will be saying it's just a tummy bug.

"Do you want coffee, Michael?" she asked, to distract herself.

"Haven't got time," he said. He thumped his mug down on the table and the tea slopped out of it. "You sure you're all right?" he

5

asked Darren. The boy nodded. "Well, hurry up then – "

Rosie put the envelopes down on the sideboard. "I don't know," she said to Michael. "He still looks a bit pale to me – " Michael looked at her as if to say, don't you start. Rosie sighed. She brushed her hair out of her eyes. "All right – but I'll take him to nursery. You just go."

Michael smiled. He was happy now, all right – now no-one was saying his son was less than perfect. He was always the same, whether it was the idea of his son being ill, or being a bit late walking or cutting his teeth: his Darren had to be the best, the first, the quickest.

Still, Mabel thought as she watched him give Darren a quick kiss on the forehead as he headed for the door, you couldn't blame him for that. There'd have been something wrong with him if he hadn't been proud of the boy.

Rosie wiped a smudge of milk from Darren's mouth. "Upsy daisy baby," she said, picking Darren up. He started to grizzle. "Maybe you're right, Mum," she said over his head.

"Why don't you leave him here," Mabel said. Rosie looked doubtful. "Michael need never know," she added. She hoped it didn't sound like wheedling, though the truth was she'd been a bit lonely since Darren had started going to nursery.

Rosie bit her lip. She touched Darren's forehead with her hand. "All right," she said reluctantly. "But just this once – and only because he's running a temperature."

Mabel smiled. She held out her arms and Rosie gave Darren to her. He snuggled into her chest.

"I'm off then," Rosie said. She gave Darren's hand a quick squeeze. "Be a good boy for Granny," she said.

Mabel, still carrying Darren, followed her into the hallway. Together, they watched as she got into her car and drive away. She stopped once to turn and wave to them. Darren waved back. He'd only just learnt to wave properly. But when he realised Rosie had really gone, he started to cry again.

"Mummy gone to work, darling," Mabel said. "Mummy be back soon." She took Darren into the kitchen, but no sooner had she settled him to finish his cereal than there was a knock at the front door.

She hurried out, smoothing her skirt and hoping that Darren hadn't got spit on her blouse. She could see a man silhouetted through the frosted glass of the door.

"Who is it?" she called, although she was already fumbling with the catch.

"Post, love," said the man.

Odd, Mabel thought. The postman had already been. Must be a parcel, then. But neither Michael nor Rosie had said they were expecting anything. Must have slipped their minds.

She opened the door a crack. She saw part of a man's body – a hand holding a parcel. She started to open the door, but before she could, the man shoved it open forcing her back. He was wearing a mask with holes cut out for his eyes and mouth.

And he was pointing a gun at her.

Mabel stumbled backwards. Her heart hammered in her chest, and her mouth had gone dry. The man followed her into the hall. He jabbed the gun at her. Two other men followed him – one in a full-face motorcycle helmet, the other masked and carrying a sawn-off shotgun.

The one in the helmet slammed the front door, while the first man forced her back towards the kitchen.

"Please don't – " Mabel said. Her hand went up to the left side of her chest. She forced herself to take a long, calming breath. Not going to have a heart attack, she told herself firmly. I. Am. Not.

But the man was shouting something. "Do as you're told and you'll be all right –" His eyes widened. He was staring over her shoulder at something. "Shit!" he said. Mabel turned. Darren was standing in the doorway, staring at them. Without thinking, she turned and scooped him up. "Put him down," the gunman said.

Mabel glared at him for a second. She wondered if they really would kill her. What would that get them? Nothing. But her heart was still thundering. She let Darren slide to the floor. He backed off a couple of paces, then stood staring at the men.

One of them grabbed the Daily Mirror off the table. He shoved it in Mabel's hands and snarled, "Hold it up in front of you." The other man raised the gun to her head. She fumbled with the paper, sure now that he was going to shoot her. "Front page out," he said. The barrel of the gun was a small cold circle against her temple. She did as he asked.

The other masked man tore open the package he had been holding, and pulled out a Polaroid camera. He pointed at her. "Smile, darlin" he said.

"What?" Mabel whispered. She realised that Darren was crying, had been crying for some time.

The flash went off as the man took the photo. There was a long, painful silence while they waited for the picture to develop. Mabel wondered what they would say if she asked them why they were doing this, and what in the world she had ever done to them. But she didn't dare.

The picture slid out of the camera. The first gunman looked at it.

"That'll do," he said. He grinned. "Come on Gran," he said. He grabbed Mabel's arm. Without thinking what she was doing, she shook him off. "Got no interest in hurting you, grandma," he said. "Unless you make me."

"Darren," Mabel whispered. They couldn't expect her to leave him here alone.

"Stick him in a cupboard or something," the man with the camera said. "He'll be all right."

"He'll be terrified," Mabel said, and wondered where she'd got the nerve. "Look at him – what's he ever done to you?"

The first gunman made a disgusted hissing sound. "All right – bring him along too – but you keep him quiet, or you'll both be sorry. Got me?"

Mabel nodded. She picked Darren up. The gunman pushed her towards the door. The quiet one – the one wearing the crash helmet – opened the door a fraction and peered into the street. He gestured to the first gunman, and a few seconds later they were in the street. The one with the handgun pushed her towards a nondescript green van. Someone will see, she thought. They'll phone the police. Someone – if she hadn't been holding Darren, she thought she might have cried out for help. But even as she thought it she knew she would never have dared.

They made her get in the van. It smelled of oil, and there was

8

only a tool chest to sit on. Darren huddled in her lap. A wire mesh screen separated the back of the van from the front. The first gunman got in the back with her. He slammed the rear doors shut, so that they were in the half-light that filtered through from the windscreen at the front.

The van drew away from the kerb. Mabel put a hand out to steady herself.

"Sorry about this," the man said. He produced a bandage and some gaffer tape. "Put the boy down and lean forward."

Numbly, Mabel did so. Darren slid off her lap but stood clinging to her skirt.

Mabel stared at the man. She licked her lips, then leaned forward. First he blindfolded her. The bandage bit into the bridge of her nose, and staring into the darkness terrified her. She felt his hands on her face, forcing her mouth open. She jerked her head away.

"Don't come it, grandma," he said, without a trace of good humour.

Mabel said, "Please – I won't make trouble. At least let me look after Darren." He didn't answer. She wondered what the expression was on his face. "He'll cry – I don't want you to get angry with him."

"All right," the man said. "All right – but any lip and it's the gag. And I'll tie you up, too, if you make me."

Mabel nodded. She stroked Darren's hair as if by reflex, and stared into the darkness.

***

A little later Michael Chater threaded the LMR Security van through the heavy traffic. His colleague, Ian McCallum sat beside him, while in the sealed-off section behind them, Robert Killigrew worked at transferring money bags from the safe welded to the subframe of the van, and into the cassettes in which they would deliver it.

"What did you think of the game last night?" McCallum asked. He nursed his helmet on his lap. He never felt really happy with it off, but regs said it was okay while they were in the cab – in fact, you weren't allowed to drive with one on – and it was just too damn hot today to wear it if he didn't have to.

Michael grunted a reply, but kept his attention on the traffic. The lights ahead turned red. Michael braked. Just then a motorbike cut them up. It slowed to a halt at Michael's side of the van. The rider was anonymous in black leathers and a full-face black helmet.

He tapped on the window. Michael looked round. The rider slapped a piece of paper against the side window. Michael's eyes went wide as he looked at it.

His mother-in-law stared out at him from a photograph. She was holding up the morning paper, and was clearly in fear of her life. And no wonder. A man's hand held a pistol to her head. The photo had been taped to a piece of paper. At the bottom, someone had scrawled in heavy black felt-tip: Follow the bike – no alarm or she's dead.

"Dear God in heaven," Michael whispered.

"Christ," McCallum said. "What are we going to do?"

"I don't have any choice, do I?" Michael asked.

The lights changed. The bike revved and then pulled away. Michael followed. The rider glanced back once, and then the bike picked up speed.

CHAPTER TWO

It was typical, Detective Inspector Charlie Scott thought. You get a plot about to go live and Bingo Tate was the one person you could rely on not to be where he should. He stared across the mess on his desk at Detective Constable Ted Donachie, who stared right back – just like Ted, Charlie thought. Never gave a bloody inch, especially not where a mate was concerned.

"Well?" Charlie Scott asked at last. He shrugged into his shoulder holster, ready for the weapon he would check out later on.

Donachie champed on a wad of gum. "I called round but he wasn't in." He found something interesting to look at in the untidy pile of papers on Charlie's desk. He was a big, raw-boned Scot, with a face like a prize fighter's and fists to match. "Then again, he never is –"

" – still seeing her?" Charlie demanded, not bothering to keep the irritation out of his voice. She was Cathy Worsley, gangster's wife and one time snout. Bingo had been sleeping with her while she fed him information about a gang she'd been involved with – she'd been screwing Slater, the gang boss, at the same time. When Slater found out she'd grassed him up, he almost killed her. All that while her husband, Dennis – as nasty a piece of work as you could hope not to meet on a dark night – was banged up, doing life for murder, plus so many bits of assorted GBH, larceny and general mayhem that Charlie had lost count. Except he wasn't banged up any more. Well, Bingo had been warned about his habits before. Maybe now he'd listen.

But Donachie was still staring at Charlie as if saying anything would be betraying the idiot. "Look," Charlie said, finally losing his temper. "Dennis is out of gaol and it's not to file a tax return." Still the passive stare and nothing else. "A clue'll do!"

Donachie pushed one of the forms on Charlie's desk with his

finger. "He said she's renting a boat, now. City Dock."

Bingo's sheer stupidity was beyond Charlie. He shook his head and pulled out his bleeper. He spoke to Donachie as he headed towards the duty room. "Ring local uniform and have armed response officers get round there now."

He didn't wait for Donachie's reply. At least there were some people he could rely on.

***

Bingo Tate wasn't asleep. Not really. He was just thinking about the night before – about the way the moonlight had silvered Cathy's back as she slipped out of her blouse. Beneath him, the boat rocked in the gentle current of the river. A little grin spread across his face as he remembered what she'd said – 'Look, even the boat wants some' – as he'd moved his hand down the gentle curve of her belly and then

– his bleeper sounded from where he'd left it in his trouser pocket, breaking his train of thought.

He sighed. Ought to get that, he thought. Sod it, though. He wasn't that late. Besides, he could hear Cathy moving around downstairs in the kitchen. Below, in the galley, he corrected himself.

The beeping stopped. That was better.

A couple of seconds later, Cathy came up the steps from the galley, carrying a tray of coffee and toast. The silk dressing gown she was wearing moved against her body, making her seem less clothed than if she'd been nude. Bingo watched her appreciatively. Last night suddenly seemed a long time ago.

"Are you going to be mother?" he asked.

"Don't be disgusting," Cathy answered, all mock horror.

Bingo levered himself up on one arm. "I'll just have the coffee, then," he said.

Cathy put the tray on the deck next to him. Then she sat down on the futon, and curled up next to him. He traced the line of her neck with the side of his thumb. The collar of her dressing gown slipped aside, revealing the creamy arc of her shoulder. She reached forward and started to pour coffee.

"You fell asleep," she said.

Well, it was hardly surprising after all she'd put him through,

12

Bingo thought. "I didn't fall asleep – I collapsed unconscious in a state of exhaustion," he said.

Cathy laughed. She raised her face to the sun. Her eyes closed and she arched her back, stretching in the heat like a cat. She had claws, too, Bingo thought, remembering the way she'd run her nails down his back, just hard enough to be painful – though they'd been far enough along then that it had only added to his pleasure.

"I like the sun on my back," she said lazily.

"You like everything on your back," Bingo answered, and thought, except when I'm on mine.

She laughed again, and this time rewarded him with the lightest of kisses. He reached for her. And his bleeper went off.

Damn, he thought. He broke away from Cathy and reached for his trousers.

"That's what I like about you," she said. "You're so romantic."

Bingo ignored her. He fumbled in his pocket for the pager. If they were bleeping him twice in ten minutes, something had to be up. Cathy laid her hand on his arm. He glanced at the beeper. The message was from the office.

"Oh shit –" he said. He leaped up and started to pull his trousers on.

"What is it?" Cathy asked.

"Nothing," he said. There were limits to their relationship – such as telling her anything at all about his work. Screwing a villain's old lady was bad enough, to say nothing of the ructions it would cause at work if it came to anyone's official notice. Letting something slip and finding it had spread through half of London's underworld would be the end of his career. For starters.

He looked around for his shirt. It was nowhere in sight. Must be below, somewhere, he guessed. Hardly surprising the way they'd been going at it. "Have you got a tee-shirt I could borrow?" he asked.

"Sure," Cathy said. She got up and sashayed across the deck, making sure he got a good look at what he was going to miss out on while she did it.

She came back a few minutes later. "Have fun," she whispered in his ear as he put on the shirt she'd given him.

He kissed her briefly then made his way carefully across the narrow gangplank that was all that connected the boat to the shore. He turned when he got to the other side. "I'll be back," he called to her.

She blew him a kiss. He stared at her for a second, then left at a run.

***

Detective Sergeant Helen Ash sipped bad machine coffee from a plastic cup as she waited with the other detectives for the briefing they all knew was coming. She looked around her, counting heads. There must have been fifteen other people in the room. Alan Oxford, a particular friend of hers in the unit, caught her eye. He was a big West Indian bloke, bald headed – Helen had never quite got round to asking him if he shaved it – with a close-clipped beard and moustache. He was fond of showing off his body-builder's muscles with sleeveless tee-shirts like the black one he was wearing today, and equally fond of heavy gold jewellery. He glanced round the room in an exaggerated way, then grinned at her.

She guessed he was thinking the same as she was – no Bingo Tate. They'd all worked together on a number of cases, and she'd never seen anyone come closer to screwing up and then pulling it all together at the last minute. Well, this time Bingo had better behave.

Her immediate boss, Detective Inspector Charlie Scott, walked in talking to his superior, Chief Inspector Uttley. Scott was clearly furious about something, and Bingo was the most likely suspect. Come to that, Uttley didn't look terribly pleased, either.

Well, sod Bingo. Helen just hoped the Guv'nors weren't going to take it out on the rest of them.

Ted Donachie walked in after them. He looked worried, but that was nothing new. Between the state of his stomach, which was always giving him gyp, and the state of his marriage, which seemed about on a par with his stomach, he was always fretting about something.

14

Charlie took up a position at the front of the room. He wasn't a particularly big man, and his mop of curly hair and the slight upward curve of his mouth always reminded Ash of a naughty schoolboy. But that was balanced by the frown he usually wore, and despite everything, he had a commanding presence.

Scott leaned against one of the desks and said, "Listen in." As he started to speak, Donachie crossed in front of him and went to a phone on the far side of the room. He hooked it towards him by the cord, picked up the receiver and began to punch in a number. Scott ignored him and continued to speak. "According to the National Criminal Intelligence Service, the raid on the LMR Security van is definitely going off this morning, although we don't know what time or which van. The whole fleet are fitted with Followplot tracking devices..."

There were a few raised eyebrows. More people who couldn't stay awake in briefing sessions, Helen thought. Not that she hadn't been guilty of occasionally drifting off, especially when she and David had yet another row about what time she got in. Like last night, when – whoops, she thought. Not that she needed to listen, particularly – as Scott's second in command on this job, she'd already been briefed. Scott was still speaking.

"...on pre-mapped routes and schedules. Soon as a van deviates from its route or fails to make a drop within the set time-frame, we jump."

Behind him, Donachie scratched his cheek with the end of his biro. Helen saw him raise his eyebrows as if listening to someone on the other end, but before he could say anything, one of the other phones rang out.

Oxford picked it up. He grinned and held the receiver up towards Charlie, but so everyone had a good view of it. "Bingo," he said, his Jamaican accent almost imperceptible under his south London drawl, "stuck in traffic." His deadpan delivery was rewarded with scattered laughter. Everyone in the room knew that Bingo only had a bad time with the traffic when he was seeing one of his women – which, Helen had to admit, was most of the time.

Donachie muttered something down the receiver and jammed his finger down on the button of the phone.

Charlie crossed the room and almost yanked the receiver out of Oxford's hand. He looked well pissed off. He listened intently to Bingo for a moment. His expression got, if anything, darker. "Your only excuse is if you stopped it with your head." The laughter was louder now. "Don't bother," he said. "Do yourself a favour – buy a morning paper. Any one will do – they're all full of a friend of yours." This time he got cheers and whistles. He put the phone down, just a little harder than was necessary.

As he turned back to the unit, he caught Helen's eye. He shook his head, clearly disgusted. Helen wondered if she ought to have a word with Bingo – maybe warn him he'd better watch it. But sod it – he'd only say she was sticking her nose in where it wasn't wanted. To Bingo, there only seemed to be two kinds of women – girls you pulled and then left when you'd had enough, and ball-breakers. Helen had no illusions about where she stood with him.

Charlie raised an eyebrow at her. She pulled the duty sheet from the folder she was carrying, and read from it, "Officers carrying are five six five, five seven six, five eight two –" she looked around, and the officers concerned nodded to her. Good. No-one wanted an armed officer on the street if they weren't one hundred percent on the ball. She reeled off the rest of the numbers.

When she got to the last one, Grace Harris's head jerked up.

"Sorry – did you say me?" she asked quickly.

"Five eight four?"

Helen stared at her. Harris was new to the squad, and Helen didn't really feel she'd got to know her yet. Harris was younger than she was, with an athlete's build and long dark hair kept tucked back under a band. Her pale skin was quite startling against that darkness, and with her wide cheekbones and wide mouth, she was attractive in an unusual way. Helen knew the lads had been talking about her ever since she arrived – but then, they talked about all the women.

Detective Chief Inspector Uttley cut in before Helen could answer. "Is that a problem?" he asked. He was a big man with a big voice, and when he spoke you paid attention whether you wanted to or not.

"No sir," Harris said. She smiled slightly. "No."

Charlie took over again. "Radios set to channel seven," he said. He turned to Donachie. "You sorted out the cars?" Donachie nodded. You might complain that he pushed the limits of the Police and Criminal Evidence Bill to make a case now and again, Helen thought; but you had to admit he got the job done. "Drivers – see Ted," Charlie finished.

Helen drained her coffee cup and tossed it at the waste bin. She missed. The cup clunked to one side, and a few drops of liquid spattered across the floor around it. She sighed and picked it up on her way out the door.

"Better not do that if it comes to it, eh?" Harris said to her as she dropped it in the bin.

"Do what?" Helen asked.

"Miss," Harris explained as they followed the rest of the squad out of the office.

Helen shoved a hand through her hair. "I won't," she said, and remembered how surprised Harris had been to be told she would be carrying. "Doubt you will either," she added by way of encouragement. Harris didn't look convinced. "Then again, I doubt it'll come to it," Helen said.

Harris smiled. "We should be so lucky," she said.

***

Something was wrong. The van lurched under Robert Killigrew as it made a sharp right turn. He reached out and grabbed the top of the safe for support. They were supposed to go straight on for a good ten minutes. Longer in this traffic, surely. Then a left, into the High Street before they made their first drop of the morning. Taking a right here would take them out into the industrial estate – or what these days was left of it.

Jesus.

He banged on the partition dividing the back of the van from the cab. Come on, Mike, he thought at Chater. Let me know what's going on.

Nothing.

He banged again. One of you bastards do something, he thought. But Ian McCallum wasn't saying anything either.

The van hung another sharp right. A few moments later it slowed down. A voice outside shouted something, but Killigrew couldn't make out what it said. There was a rumble – a mechanical sound he couldn't place. The van kept moving but very slowly. More clattering, and a loud thump.

Killigrew knew what it was then. Garage doors rolling down and slamming shut behind the van.

Christ.

He realised he was hyperventilating. He made a conscious effort to slow his breathing. Got to calm down, you pillock, he told himself. They didn't let you be a security guard because you were prone to fainting fits.

Someone outside was shouting again. Killigrew heard the cab door bang open.

This is it, he thought. This is the one you don't come back from. He licked his lips. Sorry Jen, he thought; I guess I should have married you while I had the chance...

The escape hatch in the back of the van slid open. Two men in ski masks stood there. They beckoned at him with the guns they were holding. He slid out of the van without waiting to be told.

He found he was facing a gun. The black ring of the barrel seemed impossibly large, the largest thing in the universe as he stared at it. He swallowed.

Going to get through this, he thought. Just do what I'm told. World needs dead cowards more than it does live heroes.

The man holding the gun was wearing a ski mask and white paper coveralls. All Killigrew could see of his face were his eyes, blue staring eyes ringed by white flesh. Another man, also wearing a ski mask and paper coveralls, stood further back. He had a sawn-off shotgun.

Ian McCallum was standing between him and the van. He had his hands spread out in front of him. Killigrew saw that they were trembling. Meanwhile, Mike Chater was still in the van.

"Okay," the gunman said. "Now you." He gestured with the shotgun, making his meaning plain – he wanted Chater out of the van. There was a movement behind him. Killigrew noticed for the first time that there was another man. He was dressed in motorbike leathers and a full-face helmet. The bike – a Suzuki – stood nearby; the man was holding an industrial sized angle-grinder. He noticed Killigrew watching him, and switched it on. The motor screamed. He turned it off and grinned nastily at Killigrew. Behind him, there was a white van. And next to that there was a fork-lift truck.

"I have to radio the depot," Chater said. Killigrew stared at him. The depot would already know they were late and off course – the Followplot transmitter would have told them that. What are you playing at, Mike? He thought. Don't try to be a hero, or none of us are walking away from this -

"Just do it," the gunman said. South London accent, Killigrew noted, have to try and remember that for the cops. And they're all white. He wondered, suddenly, if that was racism, coming from a black man; and was appalled that he could even be thinking such a thing at a time like this.

"Just do it!" The gunman said. He jerked the barrel of the shotgun in Mike's direction.

But Mike still hesitated.

The gunman brought the stock of the shotgun round in a sweeping arc and slammed it into the side of Ian's head. He gasped and fell to his knees, hands groping desperately in front of him. Blood glittered darkly in the harsh light. The gunman hit him again. This time, Killigrew heard bone crack. Ian slumped to the floor.

"NO!" Mike screamed. He was scrambling from the cab even as the words left his throat.

The gunman smiled beneath his mask. He bent down and rolled Ian over on to his back with as much gentleness as he'd have shown a sack of potatoes. He yanked the key chain up from Ian's belt and held it taut. The man with the angle-grinder came forward. He switched his machine on, and once again the motor hummed. He dropped to one knee, braced himself and applied the blade to the chain. It only took a couple of moments for the chain to break.

"Nine minutes," the leader said.

The man with the grinder stood up. He stepped across Ian's body without even looking at it – at the mess of blood and

19

matted hair that made Killigrew's stomach churn – and slid his visor down. He touched the blade of the grinder to the side of the van. The metal squealed and golden sparks flew through the air.

Killigrew looked from the van, to Mike. He was staring at the robbers like a rabbit caught in the headlights of an approaching car.

"At least let me see to him –" Mike said. "I didn't mean –" He was blaming himself, Killigrew realised. Maybe if he'd moved a bit faster – but that wasn't true. They're just murdering bastards, and that's all they are, he told himself firmly.

"Shut it," the leader said.

Mike slumped back against the cab door. Killigrew glanced at Ian. He scarcely seemed to be breathing.

***

Grace Harris stared at the gun that lay on the desk in front of her. It was holstered, and all she could see of it was the textured black surface of the stock. She imagined it in her hand, the darkness of it against her pale skin, the weight of it as she brought it up in front of her and found her target. The jolt as she fired – not much of a kick, but enough to let her know its power; and the flat crack of the shot ringing out – where? Some high street full of onlookers, scared and admiring at the same time. Hardly likely. A back alley, then, with assailants running from shadow to shadow as they tried to escape – but they wouldn't, not from her. As long as she hit, of course. In training, she always hit. But –

"It hardly ever comes to it," a voice said from behind her.

"What?" she snapped as she turned.

Oxford was standing behind her. He smiled slightly. Light flashed on his sunglasses which were hanging from the front of his tee-shirt. "Opening fire," he said, raising his voice above the background hum of conversation in the room. Beyond him, the room was full of officers, some trying to look busy, others not even bothering; only Helen and Charlie had any real work to do, monitoring the radio for word from the security company.

Oh for pity's sake, Harris thought. It was so typical – give a woman a gun and all the men thought she couldn't handle it.

Well, to hell with them. They'd find out soon enough that whatever the other women officers were like, Grace Harris could handle herself. And any shit the villains cared to dish out. "I'm not worried about that," she said.

Oxford looked taken aback – but not enough to stop him having another go. More fool him. "But if it does –"

"I'm worried I might miss," Harris said, thinking and you can take that and stuff it where it hurts.

This time, Oxford looked affronted. Before he could say anything, the radio hissed into life. "Charlie Mike One from Bullion Control – we have a late arrival."

Harris saw Helen pick up the mike, but by that time she'd grabbed her gun and was hammering towards the door, just like every other officer in the room.

DI Charlie just beat her to the door, but let her past as he turned to call to Helen. "Tell them we also want crew ID's and home addresses," he shouted.

Harris grinned as she headed towards the stairs. This was it. This was for real.

***

The squad raced downstairs and into the vehicle park. For a few seconds there was organised chaos as the officers found their assigned vehicles and drivers. But only for a few seconds. Charlie leaped into the passenger seat next to Donachie. A moment later, Helen Ash got in the back and they were away. It had taken two minutes, tops, for the entire unit to get underway, fully armed and with armoured vests under their jackets.

Charlie turned to Ash and grinned. Nothing pleased him more than seeing his unit working well. Ash started to brief him. Being Ash, she'd got all the information they needed, and she had it right to hand. That pleased Charlie, too.

***

Michael Chater stared into the darkness. The thieves had put tape over his eyes and mouth, then jerked his arms behind his back and cuffed his wrists around one of the iron pillars that supported the warehouse roof.

He supposed they'd done the same to Robert, and even Ian

21

– though he'd been unconscious as far as Chater could tell.

I'm sorry, mate, he thought. Over and over again, he heard the terrible sound of the shotgun stock cracking into Ian's head.

Now all he could do was listen to the sound of the grinder chewing through the sides of the van. The smell of burning metal made him feel sick. His shoulders ached. He shifted slightly, but all that did was make the cuffs bite into his wrists.

The sound of the grinder stopped. "Come on," someone shouted. "Come on!"

A motor engine started up. A diesel engine, by the sound and smell of it. The fork-lift, Chater decided. There was a series of thumps and bangs. The engine died. The darkness grew a little lighter, as if the warehouse had suddenly been flooded with light. Then a decisive click – the van door shutting, maybe? Sure enough, another engine, a petrol one this time, revved up.

It moved off into the distance, the sound growing quieter as it went.

We're all alive, Chater thought. At least there's that.

***

They were too late. Charlie went in with the first members of his squad. He took the scene in with a single glance – the empty expanse of the warehouse; the blindfolded, gagged men, handcuffed to the support pillars – two were moaning and struggling, but the third was leaning back quietly against his pillar; the fork-lift truck standing next to the wrecked shell of the security van. But not one piece of portable equipment or clothing. He'd bet his job on forensics saying the fork-lift was clean.

Uttley came up beside him. He thrust his hands into the pockets of his overcoat and stared around with a pissed off expression.

"Nice," Charlie said. "Very nice." By which he meant it was very far from nice, but a fast, professional job.

Donachie came over. "They've taken the safe," he said.

Uttley made an impatient face. "Well, they didn't come for the tyres, did they?"

As Uttley spoke, Charlie motioned to Harris to go and sort the nearest security man out. An irritated expression flashed across her face and was gone almost before Charlie registered it. He knew what it was: she hated doing anything that looked like a traditional female role. Still, she ambled toward the man. Before she got there, Helen brushed past her, knelt down by the man and quickly yanked the tape off his eyes.

Charlie's attention was suddenly attracted to what was going on around the quiet security man. He was slumped forward, and one of the officers was checking his pulse. The man's head turned, and Charlie saw blood.

"Get an ambulance," he said.

Helen tore the tape from the security man's mouth. "They've got my wife's mother" he said. He was wide-eyed and shaking, and his colour was very bad. Shock, most like, Charlie thought.

"Take it easy," he said. "It'll be all right..." He only hoped it would. He'd just caught sight of the mess of blood and matted hair on the side of the third security man's head, and it left him without any doubt: this lot were not only professional, they were totally ruthless.

***

It had gone down just as sweet as could be, the gang-leader thought. The white van was exactly right – completely nondescript. And now in the back of it there was a safe with enough money to set all of them up for life.

Still, there was one more thing to do. He pulled out his mobile phone, and punched a number with one hand while he controlled the van with the other. "Doug," he said. "Let 'em go." Not that he was going soft, but dealing with bodies would only slow them down.

He flipped the phone shut. Behind him, the other two men laughed and joked. But their voices were drowned out by the whoop of police sirens. Two cop cars rushed towards him, lights blazing. They raced past, heading for the warehouse.

"Too late," he shouted. "Too bleeding late, mate." He peeled his mask off, threw back his head and laughed.

Oh yes, Dennis Worsley thought. Life was very sweet indeed – when you were a free man.

CHAPTER THREE

Alan Oxford knelt beside Robert Killigrew, one of the security guards, trying to cut him free of the handcuffs the thieves had secured him with.

"Soon have you out of this, mate," he said. "Just see if you can stretch your arms out –" Killigrew did so, and Alan managed to get one arm of the bolt cutter between the pillar and the cuffs. As he did so, he noticed that Killigrew's skin – easily as dark as Alan's own – was ashen. He was having difficulty in keeping from trembling, too.

Shock, Alan thought. He looked around for a blanket. He caught Ash's eye, and she came over. She was a tall woman, as pale as Oxford was dark. To most people, she put up a tough front. Oxford admired her for that, but he was proud to be one of the few people she let her defences down with.

"Got a problem?" Her Belfast accent had been softened by years of living in London.

"Get us a rug, will you?" Oxford asked. He jerked his thumb at Killigrew.

"No problem," Ash said. She hurried off through the chaos of the warehouse, where the Scene of Crimes Officers were dusting the van for prints, and DC Donachie was getting the details of the fork-lift truck. Near the door, the paramedics had already made Killigrew's injured colleague comfortable. The man lay on a stretcher with a drip attached to his arm.

Alan waited till Ash came back with the blanket. Then he put his weight on the bolt cutters, and the chain of the handcuffs split with a sharp crack. Killigrew fell forward into the arms of a paramedic, who wrapped the blanket round his shoulders.

Alan picked up the bolt-cutters and stood up. He glanced around, trying to decide if there was anything else he should do.

24

Harris was on the phone. DI Scott and DCI Uttley were talking to a man in a sharp suit who looked in a right old state.

He'll be from the security company, then, Oxford thought.

"Christ," someone yelled. "Oh dear Christ." Alan turned, and realised these cries came from Michael Chater, the security guard whose son and mother-in-law had been taken hostage by the thieves. Harris was talking to him now. She patted him awkwardly on the arm, but he was crying – hard, gulping sobs that made his whole body shake. "Darren," he said. "Darren."

Alan turned away, finding he was embarrassed to watch the man's outburst. He didn't fancy being in Harris's shoes just then – but then, by the look on her face, neither did Harris.

Scott brushed past him, and he heard Harris tell Chater, "Mother-in-law and son just been picked up okay – dumped on the hard shoulder of the M25."

Just then, Bingo Tate wandered in. He was wearing a red shirt, and he was carrying a rolled-up Daily Express. He looked pretty pissed off. He'd heard about Worsley, then, Alan decided.

Bingo wandered over to him. "We catch them, then?"

Alan stared at him. "What's this 'we' white man?" he said, and grinned. Bingo grinned back and rolled his eyes in Scott's direction. They both knew Bingo had some pretty fast talking to do.

Before he could say anything else, Scott called him over. Alan grinned. Bingo scowled and went to explain himself. Lacking anything better to do, Alan drifted in the same direction. He pretended to be checking out a pile of pallets for clues while he listened.

"Traffic?" Scott asked. He wasn't exactly keeping his voice down. Bingo made a sour face. He glanced at Uttley and Ash, who stood nearby. "Everybody else got here on time," Scott went on.

Bingo looked at the van. "Obviously not," he said.

Go on, my son, Alan thought. Get yourself even deeper in the smelly stuff. He grinned. Not knowing when to stop was just part of Bingo's charm.

But Scott ignored it. "Driver's mother-in-law was a hostage.

Son as well, apparently." He paused. "Get round there. Interview the family. Take Grace."

Working with the ice maiden, that'll please Mr Drinks-With-Villains Tate, Alan thought.

Sure enough, Bingo didn't bother to hide his sarcasm. "Thanks," he said, as if Scott had instructed him to buy flowers for his own funeral.

"You're lucky I don't kick you there," Scott said.
He walked away.

Tate looked at his retreating back. Then he must have caught sight of DCI Uttley, who had listened in on the whole exchange. He unrolled his paper to display the front page. Uh-oh, Alan thought. Here we go – deeper in and deeper.

"Can we talk about this?" Tate asked, suddenly all sweetness and light.

Uttley stared at him. "Not on an empty stomach," he said. He pulled at his luxuriant moustache. "Nice shirt," he said. He grinned. Then he followed Scott.

Tate looked down at his shirt. He was obviously confused. For the moment it seemed as if he had forgotten it was one of Cathy's. He glanced at Ash, who gave him her best wry smile. Helen wasn't one for taking any shit – she was like Alan in that respect, which was one reason why they'd become such close friends.

"What?" Tate demanded.

"Nice blouse," Ash said, and followed Uttley. Tate looked dumbstruck. Alan grinned.

"No one likes a smart-arse," Tate called after her belatedly.

"Then everyone must love you," she said, without even bothering to look back.

Alan grinned at Bingo behind her back. He stared back, bewildered.

***

The thermic lance roared. Its tip was white hot, and where it touched the metal of the safe glowed cherry red. Dennis Worsley grinned as he leaned back on a pile of wooden pallets to watch. Brian Hazlitt might not have too much up top, but he was a genius with his hands. The protective clothing and helmet he wore was bulky, and he couldn't have found it easy to work in, but he handled the lance like a pro.

Dennis took in a deep breath. The air, filled with the smell of hot metal and oil, was like nectar to him. Better than it was in prison, anyway, where every breath you took stank like it had been breathed in and out by a couple of thousand other blokes. As for the rest of it – well, he was free now. He was going to stay that way, too.

He'd chosen his partners well – Hazlitt for his skills and Langley for his brains. The other two men were just meat, but they did what they were told and he didn't need anything else from them.

Langley seemed to have done a sound enough job; he'd found this place, for starters. It was an abandoned storage yard – by the look of the tea chests littering the place, it had once been used for antiques – protected from the outside by a pair of wooden gates. Dennis hadn't heard a car go by outside since they arrived, and that suited him just fine.

The tip of the lance slid forward. Hazlitt pulled the lance back and up, and the glowing tip traced a line of light in the morning air. He quenched it in the coolant trough that sat nearby. The oil bubbled and hissed.

Right, Dennis thought. He picked up a bucket of water and threw it over the safe. Steam rose in a cloud all around it. He folded his arms and waited. No point exerting yourself when there were other people around to do it for you. Langley grabbed the asbestos gloves. After a second he pulled open the safe door. It swung back easily enough.

Inside, the safe was stacked with security boxes. Langley extracted one, and set it down on the pallets in front of Dennis. The front of the thing had slumped in the heat. Dennis pulled out the keys he'd taken from the security guard, anyway. Couldn't hurt to try. He matched the number on the box to one of the keys; it slid in easily enough, but it wouldn't turn.

Well, nothing worth doing ever came easy. "You'll have to cut into this one," he said to Hazlitt.

Hazlitt pulled off his helmet. He went his tool holdall and pulled out an electric drill. He paused to select a fine drill bit, then went over and knelt in front of the security box. He inserted the bit into the lock. Dennis saw him hold his breath as he started the drill on its lowest speed. Get on with it, he thought; but he knew that the box might well be tamper-proof.

"All right," Langley said over the squeal of the drill. "Everyone here for the cut at ten." The heavies, standing at the back of the yard, nodded in unison. Langley turned to Dennis. "Plane'll be in first thing. There's an airfield in Hertfordshire we can use." Dennis nodded. "Should be okay to have you out last thing tomorrow night."

Sounded good – a day would be plenty of time to sort out an uppity copper. "Yeah," he said. "Well, I'll take my money now, if you don't mind." He paused. Langley stared at him like he wanted to say something. Bastard. "I've got a couple of things need sorting before I go."

"Dennis," Langley said, "You can't go out."

Watch me, Dennis thought. "You looking for a slap?" he demanded.

He advanced on Langley, but somehow his feet tangled with Hazlitt's legs. The other man jerked forward. The drill howled as it slammed too far into the lock.

Suddenly, orange smoke filled the air. Dennis tried to get his hands up in front of his face, but he couldn't breathe. His throat and eyes burned. He coughed, and tasted acid. Someone was shouting, and there was a series of loud clicks and bangs. He wiped tears from his eyes, but that only made the stinging worse.

Eventually the smoke dispersed. Dennis looked down at his hands. They were covered in orange dye. So were Hazlitt and Langley, and so, he supposed, was his own face.

Indelible fucking dye. That was all he needed.

"Thanks," he snarled.

***

Cathy Worsley sat in the lounge area of her boat. She was considering something very important – holidays. She stubbed out one cigarette and lit another, before flipping open yet another brochure. Florida? Maybe. Not very exclusive though. Antigua, maybe, then. That would do – white sand, warm sea and hot hot sun...

The kettle started to boil. She got up and headed towards the kitchen, but as she did so she heard a noise outside. She altered course and headed for the door, cursing Bingo as she went – she'd told him always to ring before he turned up. If it got out she was still seeing a copper -

She opened the door, ready to tell him what she thought of him.

But the man who was standing there was an orange skinned apparition in an electric blue suit.

"Remember me?" Dennis said, holding up his left hand to show off his wedding ring. "Till death us do part?"

Cathy's scream was cut off when Dennis grabbed her face and squeezed it hard.

CHAPTER 4

Charlie Scott scowled across his desk at Michael Chater. A cup of coffee, grown cold while he tried to get something he could use out of the man, sat by his in-tray. He looked at the statement sheet. It was empty, and Chater still wasn't even close to giving them anything they could use.

The man ran his hands through his hair. His thin face was pale with anger, and he'd only stopped shaking with difficulty. "I'm going to kill them," he said. He looked up and held Scott's eyes for a second. "I'm going to find out who they are, and I'm going to kill them."

It was an understandable reaction – just not very useful. "Mr Chater –" Scott said. He was still trying to be patient, though he was fast approaching the moment when he'd have to get tough.

But Chater was staring at him. "Do you have children?" he demanded.

The words cut into Scott like a knife. Yes, he thought: I have a son – a dead son, in a tiny grave. "No," he said, levelly.

"Then you don't understand," Chater said. Yes, I do, Scott thought, because I felt that way when Jack lay dying of leukaemia and there was nothing I could do for him. The only difference is, I lived with it for weeks, and you've only known it for a few hours. "They took my son," Chater shouted, leaning across the desk. Scott stared at him and he collapsed back into his seat. "He's only three years old –" he said.

Same age Jack would have been, Scott thought. He wondered what Chater would do if he told him – whether it would create enough of a bond to calm him down. Then he realised what he was thinking, and hated himself, just a little bit, for it. But that was okay. He was used to hating himself for what had happened to Jack, even though he knew – because he'd been through it a thousand times with his wife, with his friends, and

30

even, once, with a counsellor – that it wasn't his fault.

He took a deep breath. "Your son and mother-in-law are okay." Chater already knew it, but hearing it again might help him. Besides, Scott wanted to get the subject away from children. "Your wife's with them and they're being looked after by –"

Chater stood up. "I want to go home," he said, moving round the table.

Scott got up and moved to block him. He put out a hand to guide the security man back to his seat. "I realise how much you want to see them," he said, trying to sound as soothing as possible. "But I do need to get a statement from you." Chater glared at him. He made no move to sit back down again. Scott tried again. "When we've done that, I'll whip you straight home, I promise –"

"They put a gun to her head," Chater said. At least he'd stood still. "Can you believe that? They stuck a gun to an old lady's head."

"Yes," Scott said, guiding Chater back to the chair. "Yes, I can."

He thought, but didn't say, that the most surprising thing was really that the boy and old woman had been set free – when he'd seen the mess they'd made of McCallum, he'd been sure the hostages were goners.

Well, live and learn.

***

The way they were being treated, you'd think they were the criminals, not the victims, Robert Killigrew thought. He'd been brought into the room, asked – though they might as well have told him – to sit in a corner, given a cup of dish watery machine tea and then left alone to think about what had happened. It seemed to him he'd sat there for hours, nursing the tea and taking quick little puffs on his cigarette. But maybe it hadn't been that long.

He stared round at the squad room. Officers came and went, carrying important looking clipboards and files of information, or marked things off on charts, or stood talking in little knots around their desks.

There was only one black person in the room beside himself,

and that was the officer who had finally arrived to take his statement. Funny that, he thought bitterly. He tapped cigarette ash onto the vinyl, and watched the man – Oxford, he'd said his name was – read what he had told him.

Oxford looked up. He pointed to part of Robert's statement. "What kind of ski-mask?" he asked. "Full face? Just the eyes?"

Robert thought. The problem was, everything kept running together in his mind. Someone had told Mike to get out of the van, but had that been the one with the handgun or the one with the shotgun? He found he was shivering. The only thing he could be certain of was the crack of the shotgun stock against Ian's head. It had been so quick, yet it seemed to go on forever. And the way the bastard had grinned when he did it the second time. "Whole face," he said.

"Colour?"

Robert sucked at his cigarette. It did nothing to soothe him. "One mask was red," he said. The other one had been blue. He remembered sliding out of the van – staring at the barrel of the gun. It had taken all his attention. But he must have seen. He had seen, because he knew he'd looked at Mike and Ian. But the memory of it suddenly slid, so that the one threatening them with the shotgun was wearing the red mask, and the other the blue. No, that wasn't right. He was sure the one holding the gun on him had been in the red. "The one who did all the talking – his was blue." Oxford stared at him. "Navy blue, I think," he added, though in truth he wasn't sure. Anything to get them off his back.

"The guy who hit McCallum?" Oxford asked.

There it was again – that slow arc of the shotgun butt, and Ian's soft grunt as he went to his knees. The thief's look of glee as he hit him again, and that crack of bone...

"Take your time," Oxford said. Behind him, Mike walked into the office with two of the higher-ranking police officers. They spoke briefly, while all Robert could do was think about Ian going to his knees... he took a long drag on his cigarette. Mike turned and left. Robert wished he could do the same.

"My missus hates me doing this job," he said. His missus – his Jenny. He remembered how he'd thought of her when he realised they'd been hijacked – how he'd tried to say goodbye to her in his mind. Well, he'd make sure she really was his missus before very much longer.

Oxford smiled at him. "So does mine," he said. Robert tried to smile back, but the effort of it was too much for him, and he started shaking again. But there was no relief. "The guy who hit McCallum with the shotgun?"

It was too much. Suddenly he was back in the warehouse, staring at the black ring of the gun barrel. There had been the coppery taste of fear in his mouth... Ian going down to his knees... the gut-churning certainty that he would be next. Oxford very gently took the cup from his hand, and he realised that he'd been shaking so badly that the tea had gone everywhere.

Oxford put the tea down on the table, and laid his hand over Robert's. "It's all right," he said. "It's nothing to be ashamed about."

Robert tried to swallow, but his throat had gone dry. "I thought we were going to die."

"You didn't," Oxford said.

After a minute, Robert was able to nod. They were still alive, and in the end everything in the world came down to that.

***

Helen Ash stared fixedly at the wall of the waiting room. She hated hospitals – hated that smell of disinfectant that caught at the back of her throat, and the look of panic you sometimes saw in people's eyes – and she hated this part of the job. Next to her, Ian McCallum's mother sat staring at her hands. She'd cried when she heard the news. Now she just sat with a blank expression on her face, not speaking and hardly moving.

Helen was glad. She knew why she'd been sent with her – these kinds of job always fell to the women on a team. She did it without complaint, because to do otherwise would have been to set herself up as a ball-breaker, the way Grace Harris had started to do. But that didn't mean she enjoyed it.

A doctor appeared at the door. "Mrs McCallum?" The woman's head jerked round as if she were a puppet and her string had been pulled. "Your son has just come round."

She got to her feet. "Can I see him?" she asked.

The doctor looked regretful. "Not just yet. He's still in a pretty bad way."

Helen stood up, hoping Mrs McCallum would want to be taken home now. "Any idea when I'll be able to interview him?" she asked.

"I'd rather you didn't till we've had him under observation for a while," the doctor said firmly. He looked as if he'd rather have said, never.

"You keeping him in overnight?" Helen asked. The doctor nodded. "I'll have a PC posted outside his door." Again, the doctor didn't seem happy; but he didn't object – presumably he could see the dangers of having a witness to a major crime left unprotected in the hospital. "I'll be back in the morning." The doctor turned and left. Helen started to follow him. She'd already assigned a uniform constable to drive Mrs McCallum home as soon as she was ready to go. She glanced back at the other woman and gave her a little smile, knowing there were no words that could ease her pain.

"I told him people get killed doing what he's doing," Mrs McCallum said. She was already beginning to blame herself. It was written in her face.

What do you say, Ash wondered. What the bloody hell do you say? "He's a brave man," she said.

Mrs McCallum's face crumpled. "No," she said. "He's selfish. The last thing I need is him being brave."

Helen didn't know what to say. In the end, she said nothing, but left the older woman alone with her grief.

***

Dennis Worsley wanted very few things in life. He had most of them, right now – his freedom, a lot of money, and his wife back in his arms and in his bed.

Right now, she was in his arms, though he still wasn't sure whether she was to be trusted. He nibbled at the lush fullness of her bottom lip, not quite hard enough to hurt, and let his hand drift down her back to her behind.

She started to pull away. All right, he thought. If that's the way you want to play it. She went over to her dressing table and

34

picked up a bottle of nail varnish remover. She poured a drop of it on to some cotton wool, then started to dab at his face. The stuff stank. Silly bitch, he thought. Any idiot could see it wasn't working.

"I love you, Dennis," she said. "I never stopped loving you."

I'll bet you didn't, Dennis thought. All the time you spent screwing Slater, and then that filth Tate – yeah, you never stopped loving me, that's for sure. But he was careful not to let his feelings show on his face. He was good at that. "Yeah – that's what the screws used to say." It didn't sound quite as much like a joke as he wanted it to.

Cathy bit her lip. She scrubbed at his face, then looked at the cotton wool. "It's not coming off." Dennis didn't say anything. Any minute now, she'd say something, and he'd have her. He'd thought about it a lot inside, and he knew what he was going to do – first he was going to make sure she knew whose woman she was, and then he was going to make sure she never forgot it – permanently. "He said if I didn't sleep with him, he'd make sure you never got out."

That was a good one. Not something he'd thought of. It might even be true... there was just a chance. "Tate said that?" he demanded. But he couldn't look at her. He stared through the window – porthole, he supposed you ought to call it – at the boats on the river.

"Yes," Cathy said. She sounded frightened, he thought. But he expected that. The only question was whether she was afraid of losing him or of what he'd do to her if she didn't persuade him. "And he could do it – why do you think they upped your sentence on appeal?" It was possible. He looked at her then – looked at those huge, fuck-me eyes and that mouth that had been made for kissing, and he had to believe it. "I hate him," she said suddenly. Her eyes shone with anger, and suddenly he realised she was telling the truth. All that crap the screws had fed him inside – those stories about how she'd been playing around with Slater. He'd believed them, when he should have believed her. He pulled her to him. "After the first time, after he'd touched me –" oh yes, Dennis thought, he could imagine that, "– all I wanted to do was work out a way to kill him."

It sounded right. It sounded, maybe, too right. If she was winding him up... he couldn't complete the thought. He grabbed her and pulled her towards him. But he didn't kiss her. He just squeezed her arms really hard – hard enough so she'd know what she'd get if she were lying – and stared into her eyes, and hoped she was telling the truth.

CHAPTER 5

Charlie kept his promise and took Michael Chater home himself. By that time, the security man had just about calmed down. In the end, he'd even given them a fairly good description of what had happened.

It turned out he lived in Charlie's old stamping ground – Bermondsey – and as they got closer Charlie found he was ticking off several landmarks as he went past them. Not that they would ever have made a guidebook – they were too personal for that.

"You deal with this sort of thing all the time?" Chater asked suddenly.

"More or less," Charlie said. Once Chater had calmed down, he'd found he liked the man. He could certainly sympathise with his anguish over what might have happened to his son.

"What we did – me and Ian and Rob –" Chater paused. He licked his lip. "We did the right thing?"

You're alive, Charlie thought. Just about anything that gets you out alive is the right thing. "Yeah," he said. "I think so."

"It's just – when they stuck that photo on the window, I was lost, you know?" Chater said. Just as well they only showed the mother-in-law in the photo, Charlie thought. If it had shown the lad, Chater would probably have lost it when he got out of the van, and judging by what they'd done to McCallum, the lad might very well be without a father by now. "Then, when they smacked Ian..." He shook his head.

Charlie glanced at him, suddenly worried that he might be about to get upset again. But the security man was staring out the side window with a haunted expression on his face. It was going to take a long time to get over, that was for sure.

"You from round here," he asked, by way of changing the conversation.

"Yeah," Chater said.

"Me too."

That got Chater's attention. "Yeah?" he said, showing some interest. "What school did you go to?"

"Never did," Scott said. It was partly true – he'd spent a lot of time bunking off, just not as much as some that he could mention. But it made Chater laugh, and that was the main thing. "Did you say he was three – your lad?" he said after a bit.

"Yeah – three." Chater smiled. "Just the one boy. He means everything – I mean, but everything to me."

"Nice," Charlie said. "Nice..." He wasn't thinking about Jack – about how he'd have been three just about now. He wasn't thinking about that at all.

***

The Chater's home was just what Bingo Tate had expected – all dull would-be middle class respectability: exactly what you got if you settled down young and stayed with the same woman all your life. He didn't deny it was comfortable – all overstuffed dralon three piece suites and floral curtains – but that didn't stop him despising it.

He sat in the front room talking to Michael Chater's mother-in-law, Mabel. Through the folding doors that led to the dining room and in the kitchen, the Scene of Crimes Officer and the photographer took the place apart looking for any clues the kidnappers might have left behind. Not that they seriously expected to find anything – the job had been too professional by half for that.

Which left it down to him to try and get something out of Mabel. He didn't think he was going to have much luck with her – little old ladies weren't really his thing; give him one of the tarts down at King's Cross and he'd have her chattering like a cageful of monkeys in fifteen minutes flat, no trouble. But dithery little grandmas were a bit beyond him.

"Did you get a look at the gun?" He asked. He knew he sounded impatient, and that he shouldn't, but he just couldn't help it.

"Well..." Mabel said, as she'd said to every question he'd asked so far. "He had it in his hand..." Well I didn't think he wore it in his button-hole, Bingo thought, but he kept his face carefully neutral. "It wasn't very big..."

Well, that lets out AK 47s, I suppose. Bingo thought wearily, "Did it have a chamber?" Mabel's expression said she didn't follow. "A round thing in the middle for bullets," Bingo explained. "Or was it more sort of square shaped?" Mabel stared blankly at him. He changed tack. "Black? Steel colour?"

Nothing. Mabel bit her lip. Her hands worked at the bit of tissue she'd used to dry her eyes with earlier.

Dammit, Bingo thought, his irritation washed away by a rare wave of compassion. She's just an old lady. She shouldn't have to go through this.

"I'm sorry," she said.

"It's okay," Bingo said, and meant it.

"I was just so scared..."

Bingo leaned forward and touched her hand. "You didn't do anything wrong, Mabel." She was a trier. You had to admire that. "You did okay."

She smiled at him, and though it was a bit shaky, he decided she'd be okay.

***

In the next room, Grace Harris stared at Darren Chater. The little boy was lying on the sofa with his head on his mother's lap, clutching a disgusting piece of blanket. He'd been like that ever since Grace had arrived. His mother stroked his hair. She seemed to be watching something in the garden, rather than paying attention to Grace.

"Right," Grace said. She stood up.

"I'm ever so sorry," Rosie Chater said. "Let me –" she started to move the boy off her lap.

"Don't worry about it," Grace said. I can see myself out. She headed for the door that lead into the hall. It was a shame the boy hadn't been able to tell her anything, but secretly she was rather pleased. If they ever got the idea she was good at nannying small kids and old ladies, they'd make her do it all the time. She'd seen it happen often enough to women officers.

Bingo was waiting for her in the hall.

"The boy's catatonic," she said without waiting to be asked.

"Here," Bingo said. "I'm the DS – I'll use the long words."

39

Would if you could understand them, Grace thought. "Scared stiff," she explained. "Can't get a word out of him."

Bingo pulled a face. Typical Bingo, she thought. He was probably scared he might have to do some work for a change.

"Well," he said, "Mabel's got guts but she's no use as a witness. This is a waste of time."

Well, at least he'd got that right. She was about to suggest they radio in for further instructions when a man's silhouette appeared at the frosted glass of the door. A key jangled in the lock, and a second later the door opened and in walked Michael Chater. He dashed past them, almost shoving Grace out of the way in his hurry, and went into the back lounge. The Guv'nor, DI Scott, followed more slowly.

Bingo shot Grace a 'might as well' look, and went after them. Grace went too.

By the time she got there, Chater had swept Darren into his arms. "Don't worry," he said. "I'm back now. It's okay –" he rubbed the little boy's back gently. But the lad just stared over his shoulder. Slowly, Rosie Chater stood up. She put her arms round her son and husband. But Michael Chater didn't seem to notice. He just kept whispering to his son.

Eventually, Rosie Chater squeezed his hand to get his attention. The look he gave her was a mixture of rage and relief, and something else that Grace couldn't quite put a name to – guilt, most like; whatever it was, it didn't last long before he turned back to Darren.

Grace glanced at Scott. He was staring intently at the Chaters. The expression on his face was hard to read, but he clearly wasn't happy. Grace remembered the rumours that she'd heard around the office – that he'd lost a son to cancer a couple of years back. This must be hard for him to take, she thought.

Apparently she was right, because a couple of seconds later Scott turned and walked out.

***

Bingo's car was a horror story, Grace thought – flashy on the outside, a trash heap on the inside, and souped-up to the point where it probably wasn't quite safe to be in. Come to think of it, it probably quite suited him. She could understand – just –

why so many women went for him. He was really quite good looking, in an ordinary kind of way. What she couldn't understand was why he was always the one that dumped the women. Given his behaviour, you'd have thought it would be the other way round.

Since she didn't have a lot of choice, she settled herself in. There was a newspaper in the glove compartment. As Bingo pulled away, she took a look at it. There, in all its glory, was Bingo's little problem for all the world to see – Dennis Worsley's explosive exit from the high security prison where he was supposed to be residing at Her Majesty's pleasure. She grinned.

Bingo glanced at her, grabbed the paper and threw it on the back seat. "Please," he said. "Do you mind?"

Grace stared out of the side window. No, she thought – but I'll bet Dennis Worsley does. She suddenly realised they were heading towards the river. "Which way back are you going?" she asked. She had a funny feeling she was about to discover the meaning of the phrase 'stuck in traffic' as used by Bingo Tate.

"Back where?" he asked.

"Factory," Grace said, meaning the office.

"I'm not going back there. Not yet."

So surprise me, Grace thought. She had a good idea where he was going, and sure enough he turned on to the Embankment. As he parked up, he said, "Won't be a sec, but if I am –"

"We're stuck in traffic?"

Tate got out of the car. "You'll go far," he said, and slammed the door.

Grace glared at his retreating back, and at the world in general. "Not here, I won't," she snarled.

She waited almost a full minute before she got out and followed him.

***

So, the little toe-rag was hanging around Cathy.

Dennis Worsley slammed his hand against the steering wheel of the car from which he was watching the houseboat.

The only question was – did he look like a man who was

41

screwing someone else's wife; or blackmailing her and then screwing her?

Dennis didn't know for sure. But he was going to find out.

***

The trouble with houseboats was, they all looked the same. Bingo picked his way between the mooring lines. It was somewhere down here, he was sure of it.

It was a beautiful day – bright, not too hot, with just a hint of a breeze. Damn shame Worsley had to wreck it all. If he got to Cathy, God knows what he'd do. The man was a stone-cold killer, and that was a fact. He'd surely know she'd been seeing Ronnie Slater. Whether he knew she'd been sleeping with Bingo was another question. If he did, Cathy might not be the only one needing police protection. Bingo grinned – getting protection from his own mates. That would be good for a laugh.

He spotted the houseboat. Cathy was nowhere to be seen.

"Cathy?" he called. No answer. He crossed the gangplank and stepped on to the boat. The deck rolled under his feet, and he put out a hand to support himself. He tried again: "Cathy?"

Still nothing.

He went below. Inside, all was silence and shadow. He walked along the narrow corridor that was lit only by the sunlight shafting through the tiny windows. Somewhere, a fly drowsed in the sunlight. Otherwise, all was quiet.

Bingo entered the living room. A pile of holiday brochures sat on the coffee table, next to an ashtray with cigarette stubbed out in it, and a half empty coffee mug.

He thought he could smell her perfume lingering on the air. Or maybe that was imagination.

The door slammed.

Bingo whirled round, heart racing.

Harris stood there, scowling.

"What the bloody hell are you doing?" Bingo demanded.

"Refusing to be stuck in traffic," she said. She turned to leave, and there wasn't much for Bingo to do but follow her.

***

Bingo was in big trouble, Charlie Scott thought. He perched on the edge of DCI Uttley's desk and looked at the scrap of paper he'd just been handed. It had been torn from a girlie magazine, and a list of four names had been scribbled in red biro over some hapless stripper's breasts: Slater, Cathy, Tate, Willoughby.

Charlie raised his eyebrows at Uttley.

"Warder found it in Dennis Worsley's cell," the DCI said, by way of explanation. He chewed at the fringe of his moustache with his bottom lip while Charlie read the names out.

"Slater suddenly hanged himself last week," Uttley said.

Charlie looked up. He locked gazes with his boss. "Tragic," they said as one.

"Willoughby was Worsley's trial judge. He'll have round the clock protection till Worsley is under wraps," Uttley said.

Charlie grunted. "Dennis isn't going to hang around – not with half the country looking for him." He was too bright for that – if he had any sense at all, he was already on his way to Brazil or somewhere else that didn't have an extradition arrangement with Britain.

But Uttley didn't agree. "This is Worsley we're talking about – the man who put the word 'psycho' into psychopath." He said, "And that young wife of his has been a bad girl..."

Charlie knew what he was thinking – that one of their own men was on the hit list. But that man was Bingo Tate – who, frankly, might benefit from a bit of a scare. Uttley had already said as much when he first called Charlie into his office. It was risky, but it might just be their best shot. "Okay," he said. "I'll buy it. Let's give it a whirl."

***

Bingo managed to put on a bit of speed on the way back, so all in all he and Harris weren't really that late as they walked up the stone stairs that led to the station. Of course, he'd had to put up with a fair bit of moaning as he drove, but he'd managed to tune it out all right.

He pushed open the inner door that led to the reception room. He saw Cathy sitting on the bench at the side as soon as he got the door open.

A second later, she saw him. "Bob!" she cried as she got to her feet. She was just about the only person who ever called him that.

With her make-up smudged from crying and her willowy figure hidden under her raincoat she didn't look all that wonderful. She tried to hold Bingo, but he grabbed her arms and held her away from him.

Harris and the damn woman desk sergeant were looking at him like he'd crawled from under a stone. He turned to the desk sergeant. "It's okay," he said.

The uniform made a sour face at him, but when he led Cathy to into the station, she clicked the security switch to let them through without giving him any trouble.

Just as well – he had enough already.

They went inside. Bingo found an empty interview room. Before he went inside, he turned back to Harris, who was following them as if she didn't have a clue what to do next without being told. "Go and start filling the Guv'nor in on the Chaters," he said. She just stared at him. "I'll be with you in a sec."

Fat chance, her expression said. Well, to hell with her. Bingo pushed the door of the interview room open, and ushered Cathy in ahead of him.

"Nice to meet you," Harris said to Cathy's back.

Give me a break, Tate thought as he went inside. Harris just wasn't a team player, that was her problem. He slammed the door behind him, then rounded on Cathy. "What the bloody hell are you doing here?" he demanded.

"Dennis is out and you bloody knew it!" she snapped back, not bothering to keep her voice down. Anger lent colour to her cheeks and a flash to her eyes, and the soft light filtering through the windows picked out the highlights in her hair.

Bingo thought he'd never seen her look more beautiful. Not that it stopped him being furious with her.

"Shh!" Bingo said. "Keep your voice down for Christ's sake." It was pointless, he knew – he was already the laughing stock of the squad, and probably the entire station. But he had his pride, for what it was worth.

"Don't worry," Cathy snarled. "Dennis'll keep my voice down – he'll cut my bleeding throat when he catches up with us –"

She had a point. There were harder bastards than Dennis Worsley around. Probably. Holding down good jobs as torturers in some dictatorship somewhere.

"Dennis isn't catching up with anybody," Bingo said. There was panic in Cathy's eyes now, and suddenly he didn't have the heart to stay angry with her. "Look, if he's got any brains he's not even in the country any more."

Cathy didn't answer him. Instead, she fumbled in her bag for her cigarettes. She got one out, and tapped it on the packet. Her hand was trembling. Bingo covered it with his own.

"What aren't you telling me?" he asked.

Cathy stared at him for the space of a couple of heartbeats. "He..." she paused and licked her lips. "He phoned me, Bob. He said he'd heard I'd been playing around." She was almost crying. "He said if he found out it was true, he'd kill me." There was a long silence. "I'm not staying on that boat," she said. Bingo sighed. He should have seen this coming. "I'm not," she said. "Let me stay at your place. He doesn't know about you – not who you are." She laid her hand flat against his chest. "Please... let me stay at the flat." She stared up at him, all melting eyes and honeypot mouth, and he couldn't refuse her. "Just for tonight," she pleaded.

Tate stared at her. She was trouble with a capital T, and he'd always known it. So that made this as much his fault as hers. "Okay," he said. He pulled his keys out of his jacket pocket and handed them to her. "Go straight there. Don't answer the door to anyone." He smoothed her hair back from her face. "I'll have a word with my Guv'nor and see what he says about protection."

Cathy rewarded him with a quick brush of her lips against his – the barest hint of what might be to come. "Thanks," she said. "When I heard his voice I thought I was going to die –" She pulled him towards her, and this time she kissed him hard and long.

***

Grace pulled her armoured vest off, and laid it to one side. She was in DCI Uttley's office, and he had just finished briefing her. She glanced at him, and he held her look with a steady gaze.

This is it, she thought. My big chance to prove I can do anything they throw at me. Her gun and holster lay on Uttley's desk. She picked it up and put it back on, pinning the straps down tight under her arms.

"This has been cleared with the Yard," Uttley said, "But in the office only you, me and Mr Scott are in the know. Keep it that way."

"Yes, Sir," Grace said. It wasn't every day you were assigned to protect one of your own colleagues, especially without them being in on it. If Uttley wanted it kept secret, she could certainly do it. Then again, if he'd told her to jump, she'd have done it – only wondering why when it was too late. "How long will I be carrying?" she asked. Uttley made a non-committal face – the answer was obviously, 'as long as it takes'. "And what about outside work?" she asked. She thought she knew the answer, but the idea of having to sleep with a gun by her pillow excited her just a bit.

"You don't have to worry about that," Uttley said.

Grace nodded, hoping she'd managed to conceal her disappointment.

***

The trouble with making your way up the promotion ladder, Charlie Scott thought, was that you just got landed with more and more paperwork. Beyond the slatted blinds of his office window he could see the team doing some real work in the squad room. He leaned back in his chair and pushed his hand through the curly mess of his hair. He thought about phoning Steph to see how she was doing, but decided against it. Only this morning she'd told him that he had to stop worrying about her pregnancy. So he sat up and pulled another sheet from his in-tray. He'd no sooner started to fill it in than there was a tap at his office door. Charlie looked up. Bingo Tate came in without waiting to be told.

Well, Charlie thought. There were compensations. He was quite looking forward to hearing what Bingo had to say for himself.

"Grace not here?" Bingo said, as if he'd been first in that morning and would be the last to leave.

"That's amazing," Charlie said. "You said that with no sense of irony whatsoever."

That got to Bingo. It was about time something did, Charlie thought. "What is this?" he demanded. "The Flying Squad or Open University?"

Charlie stared at him just long enough so he understood that having a temper tantrum wasn't going to get him anywhere. Then he said, "She's with the Guv'nor." He let Bingo think about that for a second before he added, "I wanted to talk to you alone, anyway."

"Oh," Bingo said, seeming to cheer up. "I don't think Mabel's going to get us anywhere – saw nothing, knows even less."

Typical, Charlie thought. Trust Bingo not to realise there was a problem. Or not one he'd admit to, anyway.

"Not the raid," Charlie said. "About your friend downstairs – ." A look of desperation flashed across Bingo's face, only to be replaced almost instantly by one of injured innocence. "Look," he said, "I've not seen her in months –" Liar, Charlie thought. At the very least he'd visited her home that morning – Harris had told them as much; Charlie supposed there was a chance in a million that it had been the first time Bingo had gone there since he'd been officially warned off. But Charlie thought that was as likely as Bingo never touching another woman in his life. "She's terrified about her old man being out," Bingo continued, "and to tell the truth I'm not over the moon about it either."

Charlie stared at him. "I can understand that," he said. He knew exactly where Bingo was going with this – in fact, it would make everything much easier if he did.

Bingo was obviously weighing up his chances. When Charlie didn't say anything, he said, "Guv – what kind of cover can I have till they bag Worsley again?"

Charlie put on a thoughtful expression. He hoped he wasn't overdoing it. He wondered how long he'd have to wait before Bingo started offering to do unpaid overtime or something in return.

But before that happened, the door opened and DCI Uttley walked in. "I heard you had a mate drop in?" he said.

He was a big man – not much taller than Bingo, but far more solidly built. Bingo visibly shrank in front of him. "Look," he said, imploringly. "I didn't know she was coming –"

"I bet you hope Dennis isn't coming, too," Uttley said.

Charlie hoped he wasn't overplaying it. "Bingo wants to know what kind of protection he can have," he said.

There was a momentary silence. Then Uttley burst out laughing. If Charlie hadn't known he was putting it on, he'd have found it most convincing. Bingo was furious, but he couldn't admit it so he just stood there glowering.

Charlie shrugged helplessly, as if to say, 'sorry mate – it isn't my call.'

Bingo turned and stalked out the door.

Charlie waited for it to slam before he, too, started to laugh.

CHAPTER 6

The nursery was in shadow. Michael Chater leaned against the door jamb. He was looking at Rosie, who was fussing with Darren; but he was only thinking about his son. The sunlight that crept round the edges of the curtains caught the mobile that hung above the bed, but Darren just lay staring at the wallpaper –

Rosie stood up. Despite the worry etched into her face, she had never looked more beautiful, Michael thought – and he wondered again why she had ever chosen him. She turned, and jerked her head in surprise when she saw him watching her.

"I can't believe he was here," Michael said. "Why was he here?"

"He was sick," Rosie snapped. She breathed, deep and ragged. "What was I supposed to do?" She brushed past him into the landing and eased the door shut.

Michael grabbed her arm. "I shouldn't have rushed out this morning – I should have taken him myself." Rosie shrugged his hand away. "I wouldn't have let him stay off sick," he insisted.

"It's nobody's fault, Mike," Rosie said.

But her eyes said very clearly that it was his fault. These days, everything was his fault.

"You," he said. "I blame you." He turned and went downstairs. As he left, he heard her start to cry, but he ignored her and went and put the television on, very loud.

***

Leaving the job at the office, that was the hard part, Charlie thought as he parked outside his house. He walked up the path and let himself in. The place smelled of furniture polish and fresh flowers. Damn, he thought. Steph had definitely been working too hard, then. He wished she would take it easy, like the doctor said.

He went into the lounge. She wasn't there. "Steph?" he shouted. "Steph?"

49

There was no reply. He looked on the sideboard in case she'd gone out and left a note for him. But there was nothing there except the usual clutter of ornaments and photos – Steph cradling Jack in her arms just after she'd come of the hospital, the three of them playing in the park, Jack by himself, just before they'd found out about the cancer. He scarcely noticed them now. He didn't need to. There wasn't a day went by that he didn't think about the lad.

He wandered back out into the hall. Maybe she'd just nipped out to the shops. She might have had a fall. Or maybe her blood-pressure was playing up again and –

There was a low groan from upstairs.

"Steph!" he shouted, as he took the stairs two at a time.

He raced into the bedroom. Stephanie was lying on the bed. As he crossed the room she stretched and moaned, then turned and blinked sleepily at him.

"Oh don't do that to me," Charlie said. He realised his heart was pounding far harder than a quick run up the stairs justified.

"What?" Stephanie asked. She rubbed her eyes. "I was having a nap." Charlie sat down on the bed beside her. He stroked her hand. Her skin was fine and pale, and even in the half-light he could see the blue veins beneath it.

"Charlie," Steph said, "You've got to stop this. You're driving me mad –" Her eyes were wide set in her high cheekboned face, and she stared at him intently until he answered.

"I know," Charlie said. He looked at the floor. It was easier than meeting her eyes. "I can't help it."

"You're going to have to help it," Stephanie said. She levered herself up on one elbow. "Because it's just making me tense – and that makes it all the more likely something will happen." Charlie nodded. He rubbed her burgeoning stomach with his hand. She covered his hand with one of hers. "I'm fine," she said. "The baby's fine." She pushed herself up and sat on the edge of the bed. "Now, instead of making me tense, how about making me tea?"

***

He wouldn't have wanted anyone to find out, but Bingo

actually liked having someone to come home to. Just as long as it wasn't the same someone very many times in a row.

To prove it, he'd been shopping. He lumbered through the door with two full bags. The hallway was in darkness. "I got some shopping," he called out.

No answer.

Bingo dropped the shopping and went into the living room. Chaos met his eyes. The sideboard drawers had been emptied across the carpet, and the cushions from the sofa had been slit open and the foam trailed across the carpet. The TV, video and stereo were all missing from their places.

"Fuck," Bingo said.

He left the room at a dead run and thundered upstairs.

The bedroom was almost as much of a mess as the living room. Most of his clothes were strewn over the bed and floor. The chest of drawers stood open. He hurried across to it. There were still some things in it. That meant there was still a chance they hadn't found what they were looking for...

He rifled through the clothing. Nothing.

"The whore!" he shouted.

She'd taken the lot – nearly a grand in cash.

***

Grace Harris tapped her pen on her diary in time to the music – early Stones, just right for the work-out she'd just completed, but not for writing her diary. She put the biro down and nibbled at her ice-cream instead. Death By Chocolate – the best money could buy, or at least the best the local supermarket stocked. She let it slide around on her tongue until it melted before she swallowed it.

It was total luxury, and very bad for her. Still, she thought, eyeing the pile of exercise equipment in the corner of the living room, she'd earned it. Firstly by doing her nightly work-out in record time, and secondly by keeping control of her temper while Bingo bloody Tate insisted on dragging her off to look for his girlfriend.

Until now. She'd told her diary all about it, and it had made her feel much better. She swapped her teaspoon for the pen and started to write again. The little card table she was leaning on

51

was a bit too low, and it wobbled as she pressed on it, but that was okay. She could think of a lot of other things besides furniture to waste her time and money on.

She was just about to describe how the Worsley woman had turned up in the station when the entryphone chimed. She got up and went to answer it, though she couldn't for the life of her think who it could be – she rarely had visitors.

"Hi," said a familiar male voice when she answered. "It's Bingo – Bob Tate."

"Yes?" Grace knew she sounded frosty; she had a good idea what was up, considering the job she'd been given. But she had no intention of letting on – after all, Bingo wasn't supposed to know.

"Can I come in?" Bingo asked.

"No," Grace snapped. There were limits.

"It's an emergency." Bingo was beginning to wheedle. She hated that.

"What sort of emergency?" Grace asked, though she had a good idea.

"Please," Bingo said. He was beginning to sound a bit desperate. Serve him right.

Grace pushed the entry button. She went and stood by the front door, and listened for the sound of the outside door. When it went, she opened her door just a crack.

Bingo was standing there. "Thanks," he said.

He obviously expected her to let him in, but she didn't. "What do you want?" she asked.

"I need a favour," he said. He licked his lips. "Can I stay here?"

Bloody hell, Grace thought. It was more or less what she'd expected, given that Dennis Worsley was hot on his trail, but she still found she was furious. "I don't do bunk ups," she snapped.

"I'm not looking for a leg over," Bingo said. Really, Grace thought. It wouldn't be the first time one of her male colleagues had tried it on – just the best excuse any of them had come up with. "I'm asking as a colleague," Bingo continued.

"If I wanted a pet, I'd buy a fish," Grace said. It didn't matter what he said he wanted, she knew what it would come down to

52

– and what would get round the station, no matter what happened or didn't.

"I need somewhere safe," Bingo said. He paused. "I'm serious." There was real desperation in his voice now; and he did have Worsley after him...

Reluctantly, Grace opened the door and let Bingo in. He looked round the room – it was small and spartan with only one armchair, a stack of exercise equipment and no television. His expression clearly said he thought she was weird.

So what else is new, Grace thought.

"Anyway," Bingo said, "I make it a point not to sleep with anyone I work with."

Big deal, Grace thought. "Yeah – well, most of them are men," she said.

"You're very lippy, aren't you?" Bingo said. "For a DC..." he let the sentence trail off.

Grace glared at him, thinking, one more word from you and you're out – Worsley or not. She went and turned off the stereo, flipping her diary shut as she went. Then she started to put her tracksuit on over her shorts – just to make the point about what Bingo could expect from her. "I thought Ted Donachie was a mate of yours," she said. "Why not stay with him?"

Bingo pulled a sour face. "Cathy knows my mates," he said. "If Dennis the Deranged gets hold of her she's going to tell him where I might go – but she doesn't know about you." Great, Grace thought; she wished she'd persuaded Uttley to let her sign her weapon out overnight.

Bloody hell, thought Grace. There wasn't any getting out of it. "Tonight," she said. "Just tonight, though." She turned and went through the door that led to her bedroom. "I don't have a spare bed," she called as she hauled the rucksack that contained the spare futon out of the cupboard.

"Don't worry too much about that," Bingo called.

Now he'd got the wrong idea, she thought. Damn the man. "I don't have any bed," she said, staring at her own, much larger futon. "Not as such." She pulled the spare out of its bag.

She lugged the futon out into the front room. Bingo was staring at her diary. At least he hadn't opened it.

She chucked the futon down in front of him. It unrolled itself. He stared at it. "It's a futon," she said by way of explanation.

"Great," he said, with about as much enthusiasm as he'd have greeted Dennis Worsley with. He tapped her diary. "What's the 'B' in your name for?" he asked.

Shit, Grace thought. So far, she'd managed to keep her middle name a secret from everyone in the Unit. "Bugger off," she snarled.

"No," Bingo said. "That would be GBO – your initials are GBH." He grinned malevolently. "GBH?"

I know what you mean, thought Grace. And I'll do you some Grievous Bodily Harm if you don't let it drop. But she had better sense than to say it. "I've no spare sheets," she said.

Bingo stared at her. "Where's your telly?" he asked after a moment.

"I don't have one of those, either," she said.

Bingo was still staring at her. "What do you do of an evening?" he asked. When she didn't answer immediately, he said, "Not a dyke, are you?"

Like lesbians don't watch telly? Grace wondered. But it was too good a straight line to ignore. "No," she said, and smiled sweetly. "But a night with you might make me one."

Bingo smiled right back at her. "I was just winding you up," he said.

"Yes," Grace said. "And I'm just letting you down." She paused deliberately, to make sure she had his attention. "Tell anyone my initials – tell anyone you stayed here tonight – and I'll tell them about your houseboat detour." Bingo looked as if he were about to say something. Before he could, she pointed at the hall doorway and went on, "Kitchen and bathroom are through there." She picked up her diary and ice-cream, went into her bedroom and let the door slam behind her.

Bloody men, she thought. Then she grinned. She might be the only woman in recorded history to let Bingo Tate spend the night at her place without sharing his bed.

***

Charlie Scott lay staring into the darkness. Stephanie lay

beside him. Moonlight filtering through the net curtains barred her face, and he could feel the gentle rise and fall of the bed clothes as she breathed.

If anything were to happen to her... to the baby...

"I can hear you looking at me," she said.

Charlie grinned. "Does that mean you can see what I'm thinking?" he asked.

"I can guess," she answered. He knew it was true. Sometimes it felt like she were his second skin, and he hers. "Put your hand under my back for a sec," she asked. He did so, feeling the solid weight of her. She sighed and wriggled. He wished he could do more to relieve her discomfort. "So," she asked after a minute. "Are we going to talk about it or am I just going to lie here like a pudding?"

Charlie didn't say anything. He couldn't find the words.

"I promise I won't go into labour," Stephanie said. Her tone was light, but he knew she sometimes worried just as much as he did.

Still – she was right. He did need to talk about it. "I was interviewing a bloke today – one of the guards on that van that got slaughtered." He remembered the way Mike Chater had stared off into nothingness when he tried to talk about it. "The villains took his mother-in-law and his son hostage. The boy was only three years old." He felt Stephanie's hand touch his. "Nice bloke," he went on. "Just doing his job, you know. But one of the other guards got smashed up. He's still in hospital." He paused. "One of them's in on it –" he'd known it all the time. The job was just too slick for it to be anything else. But he hadn't said it aloud before.

"You're joking!" Stephanie said, but it was almost a question.

"Inside job," Charlie said firmly. "I'm just hoping it's not my man." He thought about Mike Chater again. There was just no telling. "More for his sake than anything." But then there was the other thing. He turned to face Stephanie. "The boy's scared to death." Stephanie rolled clumsily on to her side and put her arm across his chest. The weight of it was a comfort to him. He could barely see her face in the half-light, but he didn't need to. He knew the depths of sorrow those eyes could hold. "All I could think was that Jack would have been the same age..." Three. Dark haired, brown, laughing eyes. Curious as a kitten...

"Oh Charlie," Stephanie said. He took her hand and held it. In the dark times, that was all they'd had. But he couldn't look at her. Instead he stared up at the ceiling.

"I thought..." he started. But he couldn't finish it. After a moment he tried again. "I thought, I'd rather have him here like that bloke's boy – terrified, scared half to death." His throat closed up and he could hardly breathe. But after a moment he said, "At least that would mean he was still alive." He turned to face her again. He laughed, a horrid hard sound in the quietness. "Pretty bad, huh?"

For an answer she took his face in her two hands and kissed him. And after that, in the darkness, at least there was something to cling to.

***

Cathy was in trouble, and she knew it. Dennis hadn't wanted to have sex, and that was a bad sign.

He was sitting across from her in the shadows, staring at her with the expression he kept for when someone was about to suffer, and that was an even worse sign.

She pulled the duvet round her shoulders, wondering whether letting it slip so she showed just a bit of boob would be a good idea. It might take Dennis's mind off Bingo...

Bingo, who hadn't showed up. She'd had it all worked out – she'd let him know Dennis was around, he'd come and rescue her and, before you knew it, Dennis would be back in the nick and Bingo would be very grateful to her. Or possibly Dennis would get to Bingo before the cops got to him, and she'd be rid of both of them.

But Bingo hadn't shown and Dennis was getting more unhappy by the minute.

"I don't think he's coming," Dennis said. He played with the rug with his toe. He was a terrible sight – the orange dye had refused to come off, and his face and hands were still daubed with it.

56

"Dennis..." Cathy said, though she'd no real idea what she could say to calm him down.

"I don't think he's coming," Dennis repeated. "And I'm beginning to think you might have stitched me up..." He spat the words out.

"I swear," Cathy said, wondering desperately what she could say to convince him. "On my mother's grave. I –"

"Wasn't she cremated?" Dennis cut in. He wasn't smiling.

"He raped me," Cathy said. It was her trump card. If he wasn't buying... He just stared at her. "I didn't tell you because..." she paused, knowing she had to make it good. "I thought, if you knew you wouldn't want me any more."

Dennis stood up. Light glinted on the gun he had been cradling in his lap. He walked across to the bed. Cathy found she was holding her breath. The gun was matt black and seemed very large.

Dennis laid it on the bedside table. He sat on the bed. "Oh babe," he whispered. He drew her towards him. She lay her head on his shoulder and began to cry.

She'd always found that easy.

CHAPTER 7

Robert Killigrew had thought he'd finished with the police when they let him go after the robbery. Yet somehow here he was at nine in the morning, clutching yet another cup of coffee and watching DC Oxford read his statement. Again.

He felt like he'd been in the interview room hours. Oxford hadn't spoken in a long while, and it was making Robert nervous. Some of his coffee had slopped on the formica top of the desk, and he shoved it around with his finger.

"How's Ian?" he asked at last. "Hospital won't tell us."

Oxford looked up from his reading. "Better, apparently," he said, and went back to his reading.

It was the first good news Killigrew had received. "Yeah?" he asked. "I thought he'd been hurt really bad –"

Oxford didn't answer, but a moment later he said, "You haven't been on the van long, Rob – right?"

Best get it over with, Robert thought. "Three months. Been in security four years, though." That was three years and eleven months too long, according to Jenny, but he didn't say that.

"You live in Willesden, and you got a brother called Earnel." Oxford's tone was neutral. You'd hardly think he'd dropped a nuke into the conversation. "Is that right?" he asked when Robert didn't answer immediately.

"Uh huh," Robert said. Should have seen this coming, he thought to himself. Should have told them before they got a chance to ask –

"Who's been inside," Oxford went on. "Not been out long."

Got to make nice, Robert thought. Got to co-operate. But even as he thought it the words were coming out of his mouth. "What's that got to do with anything?" he demanded.

"The villains had help, Robbie." Oxford gave him a cool stare. "That's what we know."

That's Mr Killigrew to you, Robert thought. But he said

flatly, "Not from me."

Oxford was plainly unimpressed. "But you didn't see fit to enlighten your employers about your family ties when you put in for the job?"

Robert's hand clenched on the table top. "I thought about it," he said, trying to match the police officer's level tone. "But then I remembered I actually needed the money." Oxford just stared at him until he looked away. He shook his head. "You're unreal," he muttered.

"No," Oxford said, "What's unreal is to imagine that a security guard with a brother who's been inside should come across like the injured party." He slapped the statement down on the desk. "That's unreal."

Robert felt something snap inside him. "Earnel got done for shoplifting leather jackets," he said. "Six months! Six lousy months –"

"I'm looking at you, Robbie," Oxford said. "I think it's you. And we're talking serious time if you don't smarten up."

Bloody hell, Robert thought. Damned if I do, damned if I don't. It didn't matter what he said. They weren't going to believe him anyway. "How come you're talking to me?" He looked away and sucked through his teeth: it was the kind of thing Earnel would have done; the kind of thing that would have got him a clip round the ear from their mother. "You got something to prove round here?"

Oxford looked genuinely surprised. "Come again?" he asked.

"Whose idea was it for you to interview me?" Robert demanded. "Your boss? He think since you're a nigger you're going to get something going with me?" He thickened up his Jamaican accent. "I'm goin' to put my hands up cos we brothers – is that it, man?" he goaded. "Or is it you –"

Oxford laughed. "Oh come on – you can do better than that."

"Yeah," Robert drawled. "It's you, man. Trying to prove you can take a brother good as the next man." He glared at Oxford. Give him his due, the copper stared right back at him. "You trying to prove you can bust a nigger good as any white cop." Robert tapped his chest. "Look at me – the Bounty Bar Kid."

Oxford just stared at him.

Go on, Killigrew thought at him. Think about it. At least do that much.

***

Ian McCallum looked a mess, despite the nurses best efforts to clean him up. The sight of the drips going into his arms made Helen Ash feel slightly queasy, and she was glad there was no blood in sight, but just a surgical dressing over the place where they had shaved back his hair to suture his scalp.

He was propped up in bed on a pile of crisp pillows. Machines hummed by the bedside, monitoring his various bodily functions. No excitement, the ward sister had said. Well, Helen didn't want excitement. A simple statement would do well enough. She noted that McCallum's eyes were focusing well, and supposed that to be a good sign. But when he spoke his words were slightly slurred.

"I suppose I was lucky in a way," he said. "Being smacked unconscious – can't worry about what's happening then, can you?"

One of life's optimists Helen thought. Or a very clever inside man who trusted his mates with his life. "That's one way of looking at it," she said. The hospital disinfectant caught at the back of her throat. "The other is to say you nearly died." She stared at the man. The nurses had warned her that he was scarcely out of shock, but he was far more calm than Helen thought he ought to be. "Chater and Killigrew say there's no reason the robber should have hit you." She kept staring at him, but she could have been looking at the wall for all the response she got. "Why did he?" she asked, probing as gently as she could.

"Do nutters like that need a reason?"

"Smart villains – which that lot were – don't use nutters," Helen said. It had been one of the first lessons she'd learned on the Squad. Your petty thief or opportunistic burglar might use a knife or anything else he could get his hands on; but planned armed robbery was a different thing, by and large. Psychos were rare. Successful psychos even rarer. "They don't risk killing someone in a raid. It's too much grief – and too much extra time

60

if they get caught."

"So what are you saying?" he asked. His hands, great square workman's hands, twitched against the starched linen.

Helen gave him time to think about it. Only the whirr and click of the monitors broke the silence. "Are you involved, Ian?" she asked at last. "Was it you helped set it up?"

That got to him. He swallowed hard. "Mike's a mate," he said. "And Rosie and Darren... I wouldn't do anything to hurt them...." His face went vague, as if he were remembering something. "I mean, Rosie?" He scowled. "I'd rather –"

"What would you rather do?" Helen cut in quickly, not giving him time to think.

The scowl deepened, just for a second. He shook his head. Then his face went slack.

He fell forward into the bed just as the monitors started to squeal. Helen slammed her hand against the emergency button. Before she could do anything else, the sister raced in, followed by the doctor.

"He just keeled over –" Helen started, but no-one was listening. Other medics rushed in and started to work around McCallum. The sister kicked the brakes off the bed's wheels. She and the doctor started to push McCallum out. They were shouting instructions to each other over the clattering of the wheels.

"He just keeled over," Helen said again. Reluctantly, she followed them through the door, knowing she was, for once, helpless.

Mrs McCallum was in the hallway. She was trying to keep pace with the trolley, and Helen could see she was only getting in the way.

She hurried over and took the distraught woman by the arm. "Come and sit over here," she said.

Mrs McCallum let herself be pulled away. Her face was tear-streaked and red from crying. "What is it?" she begged. "What happened?" Her hands clutched at Helen's arm through her jacket. "He was fine till you went in," she said. "What did you do?" She wiped tears from her eyes. "What did you do," she said again.

"I'm sorry," Helen said. There was nothing else to say, so she repeated it. "I'm sorry."

CHAPTER 8

Charlie Scott paced up and down in Interview Room One reading Michael Chater's statement. It seemed solid enough, straightforward enough. But if that were the case, why was Chater so nervous?

Even as Scott watched, the security guard lit a fresh cigarette from the dying ember of the old one. He scrubbed the fag-end out in an ashtray that had been clean when the interview began, but which was now half-full. His hands were trembling.

The after-effects of shock, or fear? Scott wondered. Give me something, he thought at the man. Give me anything at all. I'm pulling for you here.

"Do you trust them?" he asked without looking up.

"Got to." Chater's voice was dull. "Ian I've known for years – he's a mate. Robbie's newish, but he's a good lad." He paused. "No problem."

Scott put the statement on the desk. "What about your boss – Davidson?"

Chater pulled a face. "Moaning git." He sucked on his cigarette. Smoke wreathed the air. "Can't see him setting this up, though." Charlie raised his eyebrows at the man. "Not got the brains for it," Chater said.

If Chater was the inside man, he certainly wasn't going out of his way to pin the blame on anyone else, Charlie thought. He pulled out a chair opposite the security man and sat down.

"Who has?" he asked.

Chater laughed. "Well, not me," he said.

That was more like it, Charlie thought. He locked gazes with Chater. "It's one of you," he said. Chater stared back at him. "I know it," he said after a moment.

Chater scowled. "Are you saying I'm going to stick up my own family?" he demanded. A muscle in his jaw jumped. "My own son?"

63

"Well," Charlie said. "I can't see it being McCallum." Though, he thought, it wouldn't be the first time an inside man had used a smacking as cover – though he doubted many of them ended up in McCallum's state from it. "And I agree with you about Davidson – not because he hasn't got the nous, but because he hasn't got the bottle," he continued. "That leaves you and Robbie."

Chater scrambled to his feet. "They kidnapped my mother-in-law and my son." He thrust his face close to Charlie's. "They put a gun against her head and scared him half to death." He sank back into his chair. "You don't understand." He rubbed his eyes with his hand. "You can't."

Poor bastard, Charlie thought. But he didn't give Chater time to recover. "They knew about the tracking device. They knew your route. And they knew exactly how long they had till your first drop."

Chater looked at him. "You think I'd put my family through stuff like that?" he said wearily. "No-one would." His fist slowly clenched. "I love my boy."

"I know you do," Charlie said. "I've seen you with him, and I know how angry and upset you are." Chater's expression shifted. Hope, Charlie thought. That's what that is. He let the silence stretch. Then he said, "I also know he should have been at nursery."

Chater's eyes went wide. "It wasn't me." He took a deep, ragged breath. "For God's sake, if you'd ever had kids, you'd know."

It was as if he'd flicked a switch in Charlie's brain. All his sympathy for Chater disappeared like a light going out. "I had a kid," he said flatly. "A boy. Me and my missus held his hands for eighteen hours while he died of leukaemia in front of us." He thought of Jack, with one drip going into his nose and another in his arm, and the terrible greyish pallor of him; and that persistent hospital smell of antiseptic and death. And little Darren Chater, curled in a ball on the sofa... "So shut up moaning about how I don't understand," he said. "You don't know what grief is." Chater just looked at him. "I tell you," Charlie said, letting the words punch the air. "You haven't even

64

begun to discover how much you can hate yourself."

Chater just looked at him. The sight of him turned Charlie's stomach. He got up and went to the window, though he could hardly see out through the reinforced glass. He found he was clenching his fists, and with an effort loosened them. He turned back to Chater. "Now – let's just start again."

Chater looked as if he wanted to say something, but before he could there was a knock at the door and Donachie put his head round the door. Scott went over to him and listened to the message he'd been sent with. He turned to Chater. "Your mate had a brain haemorrhage at nine fifteen this morning," he said, and watched the terror form in the security man's eyes. "He's in a coma."

***

Bingo Tate paced up and down the Chater's front hall. Grace Harris was upstairs doing the bleeding heart routine. She'd scowled when Bingo had said he reckoned she'd do better on her own, but there wasn't a lot she could do when he'd refused to go up with her.

Serve her bloody right after she'd made him spend the night lying on something that amounted to a doormat.

His phone bleeped. He took it out and flipped it open.

"Bob," said Cathy's voice. "It's me."

It took Bingo a second to get past his shock. "Hello, slut," he said.

"Bob, don't," Cathy said. Her voice had that whiny tone that was one of the least attractive things about her. "Please," she begged. "I just panicked."

"Panicked?" Bingo didn't bother to hide his contempt. "You don't panic long enough to unhook a telly, a video and a hi-fi. You don't take half an hour to rifle through a chest of drawers in a panic." He leaned back against the wall and looked up the stairwell as he spoke. He could just about make out the murmur of voices. Keep talking, he thought. The last thing he wanted was Ms Iron Knickers Harris walking in on this conversation.

"Bob," Cathy said.

"Not when you know there's nine hundred quid stashed there," he hissed down the phone.

"I'm sorry," Cathy answered. She did sound as if she'd been crying. "I thought I was going to need it to get out of the country." She paused. He could imagine her eyes brimming with tears, the honeyed fullness of her lips... "I was just so terrified of Dennis," she husked.

That snapped Bingo out of it. "Oh, so you thought you'd bugger off and leave me to face him alone, did you?"

"No," Cathy said. He could hear her crying now. "That's why I didn't go. I couldn't," she said. "Not without seeing you... please. I'm scared, Bob." She stopped speaking, and for a moment all he could hear was her crying. "I think I know where he is..."

"Where?" Bingo shouted. He glanced upstairs and lowered his voice. "Where is he?" he asked.

"Meet me, then," Cathy said. "In an hour or so – at the houseboat." Bingo didn't answer. "Please?" Cathy said.

"I'll be there," Bingo said. He started to disconnect, then said, "Be careful, okay?"

The line went dead. Bingo put his phone away.

All right, he thought. I've got you now, you bastard.

***

Cathy put the phone down. She looked across the tiny living space of the houseboat at Dennis.

"He's coming," she said.

Dennis's lips peeled back from his teeth in an expression that had very little to do with smiling. "No," he said. "He's going."

***

Grace was just a little bit out of her depth. She perched on the edge of the Chater's bed, watching her reflection and Rosie Chater's in the dressing table mirror. The contrast couldn't have been more marked. Rosie was wrapped in a crumpled dressing gown; her face, beneath a rats' nest of hair scraped up into a pony tail, was blotched with crying. She twisted a greyish scrap of tissue in her fingers. Grace, on the other hand, was crisply dressed in a skirt and blouse, with her mane of dark curly hair swept back under her hairband.

"Do you believe in God?" Rosie asked. It was the first thing

66

she'd said in ages.

Startled, Grace said the first thing that came into her head: "I don't know..." Sister Mary Joseph would have been appalled. All those Sundays spent in Church, all those Religious Education classes: and when it came to it, all she knew was that she didn't know.

"I mean, do you believe people get punished for doing things?" Rosie asked. She sounded forlorn.

Sister Mary Joseph certainly did, Grace thought. She'd done her best to make Grace believe it too. But when it came to it, Grace had decided to put her faith in the here and now – justice that could be seen to be done. If you were lucky. "Well," she said slowly, "I'm a policewoman, I guess-"

"No!" Rosie said. She shook her head vehemently. "I don't mean criminals. I mean people who lie, or cheat, or –"

"Cheating is criminal, as far as I'm concerned," Grace said.

"– cheat on their husbands," Rosie continued, as if she hadn't heard Grace.

What the hell was the woman talking about? Grace stared at her, willing her to continue, sure that if she said anything at all Rosie would clam up, and with a gut certainty that she was about to hear a piece of the jigsaw fall into place.

Rosie's fingers knotted round the tissue. "You're not married, are you?" Grace shook her head. "I wouldn't mind if it had been me," Rosie said, dully. "But it's worse when the people who get hurt are nothing to do with it."

"Mrs Chater," Grace said. "You're going to have to spell it out." Rosie turned to look at her – stared past her to something unimaginably awful. "I don't know what it is you're trying to tell me," Grace said gently. But she did. Motive, that was what Rosie Chater was about to supply her with. She could scarcely breathe.

"Maybe I was being punished," Rosie said, as if it all made perfect sense. "And the best way to punish me – to really hurt me – was through Darren and my Mum."

"Punished for what?" Grace could hardly keep the excitement out of her voice.

"Cheating," Rosie said. "Having an affair." Her face

67

crumpled. "And Ian got punished too, didn't he?"

"Ian?" That was McCallum, Grace was almost sure of it. But she had to be certain.

"Mike's mate," Rosie said softly. She looked at the wrinkled pile of sheets and quilt on the unmade bed. Her face softened. "We did it here once," she said dreamily.

Christ, Grace thought. The tawdriness of it repelled her. "Does your husband know?" she demanded.

Rosie's head snapped round. "I think he suspects," she started.

By the time she finished the sentence, Grace was half-way to the door.

She pounded downstairs. Bingo was nowhere to be seen.

"Sarge?" she yelled. "Bob!" There was no reply. "Bob!"

Rosie's mother, Mabel, came out of the lounge. "What is it?" she asked. "What's happened now?"

"Nothing," Grace said sharply. Then, realising the old lady looked terrified, she added more gently, "It's okay." She peered past Mabel into the lounge, but there didn't seem to be anyone else in there. "Where's Sergeant Tate?"

"He's just gone," Mabel said. "He's just gone – he said to tell you he'll see you back at the station."

Shit, Grace thought. She thought about asking if she could use the Chater's phone; but there really wasn't any point upsetting the old lady more than she had to. She turned and left.

***

Charlie Scott peered through the hatch in the door of Interview Room One. Michael Chater was sitting at the table, where he'd been when Charlie had left him. The ashtray was full of butts, and a thin blue haze filled the air. Chater held his latest cigarette listlessly between his fingers.

Charlie opened the door and went in and sat down opposite Chater. Ted Donachie followed him in and stood near the door.

"You," Charlie said. Chater stared at him. "You, Michael," Charlie repeated. He wondered if Chater could hear the sadness in his voice. He'd hoped so hard, but he'd been wrong. "You set this job up. Whether it was off your own bat or after someone put pressure on you, I don't know." Still Chater stared at him. "But you're in on the ground floor, no question."

"I don't know what you're on about," Chater said. His gaze flickered to the table and then back to Charlie.

"Mike, you put your mother-in-law up for grabs – your wife's mum." Charlie let that sink in, then feigned indifference, though he liked his own mother-in-law well enough. "Fair enough – who cares about her?" he went on. "The only problem is, young Darren doesn't get to nursery, does he?" He laid it out for Chater. "So the villains have to take him on board as well – and that's your fault, Michael." He spat the last few words out.

"You're just trying to wind me up," Chater said. He stubbed his cigarette out hard.

"And your mate Ian's ready to die any minute," Charlie said over the top of the other man's words. "And if he does, you'll be an accessory to murder –"

"Manslaughter," Donachie said from his place by the door behind Chater.

The security man looked up at Charlie. He was breathing hard, now.

"At best," Charlie said evenly.

Chater shoved himself up out of his chair. "I'm not having any of this," he said as he crossed to the window.

Charlie stayed sitting down. "And why?" he asked Chater's back. "Why'd you do it? Because you found out your best mate is sleeping with your wife." Chater slammed his hands into the window pane. "She gave it up, Mike," Charlie said. No response. "She told us. She blames herself." Still no response. "You don't deserve her –"

Chater whirled round. "She never said that," he screamed.

"She'd never say it to you," Charlie agreed calmly. "But you found out about her and your best friend and you lost it." There was desperation in Chater's eyes now, and Charlie knew with gut-certainty that he'd won. "You did a deal to get your own back. You put a gun in an old woman's face, your best friend in a coma and your son out of his mind."

"NO!"

Charlie stood up. "Mike," he said quietly. "It's over. Come

69

clean – otherwise we'll just have to go all the way." Chater's fists clenched. "You'll have to spend all that time with your son screaming in your head about what you did to him." Jack hadn't screamed, but he'd begged: for no more injections, no more doctors poking at him, no more hospitals.

"You don't know anything," Chater snarled. A muscle underneath his eye began to jump.

"I know you're a scared man, Mike – because who else would sort his mess out the way you did?" Scared? Charlie thought. Oh yes, Mike Chater was scared – and if he wasn't maybe it was time to put the fear of God in him. In Charlie's book a man stupid enough to hurt his only son deserved anything he had coming to him. "I'm giving you the chance to tell me how it goes," he said. Chater stared at him blankly. "I mean it. Otherwise..." Mike let his voice trail off. Fear would fill in the end of the sentence for him.

Chater backed away from him. "You can't touch me," he said. Charlie grinned. He took a step forward. "You can't do that," Chater said again.

"No, you're right, Mike," Charlie said. He stood still. "I can't. You're absolutely right." He waited for the relief to show on Chater's face. Then he took a couple of quick steps forward. Chater moved back until he slammed into the wall. Charlie shoved his face up close to the security guard. "But you're not on tape, you've not been cautioned, and it's getting to the point where I don't care any more." If it had started out as a ploy to get Chater's attention, it wasn't that anymore. Charlie realised he was breathing hard. Jack lying in the hospital bed. Little Darren Chater, curled up foetal style, betrayed by his father. Charlie realised his fists were clenched. He stepped back, forced them to relax. To give himself time, he took his jacket off. "Now," he said. "If you don't give me a confession, I'm going to rip your fucking neck out – got me?"

Chater looked as if he'd already been hit. He stared beyond Charlie, to Donachie. But the DC had found something fascinating to look at on the floor. Charlie arranged his jacket carefully on the back of the chair.

Come on Chater he thought; and he knew in that moment

70

that he wasn't bluffing. He concentrated on straightening the sleeves of his jacket.

There was a muffled sob. Charlie looked up. Chater was fighting back tears.

"It's okay, Mike," Charlie said gently. "It's okay – just talk to me."

Chater nodded. He collapsed on to his chair, and buried his head in his hands.

***

Bingo eased the car through the traffic on the King's Road. He'd have liked to move a bit faster, but getting nicked now would just slow him down. Not to say embarrass him.

His bleeper went. He reached down and switched it off without checking the screen. He bloody well knew who it was – Grievous Bodily Harm herself, screaming blue murder because he'd left her at home.

He grinned. Next right, he thought. He checked his rear view mirror, then hung a left. The short cut would take minutes off his journey. There was a set of lights ahead just turning from green to amber. Bingo checked his mirror again. He'd seen the Ford behind him before – it had been sitting on his tail before he turned the corner.

"Shit," he muttered, and put his foot down. The lights were red. He jumped them. There was a slow moving lorry ahead. He spotted a gap, swerved into the oncoming lane and back in front of the lorry before he had time to worry about what he was doing.

He whipped the car round the next left, then did a right.

The Ford was nowhere in sight.

***

Chater stared at the cassette recorder dry-eyed while Donachie turned it on. Charlie had been worried about the delay in getting it set up – given too much time to get his breath back, Chater might just have changed his mind about coughing.

"Interview started at nine fifty-five am," Charlie said. "Present are DI Scott and DC Donachie." Chater didn't speak. "Well?" Charlie prompted.

"Bloke called Langley threatened my family," he said. His

71

jaw worked. "I was in a pub in Peckham – used to play football for them." Charlie nodded. "He knew who I was – someone must have told him. I don't know who."

"Langley approached you?" Charlie asked.

"Yeah," Chater said. "He threatened Darren. Suddenly the old anger was back in his eyes. "Said he didn't think I'd want him to disappear..." his voice trailed off as he remembered.

"Go on," Charlie said.

"I told him he didn't have to do that – that I'd co-operate." He paused. "But I said if I set it up –"

"Set what up?" Charlie cut in.

"The raid on the van," Chater said impatiently. He went for a cigarette, but the packet was empty. "They'd have all the info they needed to do the job. But in return, above any money I got I wanted them to..." he stopped speaking. Starting again seemed to cost him something. "To hurt Ian McCallum," he said at last. Yeah, Charlie thought: well, it isn't every day you admit to a complete stranger that you're a total bastard, is it? "I found out he'd been having an affair," Chater went on. "With my... with my wife." His eyes were raw from crying, and now the tears seemed about to start again.

Charlie didn't give them a chance. "Did Langley lead the raid as well as organise it?"

Chater looked a bit surprised. He shook his head. "He didn't do either," he said. "The whole thing was put together by that bloke who broke out of Marshpoint yesterday."

Jesus, Charlie thought. "Dennis Worsley?" he demanded.

"Yeah, he was at the top end, even though he was still inside," Chater agreed.

Charlie reached over and clicked the tape off. "Interview suspended at ten-o-three am," he said.

Donachie left his place by the door. "Where are they?" he asked.

* * *

The office of the warehouse the gang was using was stacked haphazardly with furniture – tables and chairs, a couple of wardrobes and an old bureau.

Crap, Langley called it. Dirty crap at that, covered in dust

72

and filthy tarpaulins. Not to worry. They'd all be out of there soon enough.

He stared at the gang, and they stared back at them. All but Dennis. Well, sod him. If he wanted to play silly buggers instead of making a clean getaway, that was his business.

Sorting out the proceeds was Hazlitt. He'd already counted the money. Now he handed it out to the others, while Langley noted down what each one took. As for Dennis, he'd taken his the night before. Just as well. The bloke was bad news, and they all knew it.

Hazlitt picked up the final bundle of cash. "John," he said.

The lad took the wad of notes and rifled through it, obviously impressed.

"Get on with it," someone said.

John dropped the money into his sports bag. He grinned round at the others, obviously embarrassed.

"Right," Langley said.

He led them along and down the rickety platforms and stairs that let on to the yard. They'd built up quite a collection of vehicles while Dennis was putting the job together – a couple of bikes, a BMW and a Jag, among others. The Jag was Hazlitt's. Langley had picked out the BMW as soon as he'd seen it. John pulled on his crash helmet, then went and opened the gates.

John, on the bike, went left. Langley swung the BMW out into the alley but went right. Home free, he thought. Home fucking free.

***

"Go, go, go," said the spotter's voice from Helen's car radio.

"Game on," one of the others muttered from the back.

Helen had the car in motion before she had time to think about it. They screamed down into the alley from the road where they'd been waiting. A BMW came at them. Helen faked left. The other driver swerved right.

Helen slammed on the brakes and wrenched the wheel right. The suspension jounced as the car bucked to a stop and its rear end slewed round. It stopped inches from the warehouse wall, with the BMW almost touching it.

"Christ," Donachie said, "Women drivers..." but Helen was already out of the car, weapon in hand. The radio yammered, and someone was shouting. Oxford was at the BMW. He shielded his face with his arm and smashed the BMW's windscreen with his pickaxe.

Further up the alley a Jag had tried to reverse back into the warehouse, but the officers there were all over the driver.

Helen yanked open the door of the BMW. The driver shoved her in the chest and made a break for it. She grabbed his shoulder as he went past, and let his own weight swing him round. He stumbled and slammed to the ground. Helen followed him down. She jammed her knee into his back.

"Bitch," he muttered. Helen jabbed her knee a bit harder. Donachie grabbed his arms and cuffed him.

"Not bad for a woman driver, eh?" Helen said. Donachie grinned.

Scott came over. He squatted down next to the bloke. "Where's Dennis?" he demanded.

The man scowled. "Who?"

"Am I going to get bored punching you?" Scott asked, as if it were the most normal thing in the world. The man looked away. Before either of them could say anything, Oxford appeared at Scott's side.

"Guv'nor wants you, sir," he said. "Says he's got SO11 on the line – something you should know."

Scott got up and headed to his car.

Surveillance? Helen wondered. Maybe someone had got a line on Worsley. Be good to get the loose ends tied up, anyway, she thought as she pushed her man towards the van.

CHAPTER 9

Grace wasn't happy. In fact, she was massively pissed off. The special duty she'd been given – looking after Bingo – had gone wrong when he'd left her at the Chater's, and she'd had to report back what she'd learned instead of following him.

Then Scott had told her to stay here instead of working the plot like the others.

So here she was sitting by the phone listening to the Guv'nor talking to a pair of idiots from CID who hadn't been able to keep their eyes open for five minutes at a time.

"We've lost Tate," one of them admitted, his voice turned harsh by interference.

"You're winding me up," DCI Uttley's voice said.

"He lost us," the other voice protested.

Grace pondered for all of three seconds before she hit the transmit button. "Sir, this is DC Harris," she said. "I think I know where he might be..."

***

Bingo walked warily down the walkway to Cathy's boat. He tried to look casual, but he knew he wasn't very convincing. Hell with it, he thought, and stopped to give the place a good once over before he went on.

Cathy appeared on the deck of the boat. She was wearing a tracksuit. Travelling clothes, he wondered. "Bob," she called.

He went closer. There was a graze high on her cheekbone, and her lip was swollen.

"Shit," Bingo said. He took a step forward, then another. There was a movement in the shadowed entrance to the steps leading down. Dennis Worsley stepped out into the light. He was dressed in an electric blue suit, and his face and hands were daubed with fluorescent orange dye. If it hadn't been for the wicked little hand-gun he was holding, Bingo might have laughed at him.

Worsley stared at Bingo with utter contempt. "You raped my

wife, you bastard," he said. He levelled the gun.

Bingo's tasted copper. His stomach was a solid knot of ice. He spread his hands wide. "Let's just –"

He saw Worsely's finger tighten on the trigger. He swallowed. A shot cracked out. He'd dived sideways by the time he realised that Worsley had stumbled back, clutching his chest. He slammed into the rail of the boat, and toppled slowly into the water. His blue jacket billowed out around his body. His shirt was stained crimson.

Bingo whirled round. Grace Harris was standing behind the walkway wall. She was still holding her gun in the two-handed grip she'd been taught at college.

He turned to Cathy. She stared at him for a moment, then turned away and looked at the body.

***

Grace found she was shaking. She lowered the gun, then walked unsteadily back to the car. Her hands were trembling as she radioed in, and they still were when the rest of the team arrived.

Someone put a blanket round her. DI Scott came over and asked her what had happened. Something like that. She told him mechanically, letting her training take over because she felt so strange and disconnected from everything.

Oxford and Donachie were on the houseboat, talking to the woman. She was huddling in a blanket, and a drifting plume of smoke rose up from her cigarette. Off to the side, Bingo, who was also wrapped in a blanket, was talking to Uttley. Or, being Bingo, shouting. Ash stood nearby, simply listening.

"You set me up," he yelled. "You set me up as piece of bait!"

Uttley was as stolid as ever. "No we didn't –"

Bingo wasn't having it, though if he hadn't deliberately lost his tail, Grace reckoned he'd have had a better case. "You used me to trap Dennis," he said. "And gave me a bleeding novice for protection." So that's it, Grace thought: they hadn't given Bingo anyone more experienced because if they had, Worsley might just have walked away from it. Bingo wasn't the only one who'd been set up. She dismissed the thought – the job was the job, and you had to believe the Guv'nor would do his best by you. But anger snapped through her, and it made her feel more like her usual self.

76

"Oh shut up," Uttley was saying. "He's dead, isn't he?"

If looks could have killed, the team would have been looking for a new guv'nor. "I don't believe you did this," Bingo snarled.

"What you moaning about?" Uttley asked. "You wanted protection – you got it." He turned and walked away.

Ash grinned at Bingo. "No-one likes to see that," she said.

Bingo started to answer, but before he could say anything, Uttley turned back. "Oh yes, Helen – Mrs McCallum called." Now it was Bingo's turn to grin. "She says you gave her son a brain haemorrhage. Says she's going to sue – and if he dies, it's manslaughter." He turned again, and walked away.

Bingo laughed, a harsh bark. "No-one likes to see that," he said.

Grace grinned. Bingo glared at her, and she turned away. Scott was watching her. He walked over and held his hand out. Grace realised she was still clutching the gun.

"You okay?" he asked. Grace bit back a snappy reply, and simply nodded. "Helen's got the number of the Force counsellor." That sounded like Ash, Grace thought irritably. But she smiled anyway, and wondered whether Ash had ever needed the counsellor herself. "Ring her," Scott said. "You'll need to."

Grace nodded. She looked past Scott and saw that Oxford was on his way over, having finished with the Worsley woman. Scott raised his eyebrows at him.

"Some shot," Oxford said. "You aim to kill him?"

That did it. Grace had had it with being patronised. "No," she snapped. "I aimed to really piss him off."

She stalked off, so she could pretend not to see Scott motion to Oxford to ignore her outburst, but not so fast to avoid him touching her on the arm to make her wait. She turned reluctantly.

"Well, I'll take Bingo back," Oxford said. "Helen's lumbered with Miss Whiplash."

Scott nodded. Oxford smiled at Grace. She managed a quick smile back before he went over to Bingo. Her fingers knotted in the blanket.

"You did the right thing," Scott said softly. "You saved his life. That's quite a trick."

Yeah, thought Grace, staring at Bingo's retreating back. So why doesn't someone tell Bingo that?

PART TWO

COMPANY OF STRANGERS

CHAPTER 10

They were going to do it. They really were going to do it. Jimmy Gillespie could feel the cold sweat starting to prickle down the back of his neck when he thought about it. Next to him in the car, Johnny Hudson cradled the Tesco's bag on his knees.

Gillespie grinned. He knew what was in the bag. It was all planned.

Stan was driving. He was a white guy, but he was okay. Nothing wrong with white guys – Jimmy's dad had been a white guy, after all.

Got to calm down, he thought. He'd had his pills, like the doctor told him, so he knew there really wasn't anyone talking to him in his head, telling him about white guys, reminding him of his dad. Or his mum. No, he didn't need to think about that.

Not when Stan was easing the car to a standstill right near the building society, and they were really, really going to do it. Johnny nodded to Jimmy, and gave him the carrier bag, and they both got out of the car. They had to shimmy through the space between two other cars, because Stan wasn't bright – not like Jimmy – and he'd double parked.

Jimmy giggled. Soon it would be all over, and the Greek would be off their backs. But first he was going to have some fun.

Johnny went into the building society. Jimmy followed him. It was just like Stan had described it – the counter for the cashiers at the back, and the staff door with its combination punch lock at the side.

Johnny stopped, and Jimmy stumbled into the back of him. Johnny turned round and hissed at him. Anyone else, Jimmy would have killed him for that, but Johnny was a mate and you don't kill your mates.

***

It was going wrong, Stanley Callow thought. Jimmy was all

81

hyped up, and who the hell would have thought there'd be nowhere to park? So here he was behind the wheel of a bloody great BMW, double parked and drawing all kinds of attention.

And the last thing he needed was coming down the road towards him: a bloody traffic warden, all dressed up in khaki and a peaked cap, like some secret policeman in Eastern Europe, wandering down the road giving out tickets.

Got to look cool, Stanley thought. Just waiting here for my mates, that's all.

Could have been worse. He grinned. Could have been a clamper van.

***

There were three cashiers – all skirts, two of them white, one Asian. Johnny went over to the Asian woman's position; Jimmy followed him, but stood a bit further back. They'd rehearsed this. He knew what to do.

Johnny had pulled his little handgun out from under his tracksuit top. He shoved it towards the Asian woman.

Jimmy reached into the carrier bag and pulled out the sawn-off shotgun. He cradled it on his hip so it pointed at one of the white women. But he knew and they knew that he could do any of them before they could even start to yell for help. He could see it in their eyes. It was good.

They were doing it, really doing it. The Asian woman stared at them, all glazed eyes and stupid-looking.

"Give us the money, now!" Johnny shouted. He slipped the safety catch off the pistol.

"Yeah!" Jimmy added. "Move it!" Cold sweat prickled on his face, on his palms. He needed some stuff, he thought. But not before they'd done this.

The fucking bitches weren't moving. He stepped forward and slapped his free hand down hard on the counter. A security screen sliced upwards. He felt pain screaming through his hand and then his finger was pumping blood everywhere, a thin stream of it shooting out like piss and rattling against the grille.

He spun round. He couldn't think for agony. He felt himself falling – felt his fingers go into spasm on the trigger and the weapon buck in his hand. A sound like thunder and him screaming, and someone shouting. Something white drifting over him, like snow. The shotgun fell to the floor. He stared at his hand, not understanding. His finger wasn't there anymore. Not all of it.

Then someone was yanking at him. Johnny. He stumbled out after him. Quicker. Got to move quicker. There were people around – someone in a uniform. Might be a cop. Into the car, but all he could really think about was the ball of pain that was his hand. Johnny was behind him.

Christ man, Jimmy thought. Just get in and –

– there was a double crack – first a pistol shot, then the plate glass window fell in behind the guy who could be a cop.

Johnny threw himself into the car and slammed the door. Stan floored the accelerator and they screamed away, clean away.

"Fucking traffic wardens," Johnny muttered.

"What did you do that for?" Stan asked over his shoulder. "You could have killed somebody."

"Good," Johnny said. He stroked the little gun.

Jimmy squeezed his finger. There wasn't so much blood now. "Yeah, good," he said.

Johnny was his friend. If Johnny wanted to kill someone, that was all right with Jimmy.

***

Charlie Scott stood by the Scene of Crimes Officer who was searching the floor of the building society, and watched his team work. They were good, no doubt about it. Bingo and Harris were outside, trying to sort out which of the passers-by had actually seen anything.

Ash was attempting to calm down one of the cashiers. The woman was sobbing quietly. Two spots of colour stood out on her pale cheeks. As Charlie watched, her colleague, who was ashen faced but determinedly calm – and in his opinion, probably in a worse state of shock – handed her a glass of water. It didn't help. Her hands, so pale the veins stood out in blue lines on them, shook. The water slopped everywhere. Ash patted her on the arm, and she tried a smile.

Meanwhile, Oxford was having a better time. He was talking

83

to the other cashier, Sundra Matay. For someone who'd had a gun stuck in her face not fifteen minutes ago, she was doing well. Oxford said something to her, and she nodded vigorously, so that the gold at her throat and ears glittered in the morning sunlight. She was the one who had triggered the alarm, Charlie remembered.

"Sir?" The SOCO held up something with a pair of tweezers.

Charlie peered at it. It was a fragment of something bloody. "What's that?"

The SOCO turned the fragment round. Bone showed white at the end. "Looks like the top of someone's finger."

"Looks like someone's going to have trouble picking their nose," Charlie said. He never had been squeamish. The SOCO dropped the gobbet of flesh into a ziplok bag and started to pull off his transparent surgical gloves. Charlie jerked his thumb at the security camera. "How soon before I can have the video?"

"I'll get it for you now," the SOCO said. He stowed his gear and headed through the door into the office at the back.

"Thanks, Tom," Charlie said.

Ash and Oxford finished with their witnesses and came over to him. "Sounds like our team," Oxford said, "Two black guys, one much paler than the other and wearing a black leather cap. Sounded like he was right out of it, too –"

Charlie turned to Ash. "I think so," she said. "But those two are pretty shaken up."

Charlie looked at the ceiling. A chunk of it had been blown off, and the surrounding area was a jigsaw of cracks speckled with stray shotgun pellets. "I'm not surprised," he said. "These lunatics are going to kill someone if we don't get them off the streets. What's this?" Charlie went on, "Three jobs in four days?"

Bingo came in the front door and headed towards them. His eyes flicked towards the Asian cashier. "She's pretty, isn't she?" he said when he arrived. "The one on the left?"

Charlie sighed. Typical bloody Bingo. "Tate?" he said.

"Yeah?" Bingo answered.

"Shut up."

Bingo pulled a face but he didn't say anything else. He

didn't stop looking, though.

The SOCO came back. He handed Charlie the security video. "There you go," he said.

"Thanks," Charlie said. He smiled at Bingo. "Get that up to St Albans," he said, handing the box on.

"St Albans?"

"You deaf?" Charlie asked. He had the satisfaction of watching Bingo trying to suppress a scowl as he turned and left.

"You finished here?" DCI Uttley's voice came from Charlie's right. He turned and nodded. The Guv'nor was on his way to the door. "Let's go," he said, then added over his shoulder to the SOCO, "See if you can get that bullet from the shop next door."

Charlie caught him up, and they left the building society together. As they walked to their cars, Uttley said, "If Tate has a problem then he can hit the pavement." He opened his door. "I can't afford passengers." He started to get in the car.

"Tate'll be okay – he just feels bitter about the Worsley business," Charlie said. He hadn't figured out what was riding Bingo worse – the fact that he felt he'd been set up, with only Grace for protection, or the fact that she'd saved his life.

"But he shouldn't bring it to work with him," Uttley snapped. "His trouble – his brains are between his legs." He banged the car door shut, bringing the conversation to a halt.

***

Grace strode across the car park. It was good to be back – better to be back when a major plot looked just about to go down. She suddenly realised that the Guv'nor was matching strides with her.

"Grace?" he said.

"Yes, Guv?"

"How did the counselling go?" he asked.

"Okay," Grace answered. Anyone else and she'd have told him to stuff it, but she could hardly do that with the Guv'nor. She managed a smile. "I enjoyed it." It was almost true: she'd started out thinking it was a bit soft – the counsellor had even accused her of fighting the process at one point – but eventually she'd found it quite absorbing. And at least the nightmares had stopped.

"That's good," Uttley said. "Feel rested?"

"Yes, Guv. I'm glad to be back."

"Great," Uttley said. "That's what I like to hear." He patted her shoulder.

***

Alan had seen it coming a mile off, but there wasn't a lot he could do about it. Scott came up to him as he was on his way into the station from the car park entrance.

"You've got a couple of black snouts, haven't you?" he asked.

"Yeah," Alan said. He still stung when he remembered Robbie Killigrew calling him a Bounty bar – but he dealt with it the easiest way he could, by not thinking about it. Besides, a good copper used every tool at his disposal: for Ash it was her sex; for him it was his colour. As far as he was concerned, it just put him one step ahead of the rest.

"I want you to get hold of them – see what they know about these building society jockeys." Scott stuck his hands in his windcheater pockets.

"Okay," Oxford said. That would put him one step ahead, all right. "How far do you want me to push it?"

Scott shrugged. "Do what you have to – they're your snouts."

Good enough, Alan thought. That left it up to him, which was pretty much how he liked it.

***

The sodium glare of the streetlights fractured on the rainwashed pavements. Alan glanced at the building across the street – from the outside it looked like any other terraced house with an absentee landlord and tenants without the will or the cash to care about it. He checked his watch. It was gone one in the morning. Bryony had hated him going out, but she knew the score: he'd warned her when he'd married her that the job and a good family life wouldn't fit together well, but she'd just grinned and said nothing worth doing came easy.

He sighed and got out of the car, making sure he locked the door securely behind him. He pulled his collar up against the rain and hurried up to the house. As he got closer he heard the insistent throb of a reggae backbeat. He took the steps up to the door two at a time. There was no bell, and only a patch of bare wood where the knocker should have been, so he rapped on the door with his fist.

There was a rattle and thump, and the door opened a crack. A face peered out at Alan.

"Wh'appen?" said the man in a heavy Jamaican accent.

"Open the door, man," Alan said, roughening up his own accent a bit.

"You a member?" The man shifted a bit, and in the light that bled through the crack Alan saw that he was mountainous, with a torso that must have taken months of solid gym work to create. Liked to show it off, too, judging by the sleeveless vest he was wearing. Alan could appreciate that.

"Yeah," Alan said, hoping he wasn't getting into anything he couldn't get back out of.

"You don't look like no member," the doorman said.

Maybe it's true what they say, Alan thought. Maybe all policemen do look the same. "No?" he said, wondering if he dared ask for his snout by name. He ran his hand over his bald head, so that his denim jacket fell open, showing off the gold chains and tight vest underneath it. At a guess, he'd have said there wasn't much between him and the man mountain.

"No." The doorman started to slam the door.

Alan shoved it back with the flat of his hand. "Look man," he said, putting desperation in his voice. "I need something, you know?"

The doorman let out a big sigh. Come on, come on, Alan thought. The other man stepped back. The chain rattled and he opened the door. The music thundered out. He stood framed in the doorway, silhouetted by the strobing glare of a disco light somewhere deeper in the house.

"What you need, man?" he asked.

"I got to meet a friend," Alan answered, hoping he wouldn't have to give a name. Getting his snout done in wasn't part of the plan. It was true, though. He'd spent most of the afternoon hanging out in a porn shop to contact the guy in the first place.

Now he had to meet him to find out if he'd come up with the goods.

The doorman stepped back, and Alan went inside. Behind him, the other man slammed the door and secured it with enough locks, bolts and chains to see to half of the Scrubbs. Then he sat down on a kitchen chair.

"G'wan," he said, jerking his head towards the rear of the house.

Alan went through. The back room was vast, lit by the strobe light and a rack of coloured disco lights that sat on top of a waist high stack of speakers. There were a few people dancing – a black guy and a white girl, and a couple of black girls slowly gyrating while a few other men watched appreciatively. But most of the men were sitting round drinking and playing cards or dominoes, or lounging against the walls talking in small groups; as for the women, they were mostly draped around a man, or making progress in that direction.

One of the men was Alan's snout. They didn't make eye contact, but Alan knew he'd been seen – Marcus was good like that. The girl with him – the one in the satin boob tube and the pelmet skirt – would be his girlfriend. If you could call someone he pimped for a girlfriend.

Alan went over to the trestle table in the corner that had been set up as a bar. He paid an extortionate price for a can of Red Stripe from the cans stacked against the wall.

He popped the tube and took a long swig from it – not enough to get himself tipsy, but enough to look convincing. If anyone realised who he was, Marcus was in deep shit. And Alan probably wouldn't be doing so well, either.

Marcus broke away from his group. Alan made a show of watching one of the girls on the dance floor. It wasn't so hard – she had a good pair of legs, nice tits and anyway Bryony was never going to know. He sipped his lager.

Out of the corner of his eye he saw Marcus high five one of his friends, then head for the bogs. One of the lads followed him. Christ, Alan thought, he can't be more than sixteen. No prizes for guessing what was going down there: just because Marcus made some of his money grassing for Alan didn't stop him making more dealing drugs small time.

Wait for it, Alan told himself. Wait for it. He counted to a hundred slowly, then forced himself to do it again. The record changed. The girl on the dance floor started over towards him. He shook his head at her and went to find the toilets.

The place was a hole – not only did it stank of piss, there was graffiti all over the peeling plaster, and used condoms on the floor. It wouldn't have surprised Alan to have found needles there, too. Marcus and the young lad were leaning against the end wall. Alan ignored them, and went to take a pee. There were a couple of cubicles to the right, but he used the urinals instead. He saw Marcus slip the lad a twist of paper – crack, most like, he reckoned – but he didn't react.

He took his time doing up his fly to give the kid time to wander off. Once they were alone, he turned round and said, "What have you got?"

Marcus didn't answer immediately; instead he flipped open each of the cubicle doors. When he was satisfied they were alone, he turned back to Alan. He seemed a bit strung out, Alan noted; but that was nothing new – he probably needed to do some deals before he could feed his own habit.

"Those building society gigs – I checked them out," he said. "Three guys – white driver and the two shooters are black –"

Alan went to one of the sinks. "Now tell me something I don't know," he said. He spun the taps and a thin stream of water trickled out.

"It's about drugs, man." Sweat beaded Marcus's face. He licked his lips.

"Drugs," Alan said.

"They spoiled a batch of coke," Marcus said. Well, Alan thought, that would be one less load of crack out on the streets wrecking lives. But he didn't say anything. "They owe someone money for it," Marcus finished.

Alan looked around for a towel, but there was none. Marcus pulled a grubby handkerchief from his pocket and handed it to him. "Thanks. Know who they owe?"

Marcus shrugged. "Some Greek guy. Don't know his name, but he must be heavy 'cause these guys are really scared –"

"So they're pulling jobs to pay this Greek guy his money back?"

"Yeah – like, they're desperate, man." Marcus rubbed his face with his hand. "I mean, like this Greek guy will kill them if they don't pay up."

"Okay. Get me some names and an address, okay?" He pulled a twenty out of his pocket and handed it to Marcus, who made it vanish into his jeans.

All right, he thought. Now he really was one step ahead.

CHAPTER 11

Yannis Constantine rolled the dice. They rattled across the mahogany backgammon board. A five and a four. Good numbers. He cut a piece of melon and sucked it while he considered which of his pieces to move.

Across the table, his opponent, Stakis, showed no signs of impatience. A wise man, for one so young, Stakis had learned well the lesson that Constantine had taught him: it is not winning, but how you play the game that matters. Thus, his playing of the backgammon game revealed a proper understanding of the relative positions of himself and his patron, Constantine.

The door rattled. Constantine's head whipped up. He was sitting with his back to a corner, but you could never be too careful. There were enemies, always enemies – jealous men, men weaker or less clever who felt he had done them wrong.

But not this time. Constantine relaxed when he saw who was coming through the door: Gillespie, Hudson and Callow.

Fools all three of them; and Gillespie in particular was a dangerous fool. But not to Constantine, no. To Constantine they were an annoyance, like a fly buzzing around on a summer's day. They would like to think they could sting, like the wasp: but like the fly they were harmless.

Harmless but arrogant. Hudson sat down at the table. "Mr Constantine, I can explain everything." He had the good grace to sound nervous. "We've brought your guns back."

Like flies, they demanded swatting. "Why are you sitting at my table?"

"What?"

Constantine sliced another piece of melon. "Did I give you permission to sit at my table?"

"No." Hudson sounded sullen.

"Then get up!" Constantine roared. They were fools who

needed everything doing for them. "I want my money." He slammed his hand down on the table, making the backgammon pieces jump.

Hudson stood up. His face was tight with anger, but he said nothing. So, Constantine thought – a coward as well as a fool.

"You fire your gun for no reason, which means it is dirty." He put ice in his voice. Let them fear him. "I cannot use it again. I cannot even sell it." Not with police forensics working on the bullet even now. He turned to Gillespie. The man stared back at him insolently. "And you – you fire your gun at the ceiling." No reply. "Why?" He spat the word out.

"Like I said," Hudson answered for his friend, "Everything went wrong."

Ah, they were fools, Constantine thought. Not worth his anger, or even much of his attention. He let his anger drain out of him. They had their uses... yes, fools like them were expendable. "Okay," he said. "You can sit. But I still want the rest of my money, and you will have to do me a favour."

Gillespie waved his hand in Constantine's face. There was a bit of bandage round the tip of one finger. "I nearly lost my hand, Mr Constantine," he whined.

They would try the patience of the saints in heaven, Constantine thought. He picked up the knife he'd been using to cut the melon. It was a wicked little steak knife and he held it up in front of him so the blade glittered in the lamplight.

He turned to Hudson. "Tell that imbecile to shut up or I will drive this knife straight through his syphilitic heart."

"Shut up," Hudson said to Gillespie.

"Now, this favour –" Constantine said. The three men stepped a little closer.

It was perfect, Constantine thought: if they did it without being caught, they were free to try and repay his money. If they got captured, he would be rid of an annoyance, which would almost be worth losing a bit of cash for.

Though if they failed... well, if they failed he'd have someone to make an example of.

***

The house was quiet when Alan got back. The hall was in

92

darkness, except for a line of light from under the living room door. He went in.

Bryony was asleep on the sofa with a book flopped open at her side. Alan stared down at her for a second. Her plaits trailed across the back of the sofa; her eyes fluttered under her closed lids, and her hand was curled into a fist, like a child's, by her cheek. She was so damn vulnerable: and she worried about him so much... Sometimes he was just blown away by the luck he'd had in meeting her. He bent and kissed her gently on the forehead.

Her eyes batted open. She stared up at him bleary eyed. "What time do you call this?" she murmured

"Dinner time?" Alan said, also softly. He leaned down and kissed her again, this time on the mouth.

"I love you," she said.

"Why didn't you go to bed?" Bryony was an ex-policewoman herself. If anything, it meant she worried more – she knew exactly what the score was.

"I can't." She gave a little wriggle. "Not until you get home. You know that."

Alan smiled. "Yeah," he said. One or two of her plaits had fallen over her face. He brushed them back gently. "I do know."

She covered his hand with her own, then pulled him down to her. A little while later, bed seemed very much the best place to be.

***

"Hey, Thaso," Johnny said as he walked beside Mr Constantine's friend. The Greek man looked round. "You and Mr Constantine good friends, huh?"

They had found him at home, and invited him to one of Mr Constantine's card games. No-one turned down an invitation from Mr Constantine. Not if they knew what was what.

"Yes," he said. "We are from the same village in Cyprus."

"Oh yeah?" Gillespie asked. He glanced out of the window. The lights of London were spread out far below them, glittering in the darkness. How high up were they? Jimmy wondered. A hundred, two hundred feet. Might as well have been a mile. They walked towards the lift, Thaso between him and Johnny.

"Yes," Thaso said. "We are like this –" He held his hand up and crossed his fingers. Jimmy stared at his hand, not sure if the Greek man was taking the piss, but he went on, "So, is it a big game?"

Johnny nodded. "Oh yeah, it's a very big game – a lot of money."

Jimmy grinned. "A lot of money," he said, and watched the Greek's eyes. Thaso was interested now, but cautious.

So he should be. He had no idea what he was in for.

***

Just got to do what I'm told and it'll be all right, Stanley Callow thought. He jabbed a finger at the lift button again, though it was already lit.

Eventually, the door clattered open. He looked round quickly. No-one was in sight. He pulled a screwdriver out of his back pocket, and wedged it in the top of the door, jamming it.

He stepped inside. The place stank of sweat and piss. He pressed the button for the second floor, then stepped out before the lift started moving.

Done my part, he thought. That's all I have to do. He leaned back against the wall and waited.

***

They'd nearly done it, and no mistakes – no way for the Greek bastard to get at them for this one, Jimmy thought. He pressed the lift button. Got to be cool, he thought.

Johnny must have thought so too. "You like playing poker, Thaso?"

"Greek poker, yes," Thaso said. He smiled, all white teeth against his olive skin.

"What's the difference?" Jimmy asked, not really caring but just wanting to keep him talking, keep him interested.

"We play with two decks," Thaso explained. "A game could last maybe three or four days."

Johnny took out his packet of fags. "That long?"

Thaso nodded. "Sometimes longer."

Johnny offered Thaso a cigarette and lit it for him. The lift door opened. Thaso took a long drag of the cigarette, turned and went into the lift.

He vanished into oblivion.

***

Stan stared up into the darkness of the lift shaft. What was taking them so long? One bunch of clubbers coming back drunk and they'd be done for sure...

The lift shaft rang like a bell, and the cables leading up inside it shivered.

Stan grinned. He stepped back and yanked his screwdriver out of the door, which slid closed.

He wondered idly how long it would take Thaso's body to start smelling, and how long after that it would be before they tracked it down to the top of the lift.

CHAPTER 12

Alan made sure he was in early the next morning. He was rewarded with the sight of Bingo ambling out of DI Scott's office. He looked tired and pissed off.

"Guv'nor wants to see you," he muttered as he passed Alan on his way to the coffee machine. "Seems some of us have got real work to do."

Alan went into the office to face Uttley and Scott across the cluttered desk.

Alan took the photo DI Scott handed him. It had come from the security camera in the building society, and it showed a young black guy with rather pale skin and wearing a leather cap.

"Look at that," Scott said. "He's staring right at the camera."

Alan put the photo on the desk. If there were more inept robbers out there, he was going to grow old looking for them. Scott put another photo beside the first one. This one showed another black guy, this one with short dreadlocks. He was jabbing a handgun at the Asian cashier.

"Take some of these out and see if your snout recognises any of them," Scott said. "And get some to the press as well."

"Sure," Alan said. He started to leave, glad to be at the heart of the job.

"Tell Bingo I want to see him," Scott said. "And take Harris with you."

Alan turned. "What for?" he demanded. He could well do without someone who was always standing on her honour and was gun-happy with it. "I don't need her –"

"She can go places you can't," Scott replied.

"Like where?"

"Try the ladies' toilets," DCI Uttley said. He grinned.

Alan scowled. As he left the room he heard Uttley ask, "What's he got against Harris?"

What have I got against her? Just that she's gun-happy, he

thought. Don't want her getting nervous and making a sieve out of my snouts, that's what.

Not that she could, of course – they hadn't been issued with weapons.

But that wasn't the point.

***

Charlie sat back wondering if there was anything he'd missed – any line of enquiry they should be pursuing but weren't. Nothing came to mind. Uttley had already gone. The Guv'nor was a good man to work for – if he'd spotted anything, he'd have said so without making an issue of it.

There was a tap on the door and Bingo walked in. He still seemed a bit grouchy, and Charlie wondered if he really understood just how close he was to being kicked out.

The best he could do for him was to give him a chance to make good. "I want this Greek as well as the raiders," he said. "Oxford's informant says he's big –"

Bingo cut in. "Oxford's snout? I heard he's a coke dealer."

No sense of brinkmanship, that was Bingo's problem. One of them. "He's a small time street dealer," Charlie said, "and he's come across with some good information in the past –"

"So now we're buying information from scum like-"

"At least we know Oxford doesn't screw his informants," Charlie said, patience finally snapping.

"I see," Bingo said coldly. He turned to leave.

"Try and get a lead on this Greek guy," Charlie said to his retreating back. "Report back to me if you turn anything up." You had to spell things out to Bingo – otherwise he'd claim he hadn't realised what you wanted.

From the set of his back he didn't like being told though. That was his other problem, Charlie reckoned – first he acted like a child, then he got bolshie if you treated him like one.

***

Ted Donachie balanced a cup of coffee, a triangular pack of ham and coleslaw sandwiches, a packet of crisps and a doughnut on the tray he was carrying from the canteen to his desk. He was going through witness reports from the building society, and there were a lot of them.

97

Two of them had given partial number-plates for the BMW the thieves had used; Ted was wondering whether either or both were reliable when he saw Grace coming towards him, also carrying breakfast on a tray.

Ted raised his tray towards her. "Snap," he said. Behind her back the other blokes called her the ice-queen – and other, cruder, names – but Ted had never had a problem with her.

"Late night?" she asked, and smiled. Close to, she looked tired – pallid, rather than merely pale, and with dark rings beneath her eyes.

"What, you as well?" he asked.

She frowned. "Sorry?"

"I said 'snap', and you said 'late night' and..." Ted let his voice trail off, not quite knowing what had gone wrong with the conversation after all. "It doesn't matter." He shrugged, then regretted it as his coffee slopped over the doughnut.

She stared at him for a second. "Well," she said, and started down the corridor again.

"Grace?" Ted said, before she could leave.

"Yes?"

Now what the bloody hell did he think he was going to say to her? It's nice to have spent two minutes talking to each other? Something like that. "How are things?" It was all he could think of.

She turned back. "Things?"

"I mean, after the Worsley business – any problems?" Christ, he thought. This was the woman who'd bitten men's heads off for asking the time in the wrong tone of voice. They all knew she'd tried to wriggle out of seeing the counsellor, and here he was asking for it.

But she smiled and shook her head. "No, no problems. Everything's fine."

Well, that was the end of that conversational ploy. But Ted found that his mouth didn't seem to agree. "Well, if you ever want to talk," he said without any intervention from his brain at all, "You know, go for a drink, or perhaps a meal –" She was staring at him. What the hell am I saying he wondered. Mary would kill me... "I don't mean like that," he added, far too quickly.

"Like what?" Grace asked innocently.

"You know," he said. "As friends..." I'm a married man, he thought. I couldn't possibly mean anything else, now could I?

But apparently Grace wasn't sure herself. "Friends?"

Ted looked at his feet. "God, could you make this any harder?" But then he thought, all I'm doing is asking a colleague to go drinking with me. There'd not be a problem if she were a bloke.

Suddenly Grace was laughing, and he was; and he thought, she's so much prettier when she smiles.

Just then, Alan popped his head round the incident room door. "Grace," he called. "Come on – we've got to get to work!"

Instantly, Grace was all business. She hurried towards Alan. "What's up?" she asked. Before he could answer she said over her shoulder, "Yeah, I'll take you up on that, sometime, Ted." She grinned, and again Ted realised how pretty it made her. "It would be nice." Then she disappeared into the incident room.

Ted thought, I'm just asking a colleague to go out for a drink, nothing more.

Nothing more.

But if that were the case, he couldn't quite understand why he was suddenly smiling.

CHAPTER 13

Marcus lounged against the wall of the disused cinema. He took a quick little puff of his cigarette as he surveyed the punters in the street. Or, rather, the lack of them. Debbie had said she'd had a bad night. He was beginning to see why. He glanced at her. She was all right, Debbie was: she had the equipment to do the job – legs up to here and boobs out to there – and she didn't give him a hard time. Usually.

But today she was pissed off. She'd laddered her fishnet tights and her face looked pinched with the cold. She slipped off one of her stilettos. "I want to go home," she said.

"It's early yet," Marcus said impatiently. She might be all right, but she still had to earn her keep.

"It might be early for you but it's late for me," Debbie said. She rubbed her heel with her hand. Her fingers were short and stubby, but the nails were long. Her nail polish was chipped, though, and her fingertips were nicotine stained. Marcus thought he'd better have a word with her about that.

A dark blue BMW drew up to the kerb. Debbie slipped her shoe back on. A hard smile appeared on her face. She went up to the car.

"You want business, love?" she asked.

Someone in the car said, "Get out of my face!" Debbie moved back, looking cheesed off. There were three men in the car – two black guys and a white driver. "Hey, you!" the guy in the front passenger seat shouted, "Come here, man!"

"What do you want?" Marcus shouted from by the wall. He wasn't running over there like a trained dog.

The guy started to open the car door. "Just get over here."

Marcus walked over, slow as may be. He didn't want the guy thinking he'd won, or anything. "So?" he said, when he got there.

"I want some rocks," the guy said, cold as ice. 'Bout time I made some money, Marcus thought. They looked like high rollers – street hard, but with money. Could be a good deal.

The driver leaned over. "And my stuff."

"Shut your mouth," the passenger said.

Marcus pulled a packet of crack out of his jacket. "How much you want?" he asked.

The guy grabbed it and threw it on the back seat. "This'll do," he said. "Get going," he said to the driver.

"Hey man! What do you think you're doing?" Marcus yelled, but the car was already pulling away.

"You want to mess with me, man?" The passenger gave Marcus a smile like a knife edge.

"Who do you think I am," Marcus started. "I'll –" he felt Debbie's hand on his arm.

"That's all right," she said. "We don't want no trouble." She flashed the man in the car a nervous smile.

The passenger nodded. "You should listen to your woman, man."

The car finally pulled away. Marcus rounded on Debbie.

"Is there something wrong with you, or what?" he demanded.

"That's them," she said, as if it explained everything.

"What?"

"The guys doing the building society jobs – the one's who owe Constantine the money," she said. Her hand went to her throat. "The guy on the back seat's a loonie – a right psycho. He just got out."

Marcus was appalled. He grabbed Debbie by the arms and glared at her. "Constantine? You didn't say nothing about Constantine – you said some Greek guy." He rubbed his eyes. "Oh my God, and you know them?" He stared at Debbie until she nodded. "And they know you're my woman?"

Debbie nodded again. She seemed upset, but he could tell she didn't really get it. "Yeah," she said. "The guy who nicked the rocks is Johnny Hudson. I went with him round their squat. Blyton Street, it was –"

"Shut up!" Marcus yelled. "You're burying me. You're burying me..."

***

"When I meet my bloke don't get out of the car, all right?" Oxford said. He pulled away from the traffic lights.

Grace glared at his profile. "Is that an order, Detective Constable?"

Oxford glanced at her. He obviously wasn't happy. "Look, I didn't ask for you to be here."

"I wouldn't want to cramp your style," she said.

"Don't worry, you won't."

Grace stared out of the side window. She grinned to herself. Yet another opportunity to prove herself to her male colleagues. What would her life be like without them?

***

Marcus raised his collar against the thin rain that had begun to fall. The copper should be here soon, for sure. He looked around the waste ground where he had arranged the meet. He shivered, and felt the cold sweat start on the back of his neck. There was no-one in sight, only mounds of moulding furniture, rotting mattresses and a broken television staring blindly at the sky. But the place was surrounded by derelict factories. For all he knew Hudson and his cronies could be scoping him out with binoculars right at that moment. Yeah, that was it for sure. He'd started to move back into the shadow of a carton that had once held an industrial freezer, when he heard the purring of a car engine.

The car stopped. There were two people in it, but only Oxford got out. He picked his way across the mounds of rubbish to where Marcus was waiting.

"Who's in the car?" Marcus demanded. His heart was hammering, triple time. The light was too bright. It was pissing down with rain, the sky was like lead, but the light was fit to sear his eyeballs.

"Nobody, man," Oxford said. White light glared off his black skin. Maybe he didn't trust whoever it was either, because he turned round so he could see the car. Great, Marcus thought. He turned round too, but so his back was to it, for all the good it was going to do him. As he did so he got a glimpse of a white face and long dark hair.

"She a cop?" he asked. He pulled out a cigarette and lit it.

He didn't offer Oxford one.

"I just told you, she's nobody," Oxford said. "She can't even see you."

Oh sure, Marcus thought. So how come he could see her? "You setting me up?" he demanded. He kicked a box on the ground. A couple of used condoms rolled out of it. "What you doing this to me for?" Oxford didn't answer. "You're setting me up, man," Marcus said, sure of it now. Yeah, that was it – Constantine had got to him somehow. Everyone knew cops were bent as a slinky toys, no reason this one should be different. He dragged on his cigarette.

"Calm down, no-one's setting anyone up here." Oxford looked hard at him. "Are you high?"

High? That was copper speak all right. "I took some stuff. I needed to chill out, you know?"

"Well, it ain't working," Oxford said. Fucking joker, Marcus thought. The copper pulled a couple of photographs from under his jacket. "You know these people?"

Marcus stared at the pictures. The goddamn ripoff artists from the BMW stared up at him. He swallowed. His mouth felt like it was full of sand and glue. "I don't know," he said. "I got one name." Christ, he was starting to shake now. "What you want, anyway – bringing another copper here." Setting me up, that's what – going to find myself down that station, sitting in some cell. Yeah, that was it – two cops' words against just his. "It's supposed to be private," he said, and realised he was shouting. He shoved the photos out of the way.

"All right, just calm down –" Oxford said.

But Marcus didn't want to be calm. He wanted to be somewhere cool and dark while he came down, and he didn't want some scumbag copper setting him up. Best thing he could do would be to get the hell out while he still could.

But he knew the bastard cop wouldn't let him go, not that easy. "Johnny Hudson," Marcus said. He pointed at the photos. "He's the one leading the crew, okay?" He jabbed a finger at the darker of the two black guys in the photographs. "That's him."

"What about this one," Oxford said. He held out the other photo.

It was the loonie who'd been in the back of the BMW. He looked mixed-race to Marcus, now he could see him close up.

"I told you – I don't know," Marcus said. He'd had enough. He wanted to get away, maybe do a joint or three to help him come down. Anything but stand around in the rain while this copper tried to get him to sign his own death warrant.

"Okay, okay," Oxford said. "Now, you got an address?"

Jesus! Marcus thought. "They'd kill me if they knew."

"Nobody's going to kill you, Marcus," Oxford said quietly. "You've got my word on that." He touched Marcus gently on the shoulder. The place where his fingers touched burned like a branding iron. Marcus jerked back. "Now," Oxford said. "An address?"

Marcus found he was shaking. He tried to stop. Couldn't. "Blyton Street. A squat." He tried to think. He had to make the copper understand. "Listen, Mr Oxford – they mustn't know you got it from me. No-one must." He was breathing hard. His fingers closed on the copper's sleeve. "The other shooter?" Oxford nodded. "He's a nutter – he just got out from nut jail." Oxford didn't seem impressed. "They're working for Yannis Constantine."

That got him. "You're joking!"

Marcus rubbed his nose. "You got to protect me, man." He felt his lip trembling. Christ. Not tears. Not in front of a copper. But he said, "I'm frightened."

"Just chill out," Oxford said. "Somebody's got it wrong." Yeah, Marcus thought – me, for even standing here talking to you. "These people can't be tied in with Constantine."

"Have I ever lied to you?" Marcus demanded. Fucking copper – setting him up and then not even believing him. "Have I?" He sucked on his cigarette. "I got to go." He waited for the nicotine rush, but it did nothing for him.

"Yeah," Oxford said. He pulled out a wad of notes. "But stay in touch, Marcus."

Marcus shoved the money away. "I don't want no money," he said. He wanted not to have opened his stupid mouth, but it was too late for that.

He strode away, not caring whether he walked on broken

glass or used needles or whatever junk was lying around.

He was a dead man, walking around. He could feel it in his gut.

"You stay in touch, Marcus," Oxford called from behind him.

"Yeah, sure," Marcus muttered.

***

"How is Thaso?" Yannis Constantine asked.

He held a copy of the local paper in his hand, and he was not happy about what he had found in it. The three idiots were back again, and they were smiling like fools – like they had done something he should be pleased about.

He despised them, and he hated the fact that they were here, in his restaurant. They had a smell about them, a smell of failure. Constantine hated it – he imagined it lingering after they had gone, clinging to him and all he had worked so hard to achieve.

Stakis was there also. But Stakis was not a fool. In time, he would take Constantine's place – Constantine was grooming him for that very thing.

"How is Thaso?" Constantine asked again.

"Gone away," Hudson said. His voice and his eyes were the same – flat and hard.

"I'm going to miss him," Constantine said. "He was a fine poker player." It was true. If only the man had not been a fool, if only he had not thought to sneak up on Constantine like an assassin in the night, he would never have got him killed.

"He was the son of a whore," Stakis said, in Greek.

"Never speak ill of the dead," Constantine said in the same language.

"You're right – I'm sorry," Stakis said immediately. It wasn't good, this tendency of his to apologise for everything he did, Constantine thought. He should learn to stand by his word – better yet, to guard his mouth, so that the only words that came out of it were worth defending. But he let it pass, for now. At least he had not spoken in English. To lose face in front of the three idiots would be intolerable.

Constantine turned to Hudson. "You made the local paper," he said.

The fool looked pleased. "We did?" he asked.

Constantine stabbed the headline with his finger. "'Three man gang attempt to rob building society'." There was a picture of the building, and the bullet shattered frontage of the dry cleaners' next door. He sighed heavily. "I like that word 'attempt'."

Hudson smiled briefly, then scowled when he worked out it hadn't been a compliment.

Gillespie waved his hand in the air. "I almost got my hand cut off, Mr Constantine."

Constantine stared at the grimy bit of bandage. The sight of it made him sick to his stomach. "Shut up about your pathetic finger," he snarled, "Or I will sever your head from the rest of your body."

"Yeah," Hudson agreed. "Shut up." He turned to look at Constantine, as attentive as any puppy dog.

"Well now, I have a problem," Constantine said. He laid the paper carefully down on the table and smiled thinly at the three men. "You see, my problem is that you cannot organise a straight piss between the three of you." They stared back at him blankly. Stakis smothered a giggle. "What am I to do?" he demanded.

"It'll be different next time –" Hudson cut in. As always, his mouth moved faster than his brain.

"Shut your stupid mouth," Constantine said. He had had enough of them. If it hadn't been for the small possibility that he might have to still get his money from them, he would have had them dealt with. "You talk when you should listen and listen when you should talk." He slammed his hand down on the paper. "Every time you take a breath you cost me money." He walked to the window, wondering if a wise man would have known when to cut his losses. But he was a fool himself, a sentimental fool. He would give them another chance. "Now," he continued when he could bear to do so. "I have given this much thought. I will pick your next job – a nice quiet sub-post office, with a fifty grand float in it." He heard Hudson suck his breath in. Good. Now he knew he had their attention. He turned back to them. "A job even you three cannot fail to pull off." He

106

smiled at them – the smile of the wolf, though he knew they would not recognise it – and continued, "Then I will have my money and we can all go our separate ways. He gestured at the door. "Now get out and don't come back until I send for you."

"Bye Mr Constantine," Gillespie said over his shoulder. He was laughing like a child.

Well, he'd learn. Or not. Constantine really didn't care any more.

***

Alan hadn't been looking forward to reporting back to the Guv. Not with Harris along to tell him how strung out Marcus had been. But it wasn't so bad, especially since she seemed to have decided to keep her mouth shut.

"So how reliable is your snout?" Scott asked from his perch on his desk.

Alan shrugged. "He's never let me down before." He glanced at Harris. "But he's scared out of his skin," he admitted.

"There's always a first time," Harris put in.

Thanks for nothing, Alan thought, but he didn't say anything. No point getting a reputation for being difficult to work with – not with the Guv, anyway.

"It's all we've got," Scott said. He got up and went over to the area map pinned to his wall. "I think we should set up a fixed OP." That was good, Alan thought – meant they were taking his information seriously, as opposed just to thinking about it. Scott tapped the map. "Blyton Street," he said. "They've got a Neighbourhood Watch scheme. Let's see if we can set up a surveillance unit in someone's house." He turned back to them. "Get Helen for me, would you Grace?"

"Yes, Guv," she said, with none of the reluctance Alan would have expected if he'd asked her to do something. She left the room.

"What about Constantine, Alan?" Scott asked. "Is your man serious?"

Alan thought about it for a second. Marcus was definitely serious – whether he was right or not was another matter. But he certainly didn't want to admit that to the Guv. "I only know what he told me," he said at last. "He said they were working for Constantine, and he definitely ID'd Hudson."

Scott nodded. "All right. Keep tabs on your snout." He looked suddenly thoughtful. "Maybe he's telling the truth."

Thanks very much for the vote of confidence, Alan thought as he left the room. But he knew Scott was right to be dubious – you didn't get to be a DI by accepting everything every hopped-up crack-head told you.

***

It had been one of those rare days when Charlie actually got to eat his sandwiches in peace. Pity he had to ruin it by talking to Bingo. He rolled up the paper bag, lobbed it at the waste-paper bin and missed, and left his office without bothering to pick it up.

He found Bingo by the coffee machine, and decided that if his lunch-hour had to be spoiled, Bingo's might as well be too. He took the cup out of the other man's hand and put it down by the machine.

"Come on," he said over Bingo's protests. "I've got a little something for you to do." He marched Bingo down the corridor in the direction of the exit to the car park. "Oxford's man's fronted up Constantine's name," he said by way of explanation.

"Oh what?" Bingo exclaimed. He shot Scott a look that was a mixture of disbelief and contempt. Scott ignored it. "Oxford's snout again? He's obviously mouthing off for drugs money."

Scott shrugged, terminally bored with Bingo's cynical-I'm-the-only-decent-copper-here routine. "Maybe he is," he conceded. "It's your job to find out, isn't it?"

They came to the door that led out to the stairs to the car park. Bingo paused. "Constantine's a runner – a pro backer. He puts money up for big robberies. Not this sort of thing." Scott glared at him. As if I don't know this already, he thought. But again, he didn't say anything. If making out how big he was helped Bingo do a better job, he was prepared to put up with that. Up to a point.

Bingo finally seemed to realise that he wasn't going to get a rise out of Scott. He turned and started through the door.

"Just check it out, okay?" Scott called after him. "And take your own car – I can't spare a driver."

108

Bingo's back went rigid, and Scott could just imagine the look of irritation on his face. Well, sod him, Scott thought. It was about time he learned to be a bit more of a team player.

***

Ted Donachie held the camera with one hand while he tightened the lug holding it to the tripod with the other. Ash held the whole thing steady, at the same time as she kept an eye on the squat across the road.

Cyril Underwood, the owner of the house, stood near the door. He was a short, round man – round face, balding bullet head, butterball body with a floppy blue cardigan. He shuffled his feet and made a soft harumphing noise in his throat. Ted ignored him.

He supposed it was good of the man to let them use his house. He glanced out of the window. The house opposite was half-way derelict. He grinned. It must give the good folk of Blyton Street apoplexy – such a slum, sandwiched there between two neat terraced houses. It couldn't do house prices any good at all. Especially not when it was being squatted by a bunch of druggies like Hudson's mob. Not that they were anywhere in sight.

Underwood harumphed again. At this rate he'd still be there when it was time for them to pack up and go.

Ash looked round. She smiled. "Thank you very much, Cyril," she said. Ted had never heard her sound more schoolmistressy.

"Would anyone like some tea and biscuits?" Cyril asked. Neither of them replied. "Or some corned beef sandwiches, or –"

"I think we're both fine at the moment, thank you," Ash cut in. It seemed a little harsh, but at least it spared them hearing the entire contents of Underwood's larder.

"You know, I'm not one to cast aspersions," Cyril said, "but the whole of that side of the street's like a running sore. It's foul with corruption and deviance –"

He was doing a pretty good job on the casting aspersions front, Ted reckoned. Before Underwood could get even more graphic, he said, "You know I think we will have that cup of tea after all, if it's not too much trouble."

Cyril smiled, revealing yellowing teeth like tombstones. He nodded his head. "No trouble, no trouble at all," he said. "I've got some home-made scones, too."

"The tea will be fine," Ted said hurriedly.

Underwood smiled again, but at least he did leave.

Ash scowled at Ted.

"What?" he asked.

"You know what," Helen answered; her Irish accent roughened up, the way it did when she was angry. "Tea and home-made scones —"

"Well, it was the only way to get him out of the room," Ted said.

There was no pleasing some people.

CHAPTER 14

Johnny was mad, Johnny was real stinking mad. He slammed around the room. He kicked the upturned bread crate they used as a coffee table, and when he reached the end of the room he whacked his hand into the wall, over and over again, like the way Jimmy had seen some of the guys at the hospital do, only with them it was their heads and mostly they didn't stop till one of the screws came and stopped them.

But Johnny, he just started pacing up and down the room again. Jimmy lay back on the mattress and watched him. Johnny in a rage was really something to watch.

Meanwhile Stan rolled a joint, cool as you please. Maybe that would mellow Johnny out.

"That lousy stinking rotten bastard," Johnny snarled.

"Who?" Stan said. He licked a cigarette paper and added it to the others he had joined together.

"That miserable low-life little prick," Johnny said.

"Who?" Stan said again. He poured some tobacco on the skins.

Jimmy leaned forward. "Who, Johnny?" he asked, though really he knew. He just wanted to see Johnny get all worked up.

"Constantine," he said at last. "Calling us names and shouting at us." That was true. Constantine shouldn't have done that. Johnny stood still, right in the middle of the room. "After this is all over, I'm going to rip his lungs out and set fire to his restaurant with him in it." A little bit of spit flew out of his mouth. Jimmy stared at it in fascination, but then Johnny started to talk again. "He thinks we're scum. Well I'm not scum." He stopped talking.

Stan flicked his lighter and held a little lump of dope in the flame. The smell got to Jimmy.

Maybe it got to Johnny too. "He didn't even thank us for doing that thing for him," he said.

111

Jimmy knew now. He grinned, felt his lips stretching back over his teeth and the wild laughter welling up from who knew where inside of him. "You want to kill him," he said.

"Yeah," Johnny said. "Yeah, I want to kill him."

The laughter bubbled up in Jimmy's throat. He let it escape. "That would be funny." He made a high-pitched giggling sound. "That would be real funny if we killed him with his own guns." He lay back on the mattress and started pulling stuffing out of one of the holes in it. It smelled a bit of cat's pee, but he didn't mind.

"I don't think that's a very good idea," Stan said. He sounded nervous. He crumbled a bit of the dope along the length of the joint.

Johnny rounded on him. "Why not?" he demanded.

Stan pulled a face. "I just don't, that's all."

"What do you think?" Johnny asked Jimmy.

"Kill him." It was a fine idea, an idea that made the laughter come bubbling up inside him.

"See?" Johnny said to Stan.

"Well, he would say that, wouldn't he?" Stan said. He picked the joint up, licked the papers and started to roll it. "I mean, he's crazy."

Jimmy didn't like that word. That was a school word. A Dad word. He reached under the mattress, pulled out his razor and rolled to his feet. Light glittered along the length of the blade. It had been his Dad's razor once, and his Dad had shown him how to keep it nice. That had been before all the trouble at home, of course.

"What did you call me?" he murmured.

But he knew what Stan had said, and he knew what he had to do.

"Sit down Jim –" Johnny said. He took a step towards Jimmy, arms spread wide. "Take it easy."

"He shouldn't call me that," Jimmy said. He swished the razor through the air. "I was sick, but I'm better now." He had to be better, or they wouldn't have let him out of prison, would they? That was what the doctors said. He hadn't liked prison. It was full of crazy people, and people who called him names.

"He didn't mean it like that," Johnny said. "Put the blade

away." He glared at Stan. "Tell him you didn't mean it," he said.

Stan swallowed. He was scared of Jimmy. That was good. That was right. "I'm sorry, Jim," he said. "I didn't mean it, okay?"

Jimmy stared at Stan. The white boy was almost trembling. Jimmy made a fist with his free hand and raised it up to let him know that if he ever said anything like that again, Jimmy wouldn't need a razor to teach him with. "Don't you ever call me that again," he said.

"I won't, I promise," Stan said.

Fucking coward, Jimmy thought. "That's all right, then." He looked at Johnny and remembered his plan. He grinned. "I still say we should kill him." Kill Constantine, he meant.

Stan lit the joint and took a hit off it. His hands were shaking.

"Yeah," Johnny said. "After the job we take him the money and we kill him –"

"With his own guns," Jimmy said. That would teach him. That would teach him good.

***

Helen looked through the eyepiece of the camera at the squat. It was as big a tip as she'd seen – the walls were sprayed with graffiti, and there was a sofa with most of its foam torn out sitting in the front garden, along with half a dozen black rubbish bags, some of which had been torn open and kicked around.

"This is all very exciting, isn't it?" Cyril Underwood said from behind her. "Like one of those spy novels." Just another day's work, Helen thought. But she didn't say anything. Let the old duffer have his bit of fun. "Would you like some tea?" he asked. He was holding a tray with a teapot and cups, and a plate piled high with his hard little home-made scones.

It would be Helen's third in half an hour. She'd soon come round to Ted's way of thinking though – it was one sure way to get Cyril out from under their feet. "Thanks," she said, and smiled.

"I was just saying to Mrs Gardner, it's nice to have some company," Cyril said.

"Mrs Who?" Helen asked. She hadn't known of any other residents in the house – that was one reason why they'd chosen this place. It helped keep the chances of Hudson cottoning on low.

"Mrs Gardner," Cyril explained. "Nice old lady – lives two doors down." Helen knew she must look appalled, but Cyril didn't seem to notice. "Sugar?" he asked, though he knew very well by now that Helen didn't take it.

She ignored that. "You told her you had a police officer in your house?" she demanded.

"Well, yes," Cyril said. He didn't seem to understand why she was angry. "I told her you were using the bedroom."

"You were expressly told not to tell anyone of our presence," Helen snapped.

"But Mrs Gardner won't tell anyone," Cyril said soothingly. "She's a lovely woman." He held out the cup of tea to her.

Helen scowled.

***

Stan was scared. He dragged on the joint then handed it to Johnny.

The dope ought to have mellowed him out, but it wasn't working. Not with Johnny planning to murder Constantine, and Jimmy wired up like he was.

He was going to die. He knew it. If Constantine didn't get him, it would be Jimmy, and if it weren't one of them then the coppers would have him.

A sound like a shot rang out. He started forward, then realised it was someone banging on the back door.

The thumping came again. Johnny got up and inched the door open. Stakis peered through the crack at them. Johnny opened the door wider, and the Greek guy pushed his way in.

"Animals," he snarled. "Stupid animals." He stared round the room with a look of contempt on his face. "Don't you know you've been living in a goldfish bowl?"

Stan thought about that. Before he could make sense of it, Johnny said, "What?"

"You're being watched," Stakis said. He glared at them, then jerked his head at the front window. "The police are climbing all over you." Christ, Stan thought. Never mind killing Constantine, they were dead already. "Who knows you're here?" Stakis demanded.

114

"Nobody," Johnny said sullenly.

Stakis shouted something in Greek. Then he yelled, "Liar!" in English. He advanced on Johnny and shoved him in the chest with his hand. "Somebody knows."

"All right, all right," Johnny said. "I'm thinking."

So was Stan, and he didn't like what he was coming up with. "The woman," he said at last. He meant the woman whose pimp they had ripped off that morning.

The words hung in the silence for the space of a heartbeat.

"What woman?" Stakis snarled.

Johnny glared at Stan. Then he turned to Stakis. "I brought some old tart back here one night," he said. "She was stoned out of her brain. She wouldn't –"

"You brought a woman back here," Stakis cut in. He said something in Greek again. It didn't sound friendly.

"So I wanted some," Johnny said. "What's the big deal?"

Stakis sneered at him. "Find the woman and get rid of her."

"Like Thaso?" Stan asked. He was in too deep and the only reason he could find for not getting out was that he didn't know how.

"Yes," Stakis agreed. "Just like Thaso."

Jesus, Stan thought. When Johnny asked him if he wanted in, he thought he was up for a bit of dealing, something to pay for his habit. Then it was armed robbery. But murder? Jesus, he'd never been up for murder.

"It's not the woman," Johnny said.

"What do you mean –" Stan asked.

But Johnny was talking right over him. "I saw the way she looked at us this morning – she was shitting herself."

"Who, then?" Stakis demanded.

"Her pimp," Johnny said. He sounded very sure of himself.

"What?" Stan asked. "The one you ripped off?"

Stakis glared at him, then turned to Johnny. "Whoever it is, find them and cut their treacherous tongues out."

Jimmy took out his razor again. He swished it through the air. Stan hated that razor. Jimmy giggled. "Tell Mr Constantine that I'll do it," he said. "I'd like that."

CHAPTER 15

The sledgehammer slammed into the door of the Blyton Street squat. Charlie Scott shielded his face with his arm as bits of wood flew everywhere.

The constable took another whack at the door. This time the hammer went through the panel. He hooked it down and used it to lever open the door.

Darkness beckoned. Inside the house, all was quiet.

That gave him a bad feeling. Ash had been so certain they were inside – but the officers guarding the back of the building hadn't radioed in for assistance, as they would have if Hudson's mob had tried to get out the back.

Charlie gestured to the rest of the team. They poured up the garden path, all dressed in flak jackets and the Unit's distinctive checked caps, and went inside.

The place stank of sweat and rotting rubbish. Wallpaper that looked like it had been there since the war hung off the walls in tatters. The floorboards groaned as Charlie went forward.

Well, it was a bit late for subtlety, he thought. He stepped through into the living room. As he'd expected, it was empty.

A couple of filthy mattresses lay in the corner, and a table had obviously been used for rolling joints, judging by the paraphernalia lying on it.

The team spread through the house, checking it thoroughly and taking notes and photos.

Twenty minutes later, they assembled back in the front room. Thompson, the Scene of Crimes officer, joined them. He was dressed in protective clothing and wearing surgical gloves. He began to sift through the old takeaway cartons and kebab wrappers that littered the floor.

"Nice people you're dealing with," he said, holding up a used hypodermic needle. He deposited it in an evidence bag.

"Yeah," Charlie said. "Very upmarket."

"Do you know what I found in the toilet cistern?" Thompson asked.

"Surprise me," Charlie challenged.

Thompson moved a foil rice container, then picked up the crack pipe that had been underneath it. "A container half filled with perphenazine," he said as he bagged the pipe.

Ash frowned. "What's that?" She flicked her fine blonde hair out of her eyes.

Thompson turned to her. "An anti-psychotic drug," he said.

"Anti-psychotic?" Donachie queried.

Thompson nodded. "Yes. Unless the bloke's got another supply on him he's going to be one unhappy man."

It wasn't enough that a bunch of greedy, incompetent homicidal maniacs were on the loose, Charlie thought. They had to be psychotic greedy, incompetent homicidal maniacs. "Wonderful," he said.

Oxford bit his lip. "If they know they've been rumbled they'll want to know where we got our information." Charlie nodded. "I'd better find my bloke before they do." Oxford raised his eyebrows at Charlie, who told him to go and take Harris with him.

Charlie looked round. He had another job in mind. Bingo was lounging near the window. Charlie went over to him.

"They've obviously sussed we're on to them," he said. "I want you to find a fixed observation point somewhere near Constantine's restaurant."

"What, now?" Bingo complained. "I haven't eaten in –"

Charlie cut him off. "Yes, now." It was typical of Bingo to expect special treatment. "And keep in contact," he added.

"I'm in my own car," Bingo pointed out. "No radio."

Trust Bingo to have an answer for everything. "You've got a mobile, haven't you?" Charlie snapped. He walked away before Bingo could say anything.

***

Alan parked the car across the road from a porn shop he knew Marcus used as a drop. He unsnapped his seat-belt. Harris was beside him. She didn't move.

"I can't go in there," she said, staring at the blacked out

117

shop-front. Her wide mouth settled into a firm line.

"What's the matter, Grace," Alan asked. He opened the car door. "Don't tell me you're shy."

She didn't answer, but she didn't get out, either. More like a dead bloody weight, Alan thought as he crossed the road alone.

He pushed open the door of the shop and went in. The racks of magazines and sex aids were lit by the harsh light of a fluorescent strip. A bald-headed blob of a man sat behind the counter near the door. Sweat gleamed on his black, shiny face. He pulled a grimy tea towel out from under the counter and mopped himself.

A few men were browsing. Alan went over to one of the stands and picked up a magazine. It was in Swedish, but he didn't think buyers would be interested in the words. He flicked through it. Acres of not very imaginatively displayed skin stared up at him. He glanced around. The other men were all engrossed in what they were doing.

Alan strolled up to the counter, carrying the magazine. "Hey man," he said. "How you doing, Fat Bob?"

The man stared at him sullenly. "Do I know you?" He shook his head and answered his own question. "No, I don't know you."

Alan grinned. "Come on, man – you're Bob." He hoped he sounded just ingratiating enough. The man was still glaring at him. "Fat Bob to your friends, right?"

Fat Bob screwed his eyes up. "I know who I am, but I don't know who you are." He paused. Alan wondered if he should say anything. "What do you want?" Fat Bob asked at last.

"I'm looking for Marcus," Alan said quietly. He shot a glance around the shop. "I want to buy, you know?"

"I don't know nobody called Marcus," Fat Bob said. He dabbed at his forehead with his rag. "You want to buy that magazine."

"I just want to buy from Marcus," Alan insisted. "I know this is one of his spots."

Fat Bob eyed his customers. "Marcus ain't been around for days, man," he said in a voice so low Alan had to strain to catch what he was saying. "Nobody ain't seen him." He wiped his face again. "You want to buy drugs, you go to a chemist." Then

118

he added loudly, "If not, buy the magazine and split."

Alan made a sour face at him. "I don't want to buy the magazine," he snapped.

"Why not?" Fat Bob asked, in a hurt tone.

"Because you've been sweating all over it, man," Alan said. The contempt in his voice was real. He chucked the magazine down on the counter. "You fat piece of garbage."

He turned and walked out of the shop. Behind him, he heard Fat Bob mutter "Blood claat'" through his teeth.

***

Bingo was hungry, and the rain that started as he waited in the Kentucky Fried Chicken place seemed like a personal insult. He grabbed his order, paid for it and then ran towards his car.

By the time he got there he was soaking wet and his hands were so cold he could hardly turn the key in the lock. But he managed eventually. He dumped the food on the passenger seat and got in. He sat shivering for a moment, with water dripping down his back and plastering his hair to his head, then picked the bag of food up and explored the contents – fries, drumsticks, coleslaw. A large soft drink. No damn salt though. He sighed. He was so hungry it was hardly going to make a difference. He pulled a drumstick out.

He was just about to take the first bite when his pager went. He slammed the steering wheel with the palm of his hand.

Better be a good little boy, he thought as he saw that the message was from the Guv'nor. He turned the pager off and flipped open his mobile phone. As he thought, they were just checking up on him.

He told them about the old factory he'd found directly opposite Constantine's restaurant, and how he'd chatted the caretaker into letting him look round a bit later on. They made him promise to keep in contact. As if he didn't know the ropes.

He flipped the phone shut.

The chicken had gone cold and greasy. Bloody Scott, he muttered. Treating him like some bloody novice. He bit into the chicken. It was disgusting.

***

Harris had had enough. More than enough. Not that she was

going to let Oxford know that. They'd toured every place he thought Marcus might be, and then a few more. Any minute now he'd tell her they'd have to start back at the beginning again. She thrust her hands in the pockets of her bomber jacket and tried to shelter in a shop doorway, but the slanting sheets of rain got to her anyway.

Grace watched as Oxford said something to a skinny, acned lad. He towered over the boy, who shook his head. Oxford said something else and the boy shook his head again, harder this time. He took a step forward but stumbled. Oxford caught him and helped him stand up. His hand was almost large enough to circle the lad's forearm. The boy stumbled away into the sheeting rain and was lost in the darkness.

He came over to Grace and they went back to the car.

"Has he got a woman?" Grace asked as she buckled her seat belt.

"Who?" Oxford asked. He started the car.

"Your snout," Grace said, trying not to sound impatient.

"Yeah – some tart he's living off," Alan said. He started the car. "She lies on her back – he takes her money." He made a disgusted face.

Grace pushed her hair out of her eyes. The rain had made long, greasy rats-tails of it. "Well," she said, "Why don't we go and see her." Oxford stared at her. "It's worth a try, isn't it?" Grace pushed.

"Yeah, why not?" Oxford said, but he didn't sound convinced.

***

Murky yellow light from a street lamp outside illuminated the abandoned factory opposite Constantine's restaurant. Bingo picked his way around the pools of water and bits of old machinery that littered the floor. He'd hoped he would at least be dry, but rain sleeted in through holes in the roof. He stuck his hands in his pockets and scowled.

At last he made his way to one of the front windows. He found a bit of tissue in his pocket and scrubbed at the glass. Once he was done, he had a fair view of the restaurant.

***

It took a bit of searching, but eventually Alan and Harris found Debbie sitting in the bar of the Hotel Royale. Hotel Royally Seedy, Alan thought as he surveyed the damp and nicotine-stained wallpaper, and the carpet tiles slick with grease. Debbie was sitting on a high stool at the bar. She was a thin girl, wearing a pelmet skirt and laddered fishnets, and so much make-up her face looked like an explosion in a paint factory. She was so high you could have used her for a weather balloon. The barman said something to her, and she laughed raucously.

"Hey, Debbie," Alan said. She turned to them. She stared at Harris for a second, then turned her attention back to Alan. He saw that the make-up didn't quite disguise a bruise on her cheekbone. "Do you know where Marcus is?"

"Don't know," Debbie said. She flapped her hand vaguely. "He didn't come home all day, and that's not like him." She eyed Harris again. "I'm sure I seen you somewhere before. What's your name, love?"

"Mary," Harris said shortly.

Alan clasped his arm with his other hand – a gesture he'd picked up from a crack-head who was trying to control his shakes. "Can I get hold of Marcus?" he asked, making his voice tight and snappy. "You got a number for him?"

Debbie glanced round the bar. It was empty, except for the bartender, who was at the other end of the counter. "You buying," she said quietly.

"Yeah," Alan said. He bit his lower lip. Had to be convincing without overplaying it. "I need to see Marcus – I'm starting to get the jitters." He ran his hand over his bald head. "You know."

Again, Debbie glanced round the room. Then she opened her shoulder bag, revealing a stash of cocaine. She pulled one of the cellophane packages out. "Forget about him," she said. "I'll help you out." She smiled at Alan. "How much do you want?" Alan glanced at Harris. "Well?" Debbie said. She smiled her dazzling, hopped-up smile again.

There was nothing for it but to make the buy.

Afterwards, in the car, Alan held up the wrap of cocaine.

"That'll look good on your expenses," Harris said.

Alan laughed. "It'll look even better on my record – buying

coke off a known tom." He laughed again, remembering something else. "She thought you were one of her pals." He put on a squeaky south London accent. "I'm sure I seen you somewhere before."

Harris blew her nose. "She had," she said. "When I was on vice, I nicked her." She crumpled the tissue up. "And while we're on the subject, I've never suffered from shyness."

Alan didn't get it. He raised his eyebrows at her.

"Fat Bob knows me too. Did a seizure of kiddie porn," she said. From the expression on her face she was enjoying watching him squirm as he remembered how he'd simply assumed she was too coy to go into a sex shop. "He got off with a suspended and a big fine." She pulled a face. "The low life animal."

Now wait a minute, Alan thought. "Marcus just uses that place as a spot to deal in, that's all. He's no pervert."

"I never said he was," Harris said coolly. "Anyway, your snout is your own affair. Let's just find him." She brushed strands of wet hair out of her face.

Alan nodded and started the car. There was nothing much he wanted more at that moment than to get back to his nice warm house and his nice warm wife.

***

Marcus didn't like dealing around the adventure playground. Too much chance that if you were caught the filth would try and pin selling to kids on you.

But it was a stinking night, with the rain slicing down out of the leaden sky and a fierce chill in the wind. There weren't any kids around, not at this time. Weren't many punters around either. So when he got a call to meet Clifton down by the swings, he wasn't going to turn it down.

He pushed the swing. The ropes creaked in the rain. What little moonlight there was seeped through the clouds, showing the play equipment as vast dark hulks against the deeper darkness of the night. No Cliff. Damn, what if he's setting me up? Marcus thought. But he needed cash. Maybe cash to get out of town. Wait till things quietened down...

Cliff came towards him across the playground. Not that the

Rasta was a real high roller by any means. But Marcus was a desperate man and any little helped.

He did the deal and watched Cliff leave. Then he went back the way he'd come, through a place in the fence where the wire had come loose. It led directly into narrow gap between two garages. Marcus inched along it sideways – the kids who used it as a shortcut by day would have had no problem – and into the road between the garages.

He could feel his sorrows beginning to lift already, now that he had a bit of cash to his name. Course, he had a long way to go to make good on what had been ripped off that morning. But he didn't need to do that in London. He could go somewhere else. Bristol, say, or Manchester. More he thought about it the more it seemed like a good idea.

He grinned. Not even the rain that plastered his clothes to his body and put a chill right through him could wreck his mood.

A pair of headlights appeared in the distance. Marcus shielded his eyes with his hand.

"Jesus," he whispered when he recognised the BMW. "Oh Jesus." He turned and started to run. Now that he knew the car was there, he could hear its engine purring through the noise of the wind and the rain.

He'd only got a couple of paces when two shadows detached themselves from the walls. He recognised them.

Constantine's men.

One would be Hudson.

The other must be Gillespie.

As he thought it – thought of how Gillespie had just got out of nut jail, how he'd got there by cutting his own dad with a cut-throat razor – he saw a flash of steel.

Even through the hiss of the rain, he heard the swish of the blade.

He heard his own dying scream, felt a line of fire across his throat and the tarmac slamming into his knees as he went down.

And then nothing at all.

***

It was still raining by the time Alan thought of looking for

Marcus at the kids' playground. The gates were locked, but he and Harris got over them easily enough.

He remembered he'd been surprised when Marcus told him the place was often used as a pre-arranged spot for making late sales. "Where else, man?" Marcus had said. "You lot would never think of it, would you – not all shut up like it is?"

So here they were, Alan and Harris in the dark and the rain. A figure stumbled by in the dark – a tall thin West Indian guy with long dreadlocks pushed up under a woollen hat. Alan went over to him.

The guy giggled when Alan asked if he'd seen anyone around. Eventually he calmed down long enough to point in the direction of the council estate.

Alan left him laughing to himself in the freezing rain, and ran back to Harris.

"Come on," he yelled at her. They retraced their steps, left the playground and started across the wasteground that separated the playground from the estate.

The rain hammered at Alan. His eyes stung and his throat hurt. His breath came in short, hard gasps. Garages, he thought. The crack-head said Marcus was going to the garages.

His foot turned in the mud. Pain lanced up his calf as he put his hand out to save himself, but he didn't fall. He swore, but the wind stole his words. He ran on.

The rain-slicked asphalt of the garages was lit by the yellow glare of a single sodium street lamp.

Alan skidded to a halt. He didn't dare call out, and in any case he was breathing hard. He felt, rather than saw, Harris come up beside him.

"Alan?" she said suddenly.

"What?" he snapped, though in truth there was none of the usual challenge in her voice.

She touched him lightly on the shoulder, then pointed towards one of the garages. Alan squinted into the darkness. Something only slightly paler than the surrounding shadow lay there.

Reluctantly, Alan walked towards it. He had to know.

Marcus stared up him. His head lolled back obscenely, and

there was a line of congealing blood across his throat.

Oxford couldn't look at him. Instead he turned his face to the indigo sky. He knew Harris was behind him, that she wanted to say something. But he couldn't speak. The rain beat down on his face.

"I gave him my word," he said. Harris said nothing. "I gave him my word," he repeated.

There was water on Alan's face, but whether it was rain or tears he didn't know.

CHAPTER 16

Bingo was cold, wet, miserable and very, very pissed off. He perched on a crate he'd pulled up to the window and stared at Constantine's restaurant.

There was no action there. None. The only people who'd gone in and out looked like regular punters without the taste or good sense to avoid putting clean cash into Constantine's filthy hands.

Of Hudson or the rest of his merry little band, there'd been no sign.

Bingo's pager bleeped. He pulled his hands out of his pockets and fumbled till he turned it off. He could hardly feel his fingers, but he managed to dial the Station's number.

"Listen," he snapped when he got through to the squad room. "When am I going to be relieved?"

Ash was on the other end of the line. She told him coldly that Alan Oxford's snout had been killed. That turned the inquiry into a murder investigation, and meant they could almost certainly expect action at Constantine's place. And that meant they couldn't relieve Bingo for fear of tipping the Greek off. Bingo said he'd stay till morning then come into the squad room.

He didn't start swearing till he cut the connection.

***

Alan stared at the TV screen. There was a cartoon playing, but Alan wasn't paying it any attention. His son, Robert, was curled up on his lap, but Alan wasn't paying him any attention either.

Bryony handed him a cup of tea.

"Thanks," Alan said, but he was thinking of Marcus's eyes staring at the rain-filled sky, and wondering what the last thing

126

he'd seen had been; what he'd thought when he realised what was happening –

"You haven't heard a word I've said, have you?" Bryony asked.

"What?" Alan said. She was standing by his chair. He'd found her asleep on the sofa again when he came in, but at least this time she'd got ready for bed.

"I said –" she began, and then stopped. "Is something wrong?" she asked.

"No," Alan said. She wasn't impressed. "Yes," he admitted. She raised her eyebrows at him. "I don't know," he said, finally.

"Want to talk about it?" she asked. Her concern was written all over her face now.

"No, it's all right." Bryony always wanted to talk about everything. It was a standing joke between them. He tried a smile and almost made it.

"You sure?"

"Yeah." Alan rubbed his eyes. "It's okay – I'm just tired." He turned back to the TV. He could feel her looking at him, and knew she was worrying about him. But he just didn't have the energy to do anything about it. Not when all he could hear was Marcus telling him he was scared.

CHAPTER 17

It would be the last thing he ever did with Johnny and Jimmy. Stan had promised himself that. He brought the BMW to a halt outside the sub-post office Constantine had chosen for them.

He expected the others to get out immediately. That was the plan. But Jimmy muttered something from where he was sprawled over the back seat.

Johnny twisted round. "What are you mumbling about?" he demanded.

"I think we should go back to the house," Jimmy said. His head flopped back and he grinned at them.

"I've already told you – we can't go back to the house, the police have been there," Johnny said. Jimmy just grinned some more. Johnny glanced at the sub-post office. "Now we got to do this thing, hear me?"

Jimmy's grin vanished. His fingers worked against the leather upholstery. "I'm scared Johnny," he said. He swallowed hard.

Johnny frowned. "What?"

"I want to go back to the house, Johnny." He pushed himself into a sitting position. "I want my medicine," he said. "I left it in the house."

Jesus fucking wept, Stan thought. With his medication, Jimmy was a bit off the wall. Without it, he was stone crazy – not even Johnny could control him.

"You did what?" Johnny demanded. He was clearly furious.

Jimmy got a sly look round the eyes. "I hid it in the toilet," he said. He wouldn't look at them.

"For fuck's sake why?" Johnny asked.

Stan knew why. He braced himself. Sure enough, Jimmy pointed at him. "He keeps stealing it and melting it down and shooting it up," he said. No-one said anything for a second. "He does, Johnny, he does," Jimmy whined.

"Did you steal –" Johnny started. He clouted Stan hard round the face. It hurt. Stan tasted blood. "His medication?" Stan didn't say anything. Wasn't any point. Johnny hit him again, harder. This time his head bounced off the headrest. "Did you?" Johnny demanded.

"No I didn't," Stan said. Johnny raised his hand again, but this time he made a fist of it. "Well, maybe a couple of times."

"You stupid wanker," Johnny said, but he lowered his fist. He glanced at his watch. He turned to Jimmy. "Stay here. I'll do it on my own."

"But I want to come with you," Jimmy whined.

Johnny opened the door. "Well, come on then," he said. That was always the way of it – anything Jimmy wanted, Jimmy got. Johnny got out of the car. He leaned back in and said to Stan, "You'd better be here when I get back."

Like hell, Stan thought. He watched the others go into the sub-post office.

Serve them right if he did go.

But he thought about Jimmy. About Jimmy's razor. And stayed where he was.

***

The blood sang in Jimmy's ears. He knew what it was telling him, what the wind was telling him, what the rain had told him in the night.

Do the job. Then Constantine.

He followed Johnny to the sub-post office. The Asian bloke who owned it was just opening up. Johnny rapped on the door and the man opened it. Jimmy grinned. He knew what was coming next, oh yes.

Sure enough, Johnny reached under his jogging top and pulled out his gun. He shoved it in the man's face.

The man went pale. He stared at the gun wide eyed and took a couple of steps back. Johnny followed him. Jimmy went in the shop after them. It was quiet and dark. Jimmy liked that.

Jimmy got out of the way, so Johnny could kick the door shut. He kept the gun pointing at the postmaster, and almost without looking to see what he was doing flipped the sign on the door over. Now everyone would think the place was shut.

Johnny forced the postmaster to go back round the counter. He did it without speaking. Jimmy still had his gun hidden under his jacket. He thought about getting it out, but he liked having it there. It was a secret. Jimmy liked secrets.

The Asian man knelt down by the safe. He spun the dial, and the door swung slowly open. Johnny pulled a carrier bag out from under his jogging top. He gave it to the sub-postmaster, and the man filled it with money.

When he was done, Johnny picked the bag up. He backed away from the man. Jimmy followed him. They walkcd backwards to the door. The Asian man stared at them, but he didn't try to move. Johnny opened the door and they went out.

The door slammed behind them. They ran to the car.

They'd done it. But it hadn't been any fun. Jimmy hadn't shot his gun.

But next they were going to see Constantine.

***

Bingo finally left the restaurant the next morning. He felt like death warmed up. His head hurt, his neck and shoulders ached like someone had thumped him with a crowbar, and his mouth felt like something had died in it.

He blinked in the early morning sunshine. Properly speaking, he should have waited to be relieved. Well, it was tough. He needed food, coffee and a pee, preferably in reverse order, and he was damn sure he was going to get it.

He started across the road to his car. A blue BMW swung round the corner. Dark blue – matching the witness reports from the building society.

The car pulled up not ten feet away from him.

Keep moving, he thought. Keep bloody moving. Three men got out – one white guy and two black ones, one much lighter-skinned than the other.

Good enough. Keep moving.

Bingo's pager bleeped. He switched it off, but not before one of the men caught a glimpse of him. The man then turned and tapped on the restaurant door. Someone opened it, and all three of them went in.

Charlie looked round the sub-post office. Apart from the safe nothing had been touched. The postmaster, a Mr Malek, sat in one corner with his head in his hands. He was grey faced and trembling. So, Charlie thought, the Three Stooges had finally done something right. He made a sour face at DCI Uttley, who was grimly watching his team check the place out.

Charlie radioed in a report. Mr Malek had taken his life in his hands and gone to the window to get a look at the car before Hudson had driven away. If he'd known what he was dealing with he'd never have dared. That reminded Charlie to warn the local police how dangerous the three men were.

Ash came in. "We just tried to get Tate, Guv," she said. "But he's turned his pager off and I can't get any response from his mobile."

Uttley's scowl deepened. "That's it, Charlie," he said. "He's off the squad."

Ash turned away. Charlie couldn't be sure, but he thought she might be smiling. Well, he thought, she wouldn't be the only one.

***

So for once the three idiots had done something right. They stood before Yannis Constantine now, holding out a carrier bag full of money.

Constantine glanced at it, then turned back to the table. It was littered with the remains of breakfast – fruit peel, half a bowl of plain yogurt, and a pot of good Greek coffee. Constantine picked up a toothpick and proceeded to dig a melon seed out from between his teeth. It wouldn't do to let the idiots think they were of any great importance to him.

"We've brought your money, Mr Constantine," Hudson said. He jiggled the bag. Constantine looked at it again. "And we've brought your guns back," Hudson added.

He pulled the handgun Constantine had given him out of his waistband.

So did Gillespie. "Yeah," he said. He smiled.

***

Bingo punched the Station's number on his mobile. Before

131

he finished a gunshot cracked out from the restaurant. He paused. Another shot rang out.

Bingo pelted towards the restaurant.

***

They'd done it, they'd done it, they'd done it.

He'd done it.

Constantine and his pretty-boy yes-man lay sprawled at Jimmy's feet. A patch of blood stained Constantine's white dressing gown.

"Come on," Johnny said.

Stan shook his head. He'd gone pale, and his hands were balled into fists at his sides. "Not me," he said. "I've had enough. I'm not up for this – I'm just a driver."

Pissy little wanker, Jimmy thought. But Johnny just smiled. "Have it your way," he said. He raised his gun and shot Stan in the thigh.

Jimmy would never have thought of that. Stan fell to the floor. He grabbed his leg and rolled around. "My leg," he screamed. "My leg."

Johnny cleaned his gun off on his jacket, then threw it on Constantine's body. That was good. Jimmy wouldn't have thought of that, either. He cleaned his own gun, and tossed it on Stakis's chest.

"Come on, let's move," Johnny said. He ran towards the door, still holding the bag with the money. Jimmy followed him.

Behind them, Stan started to moan.

***

Bingo raced towards the restaurant. Just as he got to the door, two of the men came back out. He crashed into them and they all went down.

"Stop," he shouted. "I'm a police officer."

One of the men rolled clear. The other – Hudson, by his dreadlocks – lashed out at Bingo's head with his foot. Bingo warded the blow off with his arm. His hand went numb and his mobile phone slipped out of his fingers and crashed into the pavement. Bingo tried to grab Hudson. The other guy clambered to his feet and made a break for the Beamer. Bingo was momentarily distracted. Hudson slammed the palm of his hand

132

towards Bingo's face. Bingo jerked back and took the blow on his cheek rather than his nose, but it still hurt like hell.

Hudson clambered to his feet. Bingo grabbed at his ankle, but Hudson kicked free. He ran towards the BMW, where his mate was already behind the wheel.

Bingo got up, ready to follow. But then he realised that he'd been hearing screaming from inside the restaurant for an awfully long time. He glanced at the car. It would have to wait.

He ran inside. The dining room was carnage. Two bodies lay on the floor, and a third man was sprawled near by, screaming his head off and clutching his leg. Bingo glanced at him. It had to be Callow, the third member of Hudson's little team of incompetents.

He ignored him and went and checked the bodies. Each had taken a shot in the chest. Just to be sure, he checked their necks for pulses. Nothing.

"Help me," sobbed Callow from behind him. Bingo turned round. "Help me? I've been shot – I'm bleeding to death here..." When Bingo didn't respond, he said, "I'm dying."

Bingo glared at him. "No you're not," he said. "You've just been shot in the leg." He allowed himself a grin at Callow's expense, then raced out of the restaurant.

God only knew why, but the BMW was still sitting outside. Bingo sprinted over to it. He wrenched open the passenger side door. Hudson seemed to be having an argument with Gillespie, who was behind the wheel, but Bingo didn't waste time asking. He made a grab for Hudson.

Hudson swivelled round and kicked Bingo in the chest with both feet, causing him to lurch backwards. Hudson leapt out of the car and sprinted up the street. Bingo scrambled to his feet. He leaned on the car while he tried to get his breath back. Gillespie dived out of the far door and followed Hudson.

Bingo belted after him. Hudson disappeared down an alley at the side of the factory. Gillespie was just behind him.

Bingo's foot slid out from under him. He took the fall on his shoulder and rolled back to his feet, but he'd lost seconds. He skidded to a halt at the mouth of the alley. Neither Hudson nor Gillespie were anywhere in sight. He moved cautiously on, scanning all around. He was breathing hard and almost glad of the respite. He wondered if maybe they'd gone into one of the buildings, or – a full milk crate slammed to the ground narrowly missing Bingo. He looked up. Hudson was clambering up the fire escape outside the building.

"Ah shit," Bingo muttered. He took a deep breath and started to climb. The metal was wet with rain, and rough with rust. It bit into his palms. His feet slipped on the slick surface, but he began to gain on Hudson.

A dustbin lid skimmed past him. He dodged back.

"Nice try," he muttered, and continued climbing. Not for long though. The dustbin itself followed the lid. It turned over as it fell, spattering smelly rubbish over Bingo. He shook off the rubbish and went on.

He got to the platform where the escape doubled back on itself, and heard a sound from above him. He jerked back just in time, as another milk crate hurtled past. It slammed into the platform. The whole escape rung like a bell, and one of the bottles exploded with a sharp crack.

Bingo looked up. Hudson was peering down at him from the roof. He pulled back and disappeared, then reappeared further along. He was running.

Bingo went on up, moving a lot faster now he didn't have to worry about incoming fire.

He hauled himself on to the roof. It was slick with rain, and here and there water had formed wide pools. Hudson was in the distance. He glanced back, then ran on.

Bingo chased him. Hudson came to the edge of the roof, near a tarpaulin turret. He began to edge around it.

"Armed police," Bingo shouted. "Halt or I'll fire." It was the wildest bluff. He moved slowly towards Hudson, who backed off at first but then hesitated. "Put your weapon down and lie face down." Hudson didn't move. "Now!" Bingo shouted. What the hell he'd do if Hudson disobeyed he didn't know.

Hudson held the bag up. Bingo got ready to throw himself sideways. "I haven't got a weapon," Hudson shouted.

"Throw that bag away from you and get on the floor now," Bingo yelled.

Hudson hesitated. Then he lobbed the bag towards Bingo. He dropped to his knees, then went face down on the floor. Bingo picked the bag up but went to Hudson without stopping to look inside it. He knelt next to Hudson and put one knee in the small of the man's back, just to be on the safe side.

"Put your arms behind your back," he commanded. Hudson did so. Bingo pulled a pair of cuffs out of his pocket and snapped them round Hudson's wrists.

He leaned back and took a deep breath. Then he looked in the bag. It was full of money.

"Where's your gun, man?" Hudson asked.

"Don't have one," Bingo said.

Hudson made a disgusted sound. "Typical," he spat. "You can't trust anyone nowadays."

Bingo got to his feet. "You're absolutely right, but I wouldn't move if I was –"

There was a sound from behind him. He turned. Gillespie came hurtling round the corner of the tarpaulin turret at him. He had a cut throat razor in his hand and ran straight at Bingo.

Bingo threw himself sideways. Gillespie carried straight on. He plummeted over the edge of the roof. His scream was cut off by a sickening thud.

Bingo went and looked down. Gillespie lay on the pavement below, his head bent at an impossible angle.

Bingo backed away. He slumped against the tarpaulin turret.

"What happened?" Hudson asked.

Bingo didn't answer for a moment. He fumbled in his jacket and pulled out a packet of cigarettes. His hands were shaking. "Your pal just did a swan dive off the roof," he said at last. "It's not a pretty sight." He lit the cigarette and took a long drag. It tasted fine. It was good to be alive. "Here," he said after a bit. "You haven't got a phone on you, have you?"

"Yeah – right jacket pocket," Hudson said.

Bingo went over and found the phone. He pulled it out and punched the station number.

***

Much later, Gillespie's body was bagged up and put into an ambulance. Bingo watched Hudson being led away by a couple

135

of uniforms. He flashed Uttley and Scott his best smile.

Then he went over to Hudson. "Wait up," he said. "Your phone."

"Might as well keep it, man," Hudson said. "Where I'm going I won't have much call for it."

Bingo grinned. He tucked the phone back into Hudson's pocket. "Couldn't do that," he said. "Wouldn't be fair." He grinned.

He still had the bag. He brandished it at Scott and Uttley as he walked past them. "Evidence," he explained.

As he headed towards his car – and food, and a bath, and a warm bed – he heard Scott say, "Talk about falling in –"

"And coming up smelling of roses," Uttley finished for him.

Bingo grinned.

PART THREE

WHISPERS IN
THE DARK

CHAPTER 18

Sheena Rogers hurried down the dark streets towards home. Her school bag thumped at her side. She shoved her hands into the pockets of her blazer. There was going to be a row. She stared at the pavement. She supposed she deserved it, coming home at this time.

But then, there were always rows, always trouble. It didn't matter what she said or did.

She turned into her street. The glare of the streetlamps showed up the peeling paint and unkempt front gardens of the houses. Sheena hated the place. Then again, she hated just about everything in her life.

There were still lights on at home. It was too much to hope Mum would have gone to bed. She put her key in the lock, but the door opened before she could turn it.

Her mother stood framed in the doorway. "It's past midnight," she said. "Where have you been?"

"We went to Emma's house," Sheena lied. She pushed past her mother into the house.

"No you didn't." Her mother had obviously seen that one coming. "I phoned her mother two hours ago." She shut the door quietly, on account of the neighbours. "It's those boys, isn't it?"

Sheena didn't say anything. There wasn't anything to say. She started to go upstairs.

"Answer me," her mother demanded.

Sheena didn't. She went into her room, locked the door behind her, threw herself down on the bed and began to weep.

***

Ash stared out of the window of the flat above the newsagent's that they were using as a fixed observation point. She was watching the Rogers' house, across the road. Sonja Rogers was screaming at her daughter. The sound carried easily through the cold night air.

"We've all been there, love," Ash murmured to the woman.

Alan Oxford sat behind her at the dining table. He was going through the case notes. "No sign of the old man, then?" he asked. He put one heavy-booted foot up on a spare dining chair.

Helen sighed. He bloody well knew that Gil Rogers was keeping well clear of Sonja. "You're beginning to sound like the Guv'nor," she said. She rubbed at her eyes with the heel of her hand.

"He's got a point," Oxford said. "Three days and nights now – maybe Rogers really has dumped the family and split." Helen heard him close the notes. She turned round. "We could be wasting our time," Oxford continued.

"Rogers will be in touch," she insisted. "He thinks the world of his daughter."

***

Gil Rogers peered out of the shadowy alley into the high street. Nothing moved there, but it was illuminated by a few street lamps, and the light that glowed from the windows of the closed and shuttered shops. None of them were the target. The target was the twenty-four hour cash dispenser in the bank on the corner. It was inside, in an area customers could access by opening the door with their cash cards.

Right then, it was all but empty. But that was about to change.

"Anything happening?" his companion, Paulo Swift whispered. Moonlight glinted on the barrel of the sawn-off shotgun he cradled in his arms.

Gil shook his head. His own weapon was a silenced Smith and Wesson, sleek and deadly. He liked the weight of it in his hand.

The quiet was broken by the purring of an engine. He smiled tightly.

The van came within sight. It crossed the precinct, swung round and stopped close to the bank. A helmeted security guard got out. He looked around, then banged on the side of the van. The delivery chute opened and a money cassette slid out. He took it and went to the bank.

Here we go, Gil thought. Wait for it. Wait for it.

The security guard swiped his card through the reader machine and the door slid open. He went in, and the door slid shut behind him. A few minutes later, Gil saw the guard lock the cash machine and head back to the door.

"Standby," Gil whispered into his mobile. Eric Poulson, the man on the other end of the line, didn't acknowledge. He didn't need to. "He's coming out," Rogers said. "Go – get in there!"

In the distance, an engine roared into life.

Like clockwork, Gil thought. Just like old times. He pulled his mask down over his face. Paulo did the same.

The guard came out of the bank. He heard the engine. Hesitated.

The Shogun surged into view. The guard ran to the van and pounded on its door.

"Attack," he screamed. "Attack! Open the door!"

The driver revved the van's engine. The Shogun slewed round, blocking the street.

"Now," Gil shouted. He and Paulo ran out into the road. The guard saw them.

Instinct kicked in. Gil raised the gun. "Stand still," he shouted. "Stay where you are.

The guard hesitated for a second, then tried to make a break for it. Gil let off a single round. The gun kicked in his hand, but the noise was drowned out by the guard's scream. He staggered back and hit the ground hard.

Gil and Paulo ran towards him. As they did so, the money van lurched backwards, into the Shogun. The four-wheeler shunted backwards slightly, but that was all.

"Fucking have-a-go heroes," Gil muttered.

Paulo ran over to the van. He pointed his shotgun at the window. Point blank range. Couldn't fail to damage, even with the window up.

"Turn off the engine and nobody else gets hurt," Paulo shouted.

The driver complied. Now only the revving of the Shogun's engine broke the silence. Gil hauled the guard to his feet, pulled the man's arm round his neck and dragged him over to the van.

Eric jabbed the shotgun under the guard's chin. He was

142

ashen with pain and shock.

Great, Gil thought. So he'll do his best to make his mate hurry up.

"Please," the guard whispered. "I've got kids."

Big bloody deal, Gil thought. No-one had ever given a toss about what might happen to his Sheena if he'd copped it when he was in the army. "Yeah, me too," he said. He turned to the van. "Open the chute," he yelled. The driver stared at him. "Do it – or I'll blow his head off," Gil shouted.

The driver did.

***

Gunfire rattled out. Sheena's finger squeezed on the trigger of the joystick, and a demon died in a bloody hail of machine-gun bullets.

A thousand points. Two thousand. All the monsters going down in front of her weapons.

"Sheena!" her mother called. Sheena realised she'd been hearing thumping on the wall for some time. "Go to sleep," her mother shouted. "It's nearly one o'clock in the morning."

Sheena sighed. She saved her game and turned the computer off. Anything to keep the old witch happy.

At least she didn't feel like crying any more.

***

Helen sat at the dining table in the observation flat. She finished writing out a party invitation – all balloons and teddy bears wearing paper hats – folded it and put it in an envelope.

Oxford was watching the Rogers' place. "Kids, eh?" he sighed.

Helen licked the envelope and stuck it down. "Tell me about it," she said. "I've got eighteen of them coming round next weekend."

"You reckon you're this big tough copper," Oxford said. "They can do it to you every time – reduce you to..." he thought about it. "I don't know..."

"Family problems?" Helen asked. "I thought that was my area." She wouldn't have told just anyone – but then, Alan Oxford wasn't just anyone: which, according to her husband, was most of the problem. "Time not spent, and all that," she clarified. There, he maybe had a point. The rest of it was nonsense, just nonsense.

"Terrible twos," Oxford said. "I was dressing him this morning. He had a tantrum – worst it's ever been." He stopped. Grinned, though he didn't seem amused. Helen had to stop herself from smiling – not because the thought of a friend having problems amused her – but with affection, at the thought of a big bloke like Oxford with a wee scrap of a lad. "Wouldn't have his shoe on. Peed on my leg." He pulled a sour face. "We're standing there screaming at each other. In the end I lost it – let one go." He chewed his bottom lip.

"It's going to happen," Helen said. She was a great believer in not worrying about what you couldn't change. "Helps if you've not been up all night on an obbo."

"Yeah," Oxford said. He didn't sound convinced. He stroked his bald head. "How are your kids taking all this night work?"

"They're okay," she said. "It's David – he's worse than he ever was." Her Irish accent sounded thicker than usual, even to her own ears, as it always did when she was upset. "Says I'm short changing the kids – that we're no longer a family." David had actually said that she was having an affair: almost certainly with Oxford, but if not him then with someone else. But she wasn't about to tell Oxford that. "He wants me to transfer out," she finished.

Oxford looked properly shocked. "What?" he demanded.

"Every time we have a row, I can feel an ultimatum coming," Helen said. It was true. Lately she'd lived in fear of what David might say next.

"Hell of a choice," Oxford said. He leaned back in his chair, his big frame silhouetted in the moonlight. "What are you going to do?"

Helen looked away. "Maybe he's right," she said. "I used to think I was born for this – that this was one way I could make a real difference." She paused, trying to put into words what she had never really needed to articulate to anyone before. "Do something worthwhile. Now there's the kids I'm not so sure." She'd thought she was making the world a better place for their

144

future. If David was right, she was ruining their present to do it. It was useless, anyway – just words that didn't mean anything, only trapped you. "Oh, come on," she said. "This is a waste of time – let's go and get a drink."

***

Sonja lay half asleep, thinking about Gil, almost dreaming about him, about his arms holding her; his smile, just for her; the touch of his mouth on hers...

The phone rang. Her eyes flicked open. She stared into darkness. The ringing stopped. A moment later it started again, then stopped.

Sonja smiled. She closed her eyes and went to sleep. And dreamed about Gil.

***

Helen got undressed in the dark. The bedside clock said ten past two. David was in bed, asleep. She got in beside him.

"Have you thought any more about what I said?" he asked without opening his eyes.

"Yes," Helen said. She was so tired she ached, and her nerves felt as tight as a bowstring.

"And?" David persisted. He opened his eyes.

Helen sighed. The perfect end to a perfect day. "I need more time," she said. "It's asking a lot."

"In case you hadn't noticed, there's a lot at stake," David said. His eyes searched her face.

How could I forget, with you to tell me every minute of every day, Helen thought. Suddenly, she couldn't bear to look at his face. She rolled over and glared into the darkness instead.

CHAPTER 19

If they didn't get a lead on Rogers soon, they were buggered, and Charlie Scott knew it. He paced nervously around his office as he planned strategy with Ash and Bingo. Beyond them, the squad room was only half full – and even then Donachie was reading the paper and the phone conversation Harris was engrossed in didn't look much like work.

Bingo stood by one of the pinboards. "The uniforms found the getaway car in a factory car park. Nobody saw the changeover vehicle," he said.

He looked about as pissed off as Charlie felt, and that was a lot. "Brilliant," Charlie said. "Four robberies and we still don't know where Rogers is living." He turned to Ash. "What about your obbo, Helen?"

She shrugged. "No contact so far with his wife and kid, Guv." She looked pinched and pale with tiredness, and there were dark circles under her eyes.

"Look, the bloke hasn't been home in five months," Bingo cut in. "Face it, Helen – he's bailed out."

"In the absence of any other lead, Sonja and the girl are our only chance," Helen said. She sounded icily determined, as only Ash could be. "We know he's very attached to the daughter."

"Yeah, so you keep saying," Bingo answered contemptuously.

"Back off, Bob!" Ash snapped.

"That's enough," Charlie said sharply. Both the others stared at him as if he'd said something outrageous. "Put some of that excess energy into chasing up new strategies." He went to his desk and picked up a sheaf of case notes. "Because as of now these blokes are murdering us."

"Come on, Guv – it's only been three days," Ash said, cajoling. "Without reliable information it's all down to good surveillance – house him, follow him, draw a pattern of activities, catch him recceing the next job." She pursed her lips. "What's changed?"

She had a point, Charlie thought, though he hated having the textbook quoted at him. "The phone checks you requested on Sonja's place – what did you get?"

"Call frequency breakdown for home phone and mobile," Ash said. Bingo sighed heavily. "He must be staying in touch somehow," she went on determinedly.

It might be all they had to go on, but at least it didn't involve taking officers from other aspects of the case. "All right," Charlie said. "Two more days – then I want you back on other things."

"Thanks Guv," Ash said. Bingo merely scowled.

Charlie grabbed a memo from the desk and went into the squad room. He pretended he hadn't heard Bingo mutter "What's up with him?" as he left.

He went over to Harris's desk. She'd had her problems, but Uttley thought a lot of her and, at the very least, Charlie thought she showed a lot of potential.

She was still on the phone. He circled till she could see him. She looked up. "Wait one," she said into the mouthpiece. "Guv?" she asked.

She wasn't going to like this, Charlie thought. "Memo from SO19 – you're due another requalification shoot." He handed her the memo. "Seems the last one was borderline."

She glanced at the piece of paper. "Tendency to snatch the trigger," she said. Her voice was tight. She rubbed the side of her nose with her thumb. "Apparently." Her tone said she didn't believe it.

"That's a recent development," Charlie said. Recent as in, since the Worsley shooting, he thought. But he didn't say it. "Need any help?"

"No, sir," she said. That sir gave her away – she was definitely worried. "I'm fine."

"Good." Charlie knew it wasn't quite true. He also knew that helping Grace required a deft hand. "Get some practice in beforehand." He paused. "Get one of the lads to show you a bit of ball and dummy."

"Yes, Guv," Harris said as if she understood. Her face gave her away, though. That was the idea – with a bit of luck she'd be intrigued enough to go and do it.

He walked off, noticing as he went that Donachie was smiling at her. That was good – it wouldn't do her any harm at all to make a friend or two on the team.

***

School was over for the day. Shame, Sheena thought as she went through the school gates. The little kids were milling round an ice cream van parked nearby, and a whole crowd of parents were waiting patiently for them.

"Come on," Emma said. She tugged Sheena's sleeve.

Sheena shook her off. She looked at the crowd of adults. There were no familiar faces there.

Good, Sheena thought. She thought it was good, anyway.

Emma grabbed her arm and started prattling about some group she'd seen on MTV. Sheena let herself be pulled down the road.

***

Sparks flew from the grinder. Rogers kept up the pressure till the metal of the container gave way. Then he flicked the switch. The roar of the motor died, but the stink of hot metal filled the air.

Rogers pushed back his face mask and pulled off his gloves. He waited a minute or so for the metal to cool, then pulled the cassette apart. Inside was a wad of cash.

He turned round. Eric and Paulo were standing behind him, next to a blue minivan. It was clean, stolen that morning.

"Right," he said. "Let's have that suitcase over here."

Eric reached into the van and brought out a suitcase, which he threw to Paulo, who started packing the cash into it.

Rogers wasn't done yet. He pulled his face mask back down. There were several more cassettes on the floor. He picked one of them up and flicked the grinder back on. It roared, and he applied it to the metal. It bucked slightly as it touched, and sparks flew.

Soon be done, he thought. Done and out of it.

***

148

Sheena pulled her blazer round her more tightly. The wind that whipped across the park and ruffled the water of the duckpond knifed through her. The ducks swam up close to the edge of the pond and looked at her expectantly. She fumbled in her pocket for more bread. She'd saved it from the horrible sandwiches that Mum gave her for school lunch, but it was nearly all gone.

Just a bit left. Lucky duckies, she thought, and it almost made her laugh. She threw the scrap on the water and the ducks squabbled over it.

A shadow fell across her. She turned. Her father stood there. He smiled. She knew she should smile back, but she couldn't. He reached out and stroked her hair. She felt her shoulders go tense.

She felt moisture on her cheeks, but she wasn't crying. It was just the wind making her eyes water, that was all.

***

Gil pulled on a dark jumper. He felt lazy, in that after-brilliant-sex state that would have let him sleep the clock round if he had let it. But there was business to attend to. He looked at the thin figure on the bed, knowing he should at least say something to her.

"How was school?" he asked at last.

Sheena pulled the sheets up over herself, covering the pale buds of her breasts. She shrugged and looked away. She always could be a bit sullen when she didn't get her own way.

"Here," he said. "I got you a present." He handed her the package of toiletries – real, grown-up stuff, not your childish rubbish – that he'd got the sales-girl to wrap in the department store. She stared at the glossy paper and the pretty ribbon, but she didn't even start to undo it.

Come to that, she didn't even say thank you.

"Dad," she asked after a bit. "When are you coming home?"

"Soon," Rogers said. He hated to disappoint her.

***

"No, of course you're not wasting anybody's time –" Charlie said into the phone, "–that's what the doctors are there for." He doodled on the front of the folder on his desk, hoping he sounded less worried than he felt. He was pretty sure such intense headaches during a pregnancy were a bad sign; the books all said it could mean toxaemia, and that might damage the foetus or even worse.

Bingo came into the room and stood near the window. On the other end of the line, Stephanie said something about it not being anything much. Charlie tried to concentrate, but all he could think was that they might be about to lose the baby. God, he might be about to lose her. "Look," he said, "I still think we should get it checked –"

Bingo caught his eye, and turned to leave. There was sympathy in his eyes: it was easy to forget sometimes, Bingo was actually a good bloke for all his skiving ways. Charlie snapped his fingers at him – he didn't dare let the case get away from him.

"Look, Steph, I'm going to have to go," Charlie said. "Make that appointment, okay? I'll speak to you later." Stephanie said goodbye. Charlie wished the fear hadn't been so evident in her voice.

He put the phone down and looked at Bingo, who said, "We've got a woman who says she saw a blue VW van parked in the same place we found the getaway vehicle."

It wasn't much. In other circumstances it would have been almost nothing. "It's a start," Charlie said. He remembered something that had occurred to him earlier. "Do you still see that mate of yours – the staff sergeant from SIB?" That was the Special Investigation Branch of the Military Police.

"The odd drink," Bingo said. He frowned. "Why?"

"Still having trouble getting the full SP on why Rogers left the army," Charlie answered. It might give them an idea what he was likely to do, who he would turn to in a crisis. Something. He stared at the folder on his desk, and realised he'd doodled the name Jack on it over and over again.

Bingo said something. "Huh?" Charlie said, realising he hadn't taken it in.

"Not bad news, I hope, Guv?" Bingo said.

Charlie realised Bingo had changed the subject, but he couldn't be bothered to argue. "No," he said. "Everything's fine." If Bingo were as good as he thought he was, he'd catch the lie – but if he did, he didn't say anything.

There was a sudden cheer from the squad room.

"What the hell is going on?" Charlie muttered. He went outside. Bingo followed him.

Ash was just coming in the door. She had a sheaf of papers in her hand. "The phone records, Guv," she said waving them in his direction. "We've housed Rogers." She shot Bingo a triumphant look. "He's in a flat in the city," she said.

Charlie glanced from her to Bingo, who seemed distinctly pissed off. "Start surveillance now," he said. "If he leads us to the other gang members I want them all taken out today."

Finally, he thought. Finally something was going right.

***

Gil hauled himself up on the bar he'd fixed to the kitchen door frame. The superior man is fit physically and mentally, he told himself as he pulled up, did a slow count to twenty, let himself dangle, counted and pulled himself up. He felt the sweat bead on his body and the tendons in his arms and neck work. It was good. Nothing worth doing came easy.

The phone rang. He dropped to the floor, picked up his towel and went to answer the call.

"Gil?" said Paulo's voice.

"Yeah," Gil answered, drying himself on the towel. "What's up?"

"It's Eric," Paulo said. "There's been some uniforms round the estate asking about a blue VW van. He wants to move the suitcase."

Gil thought about that, but only for a couple of seconds. "All right. Burn the van. I'll see you about lunchtime." There was no need to say where or, precisely, when. You never knew who might be listening.

***

A little later, Gil left the flat. He sauntered down the driveway of the apartment block, checking the scene as he went. There seemed to be the same number of cars parked as usual. No-one loitering on the corner or making an unexpected delivery.

Safe enough.

151

He headed to the underground car park.

***

Helen sat in the back of a radio car. Alan was driving. With a little luck, anyone watching would assume they were a mini-cab. They were parked well back from the vehicle entrance to Rogers' block of flats, with several cars on either side of them.

Helen leaned forward. The officer watching the street entrance had already told them he'd eyeballed Rogers, who had been heading for the underground car park. He had to be coming out soon, unless he'd clocked someone watching him.

The radio crackled into life. "Moving off," said the officer without preamble. "Coming out of the car park, inclined for the off-side. It's a right, right, right."

Sure enough, a white BMW pulled out of the driveway and turned right. It came towards them. Oxford twisted round, as if he were asking Helen where she wanted to go. The BMW passed them, no problem.

Helen spoke into the radio. "Nine-o from seven-two – you take up eyeball, Chris. Rest of you stay well back."

Oxford turned back and started his engine.

***

The white BMW pulled out into the street. A little later, a blue Sierra followed it.

A little after that, a brown Carlton started down the road, hanging well back from both the other cars.

Only then did Oxford, in the blue Granada, pull out.

Helen took in-coming radio messages from the other drivers. She leaned forward on the back of Oxford's seat. Game on, she thought.

***

Charlie put his pint down on the coaster. He leaned back on the red leather banquette. There were a few people in the pub, but none of them were sitting nearby. Opposite him, Bingo sipped a Scotch. Smoke from his cigarette wreathed the air. The burly man next to him with the military haircut was his mate Sutton, from SIB. The Staff Sergeant took a long pull on his bitter.

"Ordered to resign?" Bingo said, as if he hadn't heard Sutton clearly the first time he'd told them.

Sutton looked impatiently at Bingo – he obviously wasn't a man who was used to having his words questioned – so Charlie cut in. "What exactly did he do?" He picked his lager up again.

Sutton leaned back. "Corporal Rogers was one of a three man team trained for covert observation in South Armagh," he said as if he were reciting something he'd memorised. "Plainclothes patrols, static OPs." Pretty much what we do, Charlie mused. That would make him a tough opponent. "The other two men were Paulo Swift and Eric Poulson." He pulled three photos out of his jacket pocket and passed them to Scott. They were official photographs. The men were uniformed, and they stared with fixed intensity out of the photographs. Hard eyed, they were, Charlie thought: he supposed a stint in Northern Ireland might do that to you, if you were a certain kind of person in the first place. Then he thought of his own passport photo – portrait of a serial killer, Steph called it – and realised that the pictures probably said nothing at all about the men's personalities.

Sutton waited till Charlie and Bingo turned their attention back to him, then went on, "It was their job to report the movements of known players." He took another sip of beer. "Two of the IRA men they were watching were assassinated."

"You think these three were involved?" Bingo asked.

"At the very least they were guilty of fingering the targets for a loyalist hit squad," Sutton said. "Unfortunately, we couldn't prove it."

"Not the kind of thing the government wants splashed all over the papers," Charlie agreed.

"Hence: ordered to resign." Sutton finished his beer.

Bingo swished the last of his Scotch round in his glass. The ice-cubes clinked. "Covert observation. Special Forces. That means he'd be surveillance conscious." He knocked the Scotch back in one mouthful. "He'd have made a special study of it?"

Sutton nodded. "Where he's been, it was a matter of life and death," he said sombrely.

***

The Sierra was two cars behind Rogers' BMW. Traffic was too heavy for it to risk staying further back. The traffic slowed to a halt at the entrance to a big four-way roundabout. The BMW pulled to the left.

"From nine-o," said a voice down Helen's radio. "Junction ahead. He's inclined for the nearside."

Okay, Helen thought. They were staying with him, that was the main thing. "From seven-two," she said. "You go with him. Others hold your positions until he's committed." She turned to Oxford. "You pull in."

Oxford did so.

The radio crackled back into life. "From nine-o. He's on the roundabout. It's a left, left –" There was a pause. Come on, dammit, Helen thought. "No, he's refused. Continuing on."

Shit, Helen thought. He knows we're on him. Sure enough, the eyeball vehicle came back on. "Not the second exit. Not the third." The officer sounded as if he were starting to panic a bit. Hold it together, Helen thought at him. "Damn," said the voice. "He's going all the way round. I'm pulling off – eyeball lost."

Helen sighed. They must still be in with a chance. Maybe he was always this cautious. "From seven-two," she said into the radio. "John, you take up the recip." Had to be worth a try.

"Already covered," said the officer in the Carlton.

"Coming back this way," Oxford said. "He's looking for escorts," he added warningly. He pulled a roadmap out of the glove compartment and made a show of opening it. Helen peered over his shoulder to look at it.

A second later she saw the BMW go past, followed a couple of cars later by the Carlton.

"Okay," she said to Oxford. "Let's give 'em some back up."

Oxford pulled out and turned the car round. They were so far behind that with any luck Rogers wouldn't notice them.

Rogers led them out of town. Helen began to relax. Maybe he'd just been being careful at the roundabout. He certainly wasn't taking evasive action now. In fact, he'd got himself on a long, straight stretch of road – nowhere for him to go but forward.

The road started to climb a hill. The BMW put on speed.

The Carlton did the same, but this was a good, fast road and there was enough traffic around that it wouldn't seem out of place.

Helen hoped.

Oxford accelerated to keep up, though the Carlton was about a third of a mile away and the BMW some way beyond that, approaching the crest of the hill. It put on more speed.

"I don't like it," Helen said.

"What's wrong?" Oxford said, without taking his eyes off the road.

"Accelerating to the brow of a hill – classic anti-surveillance." The BMW disappeared over the crest. "Seven-two," Helen said into the radio. Her blonde hair swung over her face. "All units be alert – I think he's going for a pull through."

Helen peered at the road ahead. They were halfway up the hill themselves now, and the Carlton had just crested it.

The driver came back on the radio. "Six-eight, he's out of the car!" Suddenly there was panic in his voice. "He's pointing something down the road – could be a weapon!"

Helen's car made the top of the hill. Sunlight flashed silver on metal. Christ, she thought, as she saw that Rogers was holding something up to his eye. Uzi, maybe, or an Ingrams... a thought of bullets lacing the road with thunderous fire flashed across her mind. He swung round to catch the Granada in his sights.

This is it, Helen thought. Her belly was like water. David, I'm sorry...

"Correction," said the Carlton's driver. "It's a video camera, that's a video camera." Helen felt the tension drain out of her. She realised she'd been holding her breath. "I'm going through," the voice said.

"Seven-two to all units," Helen said into the radio. "It's no good, he's blown us out. Peel off. Terminate." She slammed her hand into the back of Oxford's seat in frustration. "Terminate."

CHAPTER 20

Gil stood back from the window and twitched the grubby net curtain aside. The street outside was empty – nothing but dull houses converted into dull flats where dull people would live out their dull lives.

Let them, Gil thought. He was still buzzing from his skirmish with the police. They'd been good, he knew that. But he was better. He only wished he could have seen the looks on their faces when they thought he was training an anti-vehicle weapon on them. Or when they realised it was just a cheap Japanese video camera – and then when they stopped to figure out how many of their cars they wouldn't be able to use to tail him again. All caught on tape so he'd know them again.

He grinned. But there was business to attend to.

He turned away from the window. Eric was standing in the middle of the room. He was almost, but not quite, at attention, and he looked as sorry for himself as any squaddie who'd ever had to answer to his commanding officer.

"You parked a dirty vehicle outside your own place?" Gil demanded, though he knew the answer. The van would have been identified by the security guards, and it should have been dumped miles from anywhere. "Where's the van now?" He'd told them to torch it. If they hadn't, there might be a problem.

"Taken care of," Paulo said. He lounged on a grey leather sofa at one side of the room. "We made sure it was well cooked before we left."

Good man, Gil thought, but he didn't say anything. He believed that too much praise sapped a man's spirit – you had to have something to kick against, or what was the point? He turned to Eric. "I'll be taking care of you, boy, if anything like this happens again."

Eric looked away. Gil glanced at the suitcase, which was lying open on the dining table. It was a lot of money. But not enough. Not enough to set him and Sheena up for life. And Sonja, of course.

He went back to the window.

"What's the matter?" Paulo asked. "You wearing a tail?"

"Not going to know, are you?" Gil said. It still rankled that the coppers had managed to tag him at all. "Not if they're any good." And they had been good – just not good enough. "Most you can do is make sure they can't stay with you." Well, he'd done that all right.

"This isn't bandit country, Gil," Paulo said. He pushed his spiky hair out of his face. He was wearing it a bit long for Gil's taste – where the hell was the discipline in worrying about your hair? Complacency, that was what it was. "They're only coppers –"

"We can still do fifteen years," Gil snapped. "I want to see my kid grow up. Spend some of what we've earned." And he didn't mean the little bit the army had paid them off with, either. Pension, they called it. Gil had another name for it.

He crossed the room and closed the case.

"What now?" Paulo asked.

"You two keep your heads down," Gil said. "Only don't get too comfortable." Or lazy, he added to himself. But he'd given them their bollocking and enough was enough.

Paulo raised his eyebrows. "Another job?"

Gil nodded. "That's right."

"When?" Paulo seemed keen.

"A few day's time," Gil said. He needed to suss out a good spot first.

"Bit soon, isn't it?" Eric asked. He sounded a bit nervous.

Gil rounded on him. "What was it we used to say about the life expectancy of an observation point in hostile territory?" Backbone, that was what Eric needed.

The man nodded, reluctantly.

"One more job," Gil said. "Then it's sunshine all the way."

***

Helen took the photo Bingo handed her. They were in Scott's office, where she had already briefed the Guv'nor on their failure to tail Rogers. He hadn't been pleased, though he did say

157

that they were dealing with men as professional as themselves.

That was when he'd called Bingo in. Now they sat around Scott's desk, planning strategy.

Like the two photos Helen had already seen, this one showed a man in his early thirties, in army uniform. A service number was printed underneath his picture.

Bingo had already told her something about the men. He continued, "They resigned back in 1992. Seems they decided to stick together in civvie street."

Helen considered. A lot of Rogers' behaviour made more sense now – and what she'd heard certainly accounted for his knowledge of surveillance techniques. "Did you get last known addresses for Swift and Poulson?" she asked.

Bingo gave her a look that told her not treat him like an idiot. "Yeah," he said. "But they date back to just after they left the army. All three applied to the same private security firm." He paused to take the photos back. "Because the cloud hanging over them was considered political, the army gave them a clean bill of health to escort cash in transit."

Helen was appalled, and didn't bother to hide it. "Conspiracy to commit murder – political?" she said.

"These men operate security like a terrorist Active Service Unit," Scott said.

She knew he was trying to calm her down: surveillance was one of her specialities, and she hated having screwed up.

Well, there was no point brooding on it. All they could do now was try a different trick. "We're going to have to stand off and go technical," she said. "Plumb up his vehicle. Put a bell on his phone and a listening team in the flat next door." Scott nodded. "We already checked, and it's empty," she said, forestalling his next question.

Security like an ASU or not, it was the first thing that had occurred to her when they housed Rogers – she'd realised long before that she was dealing with the best.

But then, she told herself, so was Rogers.

Scott considered. "All right – go for it," he said. "I'll talk to SO11."

Helen got up and went into the squad room. Bingo followed her. As they split up, he turned and said, "More late nights,

Helen? That bloke of yours is going to love you."

Sod you, Helen thought at Bingo's retreating back. The only trouble was, he was right.

***

A midnight blue Volvo drew up outside Rogers' apartment building. This late, it was deserted. A pool of light from the lobby illuminated the forecourt, but most of the windows were in darkness.

Two men and a woman got out of the Volvo. Without speaking, they approached the building. Each one of them carried a metal case. The woman arrived at the entrance first. She held open the door for the two men. She glanced around. No-one was watching. The men went inside. So did she, closing the door softly behind her.

They waited for the lift in the lushly carpeted lobby. One of the men stabbed at the button again, though it was already lit. The other man stood near the door, trying to look casual.

Eventually, the lift came. They got in and the woman punched the button for the sixth floor. The lift moved smoothly upward, and opened on a corridor only marginally less plush than the lobby.

The three people walked in silence down the hall. As they approached their destination, the sound of Pavarotti singing *Nessun Dorma* filled the air. It wasn't loud, but it was enough to mask the noise of their entry into the flat next to the one from which it emanated.

They moved through to the lounge. The music was quieter now, but still audible. One of the men took a torch out of his pocket and flicked it on. He flashed it around. The apartment was luxuriously appointed, but there were dust covers over most of the furniture.

The other man laid his case on the floor. He began to unpack it. The sleek, efficient audio equipment made a dark silhouette against the pale carpet.

***

The glare of the overhead halogen lamps bounced off the grey concrete walls of the underground car park.

Two men worked on a white BMW. They had it up on jacks.

159

The bonnet was open, and the wires connecting the battery to the alarm system had been disconnected.

One of the men took a small device from a compartment in his toolkit. He placed it under the car and fiddled with it for a few seconds. Then he stood up.

"All done," he said.

The second man began to lower the jacks.

***

Gil sprawled on the sofa, listening to *Nessun Dorma*. He had the CD player set to loop, and he'd forgotten how many times it had gone round. Must be driving the neighbours crazy.

He grinned at the thought. He was knackered, though. Too tired even to read – not that Nietzsche's *Beyond Good and Evil* was exactly light material for bedtime. He considered getting up and finishing the Jack Daniel's and soda he'd left on the side, or at least turning the music off.

But he was too tired even for that.

The phone rang. The only people who had this number knew they could only phone him here in an emergency. He rolled to a sitting position, reached over and picked it up.

"Gil," Sonja's voice said. "It's me."

He checked his watch. It was gone one in the morning, and he knew she wouldn't have phoned him unless it was important. "What's up," he said. He reached for the remote control and turned the music off.

"It's Sheena," Sonja said. That got Gil's attention. If anything had happened to her –" I can't sleep," Sonja continued. "I'm worried sick. There's something going on –"

So Sheena hadn't said anything to her. That was his other worry, the great fear he rarely let himself dwell on. "What do you mean," he asked.

"She's coming in all hours," Sonja said. "Acting strange." Her voice caught. He longed to reassure her, to tell her that there was nothing wrong – that teenagers in love behaved that way. "I think it might be drugs, Gil," Sonja said. She breathed raggedly into the phone. "I don't know what to do."

***

Helen felt totally vindicated. Her hunch about keeping tabs

160

on Sonja was obviously right. She held the headset as she listened to the conversation Gil was having with his wife. She turned and exchanged a significant look with Oxford. He grinned at her. She would have said something, but they were running silent – and though speech was allowed, she preferred they stay as quiet as possible.

She leaned back in her chair.

"Leave it with me, love," Gil said in her earphones. "I'll sort it out."

Helen glanced at the cassette machines, just to check they were still working. The two SO11 operators who were working with them had done a good job, she was sure – but she still wanted to be certain.

"I just wish it was all over," Sonja said. Only a faint hiss behind her words betrayed the fact that they were being relayed by the spike microphone that had been driven into the partition wall.

"Not for much longer," Rogers said soothingly. Hell, Helen thought. He was an armed robber but there was more concern in his voice for his wife than she'd had from David for months. "Don't worry," he said. "When it's over, I'll take her away for a while – Disneyland, maybe."

Sonja sighed. Helen shifted in her seat. In her peripheral vision, she saw John, one of the SO11 operators, note something down in the Occurrence Book they always maintained on a fixed obbo.

"She'd like that," Sonja said. "I think she really misses you." She sighed again. "I just want us all to be together again."

"Yeah," Rogers said. "But not yet." Come on, Helen said. Give it up. Tell us when you expect to do the next one. But he didn't. "It's too risky. Now, go back to bed and try not to worry." Damn, Helen thought. She supposed it had been too much to hope for. "I'll take care of everything," he finished.

"Good night, Gil," Sonja said. The line went dead.

Helen pushed her chair back. She grinned triumphantly.

***

Charlie had had a bad night. Or, rather, Stephanie had, and that meant he'd sat up with her. Still, the investigation was going

161

well, at last. At least they had some real leads to follow up and some real work to do.

He walked quickly down the corridor towards his office, exchanging hellos with various officers as he went. His route took him through the squad room. Ash and Oxford were both there. They both looked about as knackered as he felt.

Oxford rubbed the back of his neck, then went back to writing up his notebook.

Ash was cradled a cup of coffee in one hand and typed out her report on the word processor with the other. Charlie went over to her.

"How'd it go last night?" he asked. He didn't stop, but continued over to his office.

Ash pushed the print key. She grinned at him as she went over to the laser printer. Charlie put his case down.

"Sonja called," Ash said.

Charlie went and stood in the doorway between his office and the squad room. "They're still in touch then. Seems you were right."

Ash grinned. Her smile lit her face, and took away the pinched look she got when she was tired. "Let's not be humble about this, Guv," she said. "Yes – I was." She pulled the papers from the laser printer and clipped them together.

Oxford looked up. "When she's right, she's right," he agreed.

"Soon as Rogers starts recceing the next job, we'll be along for the ride," Ash said. She handed her report to Charlie.

"Good," Charlie said. Finally, they were moving. Now if Stephanie was just okay, his life would be perfect. He dragged his mind back onto the job. "Who's covering now?" he asked.

"Ted and Grace," Oxford said. He suppressed a yawn.

"Right. You two better get some sleep if you're back on again tonight," Charlie said. He only wished he could do the same.

***

Grace sat with a map book open on her lap. She and Donachie were with two officers from SO11, sitting in a car parked opposite a council car park.

They'd trailed Rogers and his men there, using the bug SO11 had planted on his car. The three men had been in the car park for a while. It looked to Grace as if they were looking for a car to steal, but without much luck.

"So, Ted," she said. She was suddenly acutely conscious of the two officers in the back seat, and hoped they were too busy with their electronic gizmos to pay any attention to what she was saying. In any case, Donachie was looking at her and it was too late to back out. "What do you know about ball and dummy?"

Donachie smiled at her. Dammit, she thought. We were supposed to be friends. If he were going to take the piss out of her, she was going to tell him what she thought of it – though if she had to take a bit of winding up to get herself requalified to carry a gun, so be it. At least the technicians hadn't said anything.

Donachie looked as if he were going to say something when the BMW and the Audi the other men had arrived in pulled out of the car park.

"Heads up – moving out," Donachie said. "Still only two vehicles." He sounded bored. Grace wondered if she'd get to the point where a moving obbo was just something else to do. "Come lads," Donachie muttered. "Three car parks. Surely you can find one worth nicking." He put the car in gear and pulled away.

"Got a fix," the SO11 tech confirmed from the back seat.

***

Gil wasn't in a good mood. His hands gripped the steering wheel so tight that he could see his knuckles turning white. He drove at just the right speed for a built-up area – no point attracting attention.

They had to have another vehicle, and they needed it fast. The longer they hung around before they did the final job, the more likely the cops were to make their move. He was ninety percent certain they were on to him – but being on to him and having the evidence were two different things: and he'd made sure they didn't. Like he'd said all along, the cops had to catch them on the pavement before they could nick them. And so far, they were one step ahead. He planned to keep it that way.

Eric, though. Eric was beginning to be a problem. He

seemed to have lost all sense of discipline.

"So the alarm goes off," Eric said. "Who's going to challenge you? Nobody."

No bloody wonder he'd only ever made private, Gil thought. "It's a trigger point – someone might remember," he explained, though Eric should have known. Maybe the wonder was that he'd got out of Armagh in one piece. "We find one without an alarm," he added. Eric nodded. At least he still knew who was in command. "Now," Gil added, "Shut up and put some music on."

Eric fumbled in the glove compartment, looking for a tape. Gil made a conscious effort to relax. The superior man, he told himself, has a superior mind and a superior body. But the body must be under the command of the mind, not the other way round.

"What's the code?" Eric asked.

Roger frowned. He glanced at the dashboard. The cassette player was requesting a security code before it could be used. Without speaking, he pulled in to the kerb. He looked more closely at the display, but there was no mistake.

A moment later, Paulo appeared at the window. "What's the problem?" he asked. "Why've we stopped?"

"Stereo's asking for the security code." Eric looked blank.

"Means the power supply's been interrupted," Gil explained. "It was fine last night."

Paulo looked impatient. "Forget it," he said. "Mine's always on the blink."

Maybe, Gil thought. But he didn't want to take any chances. Not when they were so close. Not when he was almost sure the police were snapping at their ankles.

***

Helen unlocked the door and walked into her house. She headed straight for the kitchen: a decent cup of coffee and then sleep, those were the limits of her desires at that moment.

But when she went in, David was sitting at the kitchen table. He was wearing his uniform trousers and reading the paper. The radio was playing quietly. He glanced up at her, and without saying anything got up and unplugged the kettle.

"What are you doing here?" she asked, and immediately regretted her tone, which was strident. "I thought you were on eight till four today?" Her attempt to soften it only made things worse.

"No, late turn," David said, turning back from the sink to talk to her.

Helen frowned. "I thought that was Thursday," she said. A horrible thought crossed her mind: he couldn't – surely wouldn't – be checking up on her? After all, he'd know she'd be back about now – if she'd really been out on an obbo.

"No," he said patiently. "I switched, remember? So I could get a piece of that AMIP enquiry?" Helen stared at him blankly.

"The murder?" he insisted.

Helen rubbed her eyes with the heel of her hand. Of course. The little girl who'd been found dead in Alexandra Park. "Damn," she muttered to herself.

"You'd forgotten," David said. His voice was tight with anger.

It was true. And there was worse to come. "I'm meant to be supervising the late obbo again," she said.

David slammed the kettle down. He turned to the window, as if he couldn't bear to look at her. "Again?" he demanded. "Who's going to look after the kids?"

"I'll call the sitter," Helen said. She knew well enough that nothing she said now would be right.

"You off your head?" David asked. "No babysitter's going to want to stay here till three in the morning–"

"There must be something –"

"Christ, I spend half my life holding this house together." He turned to face her. "I mean, this is my whole point about that bloody job of yours."

As if that didn't mean she spent half her own life doing the same thing, Helen thought. She knew damn well that if he'd had to do a late shift unexpectedly, he'd have expected her to cover for him – and no arguments. "Forget it," she said, still determined to be conciliatory. "It's my problem. I'll sort something out."

But David wasn't in the mood to listen to it. "What's the big draw that keeps you out till all hours?" he demanded. Lately,

Helen thought, getting away from you. But she didn't say it.

"Come on, Helen – what's so special about it?"

Here we go, she thought – it was David's favourite topic: the affair she was supposed to be having with Alan. "Look, I'm not in the mood for this, David," she said. It was true. She could hardly think straight, and any minute now she'd say something she could never take back. "I'm going to bed."

She turned and went into the hall.

"Don't you want your tea, then?" David called after her.

She ignored him.

CHAPTER 21

The BMW was brand new. It stood in the middle of the wrecker's yard gleaming in its perfection. Swift and Poulson stood some way off from it. Rogers was a little apart from them. All three men were watching the car.

And Ted Donachie was watching them. He stood across the road, pretending to read the sports pages of the newspaper. Harris was in the car, parked round the corner.

A crane swung across the yard. It inched slowly down, and then the jaws of its grapple opened. It grabbed the BMW and hoisted it up as slowly as it had come down. Then the crane moved across the yard with surprising swiftness.

The grapple opened. The BMW fell into the open maw of a metal compactor. Even from where he was, he could hear the whine and groan of the crusher.

"Jesus," he whispered to himself. Then he said into his concealed mike, "Grace, it's Ted. They've crushed the Beamer."

"You're joking!" She sounded shocked.

"Oh yeah," Ted said. "I should have my own show."

"They've found the tracker?" Grace asked.

"I don't know," Ted answered. One thing was for sure – they weren't taking any chances. "Better warn the OP. See what she's going to do now."

There were times Ted was glad he was only a Constable – he didn't have to figure out what to do when there didn't seem to be any choices left. Like now, for instance.

***

The doctor pumped the bladder attached to the blood pressure cuff Stephanie was wearing. Charlie leaned forward to see the dial, but it was pointless – he didn't know what the numbers meant anyway. The room was spotless and soulless, and it smelled of disinfectant. Charlie hated it.

Stephanie gripped his hand. Hers was warm and dry. She

167

smiled at him reassuringly.

God, he thought. It was so typical: she was the one in trouble – their baby, but her body, after all – and yet she was the one doing the reassuring. But he couldn't help himself.

The doctor harumphed to himself. He made a note on his pad and started to take the pressure cuff off Stephanie's arm. He was quite old, and the veins stood out on his hands like ridges on a relief map.

"Well?" Charlie demanded.

"Everything seems fine to me," the doctor said. "Blood pressure maybe a bit high, but nothing that could threaten the baby."

"You're sure about that?" Charlie startled himself with his own intensity. He felt himself scowl, and tried to force himself to relax, but without success.

"Charlie," Steph said. She squeezed his hand again. "Sorry, doctor. It's just –"

That was typical of her, apologising when there was no need. He cut in and said firmly, "We were concerned. We thought it might be toxaemia."

"Toxaemia," the doctor murmured as if it were the first time he'd heard the word.

"The headaches," Charlie explained. "It's supposed to be a symptom."

"Mr Scott, if you want to keep your sanity during this pregnancy, stop reading medical dictionaries," the doctor said.

Patronising bastard, Charlie thought. "You don't have to treat us like morons," he snapped. "This is our child we're talking about"

"Charlie, please," Stephanie cut in.

"That's all right," the doctor said. He patted her arm. "I'm used to parental anxiety. Especially with first babies."

Steph sucked her breath in sharply.

"You haven't even read the notes, have you?" Charlie snarled. He got up and stalked out of the room.

Behind him, he heard the doctor say, "Oh, I'm so sorry –"

Bastard, Charlie thought.

***

Stephanie caught up with him outside. He was just about to

168

get in the car when she touched him on the arm.

He turned. "I'm sorry," he said. His eyes searched her face. Her pale skin was almost translucent with weariness, and when she touched his arm her hand trembled.

"We can't keep falling apart at every murmur because of what's happened," she said.

Charlie looked away. How could he face her, when he couldn't help her, couldn't take the pain away, help her sleep or anything? "You're right," he said. "I'm not much good at this, am I?" She smiled. He loved her smile – would have done anything to make her smile. "Too used to being in control," he admitted finally.

"The doctor was right about the medical dictionary, Charlie," she said. She laid her hand on his chest. He put his arms around her, wishing he could shield her from anything at all that might hurt her. "We've just got to get through this as best we can," she said.

"I know love," he said. He stroked her face with the side of his thumb. "I know."

***

Gil tugged at the sideboard in the living room of his flat. It took a bit of doing, but he managed to yank it away from the wall. There was nothing there – nothing on the wall, or the skirting board, or even on the back of the sideboard itself.

He turned round. Eric and Paulo were searching the rest of the flat. Between them, they'd lifted all the carpets, moved every rug and piece of furniture, and looked behind every picture.

The flat was clean as a whistle.

Eric kicked the armchair and it rolled back into place. "There's nothing," he said.

Maybe he was right, Gil thought. And maybe not. "Something in here tells me maybe it's time to foxtrot oscar," he said. He pointed at his gut. His instinct had saved all their lives more than once in Northern Ireland. He wouldn't be surprised if it did again.

Paulo scowled. He perched on the arm of the sofa. "I thought we agreed on half a million a piece, or it wasn't worth getting started?" he said.

169

Gil glared at him. The superior man knew when to fight. And when to make a tactical retreat. He considered, then added, and when to move faster than the enemy anticipates to the list.

**

The lounge of the observation flat was littered with takeaway cartons and wrappers, and used cardboard coffee cups. The place was beginning to smell a bit, of old food and urine – the toilet hadn't been flushed since SO11 had started using the flat, just in case it alerted the target. All that was standard silent running procedure.

One of the men on duty, John, munched a chicken tikka sandwich while he monitored next door's conversation through headphones. The whole conversation was being taped anyway, but there was always the chance of something urgent coming up.

"I haven't forgotten," Rogers said. There was the faintest of hisses on the line.

"Still got my eye on that apartment in Orlando." That would be Swift, John thought. He sounded royally pissed off.

"We're not cancelling it," Rogers said, placatingly, "Just bringing it forward to tomorrow night."

John turned round, caught Chris's eye and jerked his head at the other set of headphones. Chris put his paper down and hurried over.

Meanwhile, Swift said, "Tomorrow night?"

"Sooner it's done the sooner we're away." There was a pause. Come on, John thought. Give us something real to go back to our lords and masters with. "Long as they don't catch us on the pavement, we're still honest citizens, right?"

Arrogant bastard, John thought.

"Right," Swift said. "Does Sonja know about it yet?"

So Sergeant Ash had been right all along, John thought. That would please her. He glanced at Chris and saw that he had clocked it as well.

"I sent her out to pick up the second motor on that nicked driving licence."

Thank you very much, Mr Rogers, John thought.

**

Emma was chattering again. That was all she ever did,

Sheena thought. You'd think she'd get bored with the sound of her own voice, but she never seemed to.

They were walking along outside school. Emma wanted to go to McDonalds, but Sheena had decided to go straight home. That would shut Mum up, at least for a while.

There was a road crossing ahead. They were half way across when a familiar voice called out, "Sheena!"

She turned. Her dad was there, lounging against a new black BMW.

Oh no, she thought. But there was nothing else for it. She turned to face him.

"I got you a present," he said. He opened the back door of the car and brought out a Winnie-the-Pooh teddy bear.

Sheena stared at the bear. Just for a second, she was six years old again. Lying in her bed and listening to the rain patter against the window. The hall light was on, and she could see Winnie sitting on the chest of drawers. Looking after her, Mummy said. The door opened and Daddy came in. He sat on the bed with her, and they started to play her favourite tickling game. But then she wanted him to stop and he wouldn't stop. He touched her down below, where she knew she shouldn't. She wanted him to stop now, please Daddy. But he said a good girl wouldn't say that. She was a good girl, wasn't she? She wanted to please her Daddy, didn't she? Of course she did, of course she did. And a good girl wouldn't cry. A good girl wouldn't tell Mummy...

Sheena shook her head to clear it. Daddy was calling her name. She glanced at Emma, who grinned at her. Lucky Emma, who just didn't understand.

There was nothing she could do about it, not without making a fuss. And good girls didn't make fusses.

She went over to him. He pushed the bear into her hands. "Been talking to Mum," he said. "You and me got to have a little talk, sweetie." He opened the passenger door for her, and she got in.

Her fingers clutched tightly at the bear as Dad got in the driver's seat. She stared out at Emma, who was grinning at her. But Sheena was a good girl, and she didn't make a fuss.

***

Dressed in her scruffiest jeans and a tee-shirt, Helen was lounging on her bed. She was off duty but that hadn't stopped Alan phoning her with news of the latest developments.

She held the phone in one hand and held her other hand over her free ear – the kids were creating their usual bedtime havoc in the bathroom.

"There's no way Rogers could have found the tracker – they're too well concealed," she said into the mouthpiece. "Either he's guessing or SO11 screwed up."

"How come?" Oxford said. He sounded genuinely puzzled, though he should have remembered a little of this from college.

"By leaving signs of intrusion," Helen said. "Scuffs and scratches. Sweat on the steering wheel. Maybe even a whiff of aftershave."

Oxford made a disbelieving noise. Then he said, "So, what do you want to do next?"

Helen pushed her hair out of her face. "What choice is there? We need that next attack point."

"What time do you want picking up?"

Helen bit her lip. "Sorry," she said? "Tonight's no good. You'll have to cover." She owed him some explanation, but she couldn't even face talking about David just then. "I'll explain when I see you," she said at last.

"No need," Oxford said. "I think I know the score." Helen muttered a thank you. "Look," Oxford went on, "I'll call you later if we get anything – otherwise tomorrow." That sounded good to Helen, and she said so, then hung up.

The kids were still creating mayhem in the bathroom. She went out to see to them.

The bathroom floor was swimming in water, and the towels had landed in a heap and become soaked. Helen put her hands on her hips.

"Who's been making all the noise?" she demanded sternly. There was silence for a second. Her lips twitched.

"Me!" Jane shouted.

"No! Me!" Andrew said.

Helen reached forward and grabbed the can of shaving foam from the sink. She fired it at the kids, and they were instantly

172

covered in foam. Jane giggled and splashed water at her. So did Andrew. He scooped his water pistol out of the bath and squirted it at Helen. He got her square on the chest, so what could she do but foam-bomb him back? He giggled, and sat down with a thump. Helen reached for him and helped him up. Then she gave both of them a big wet bear-hug.

She laughed and laughed. It was the best fun she'd had in days.

***

Gil sat on the edge of his bed, smoking. He didn't do it often, but by God he needed it now.

"Dad?" Sheena said. She sounded worried.

He turned to her. She was sitting up in bed, clutching the sheet to her the way a child would hold a cuddly toy. "What is it?" he asked. He hated to see her frightened.

"Dad, I'm scared," she said. "What if I get pregnant?"

Gil blamed the school. She'd had a sex education class again. She always got worried after one of them. "Don't talk stupid," he said. "I look after things, don't I?" It was true. He always made sure he used a condom.

"But if I did?" she persisted. Her fingers wound round the sheet. Her skin was pale as milk in the moonlight. "What about Mum," she said. "She'd hate me." That was true. He'd made sure she understood that – that no woman would stand by and watch her own daughter steal her husband away. "I couldn't face her," Sheena said.

Well, you know the answer to that one, Gil thought. Make sure she doesn't find out.

***

John lobbed a screwed up bit of paper at the mini basketball hoop they'd fixed to the far wall of the obbo flat lounge. He missed. Chris had a go, and missed as well.

A voice crackled softly from the headsets, which were lying unused but plugged in on the desk. Properly speaking, either he or Chris should have been monitoring at all times. But Rogers had brought some girl back, and unless you liked getting cheap thrills from hearing him go at it, there wasn't a lot to listen to. In any case, the tapes would get it all.

John crumpled up another bit of paper and chucked it at the hoop. It dropped in, but not being able to cheer took all the fun out of it.

There was a soft tap at the front door. John went and opened the door. DC Oxford stood there, silhouetted against the light from the corridor. He stepped inside and gently closed the door behind himself.

He looked around. "Run off your feet, I see," he said.

Chris tried one more basket, and missed again. "Glad you're here," he said. "I'm due off." He picked the bits of paper up and dumped them in the carrier bag they were using for rubbish. "Where's DS Ash, by the way?"

"Got some bits to sort," Oxford said. He sounded evasive. Personal problems I guess, John thought. "Probably be down later."

Oxford went over to the desk and looked at the log. "What's doing?" he asked.

"They were talking about tomorrow night earlier on," Chris said. "No mention of a target yet, but Rogers' wife appears to be involved."

Oxford nodded. "It was always on the cards."

"Quiet now, though – apart from the opera," Chris added. "He's got some bird in there."

Oxford pulled a face. "Know what they say – all work and no play." He paused. "When was the last time the loo was flushed in here?"

"About two days ago," Chris admitted.

"Animals!" Oxford said.

Charmed I'm sure, John thought.

"You know the rules for silent running," Chris said.

John thought, the trouble with Chris was that he had a rule for everything. "There's nothing says we have to die of asphyxiation," he said.

Oxford grinned at Chris. "Go on, get off."

Chris picked his jacket up off the sofa and headed out of the door. "Cheers," he said, and left.

With Oxford around, there was nothing for it but to do some proper work. But Rogers' girlfriend soon left, and after that there was nothing much to do.

The night ground slowly by.

Eventually, John got so bored he started stripping down the backup equipment, just for something to do.

Sometime around midnight, he realised he wasn't just hungry, he was starving. There'd been no activity from next door for hours; in fact the only sound coming out of the headphones was the rhythmic sound of Rogers' breathing.

"I'm starving," John announced. "Fancy sharing a pizza?"

Oxford looked up. He'd just finished writing up yet another 'no activity' log report. "Go on then," he said. "Should be somewhere open."

"Fancy getting it?" John asked. He'd no desire to go wandering about in the dark when he could be in the warm.

Oxford looked dubious. John waved his hand at the equipment he was working on. Oxford pulled a face. He obviously knew John was putting one over on him. Despite that, he grabbed his jacket and made for the door.

"My shout, my choice," he said.

"Whatever," John agreed, glad to have got out of going for it himself.

Oxford turned when he got to the door. "Keep this door locked while I'm out, okay?"

Yes Mum, John thought; but he just nodded. Oxford left, easing the door shut behind him. John got up and locked the door. The bolt clicked loudly in the silence.

John stared at it. He was dying for a leak. He went to the bathroom. It smelled putrid. The door banged behind him in his hurry.

What the hell, he thought.

***

Gil's eyes flicked open. He'd fallen asleep in his clothes on the sofa, but he was fully awake now. He couldn't place what had woken him.

A bang, he realised. From next door. From a flat that was empty. So he'd been told when he rented this place.

He went to the party wall and put his ear against it. He heard the gurgle of a cistern filling.

Several things snapped into place.

Gil's lips skinned back from his teeth, but it wasn't what you'd call a smile.

***

Helen sprawled on the sofa, dozing. Some old film droned on the television, but she wasn't listening; she just wanted it on for the company.

A key turned in the front door. Helen wriggled upright just as David stumbled in. His tie was loose and the top button of his shirt was undone. He stank of alcohol.

"David?" Helen said.

"Make us a cup of tea, love," he said, slurring his words. He put his hand out and supported himself on the nearest armchair.

"Where've you been?" Helen said. Not work, that was for sure.

"Don't start," he said. "Just don't start – I'm not in the mood."

Well screw that, Helen thought. And screw making him a cup of tea, too. "You said it was a murder inquiry," she accused.

David glared at her.

***

Gil stood outside the door to the flat next door to his own. He'd put Tosca on the CD specially, and the music boomed out. Nothing surprising in that – everyone knew he loved opera.

He held his sawn-off shotgun loosely in one hand.

He steadied himself. Waited for the music to crescendo. Pivoted on the ball of his foot and brought his other leg up and round in a perfect karate kick that smashed straight through the door.

He stepped through. The light of a table lamp beckoned him into the lounge. He was there in two strides.

There was a police officer there, face turned ghostly by the flickering of his equipment.

Gil raised the shotgun. But he waited for the next crescendo in the music before he used it.

***

Helen got up. She glared at David. "I don't give a damn about your drinking," she said. "It's the fact that you lied to me – ."

176

"You want to talk about lies, Helen?" David demanded.

"Tonight's job was important," she said, struggling not to shout.

"Yeah," David said. He stepped towards her. "I'll bet it was." Anger made his face ugly.

"It was my responsibility," Helen said, determined not to let him shift the blame.

"You think I don't know what goes on at these all night obbos?" he said. "You and the chocolate soldier."

"Grow up, David," Helen said icily.

He took another step forward. Now he was so close she could smell the booze on his breath. "You've been going with him, haven't you?" he demanded. For a second she thought he would hit her. "That's why there's never anything left for me – ."

"Not that again," Helen cut in. "Look, when I finish work I've a house to run and two kids to look after." He wasn't impressed. "Forget sex," she snapped. "It's as much as I can do to keep up with the ironing.

David grabbed her shirt. "Don't lie to me, Helen," he shouted. He pulled her in close to him. "I'm not stupid." He pushed her away.

"Yes you are, if that's what you think," she yelled. "Get it through that thick head – I'm not screwing anyone."

He slapped her, open handed but very hard. It hurt. She stumbled back and crashed into the sofa.

David stared at her, evidently appalled at what he'd done.

Too bad. "That's it," Helen said. "I'm going, and I'm taking the kids with me."

She turned and left. As she went upstairs, she wondered if he would try and stop her. She didn't know if she wanted him to or not.

But in the event it wasn't important, because he didn't.

***

Alan came out of the service stairs on to the landing. He closed the door quietly, but with difficulty, because he was balancing a pizza box and doing his best to keep it flat.

He walked along the corridor until he came to the door of the obbo flat.

It had been kicked in. The wood round the lock was splintered, and the door stood open.

Alan dropped the box and drew his handgun.

He went inside, keeping his back as much to the hall wall as he could. Light from the front room barred the hall floor. There was no sound. Nothing moved.

He kicked the door open.

John was lying unconscious on the floor. His head was a bloody mess. So was his equipment, which lay scattered in pieces all over the room.

Alan walked cautiously into the room – no telling who could be hiding behind the sofa – and went to John. He checked the pulse point in his throat.

The man was still breathing.

Thank God, Alan muttered.

CHAPTER 22

Gil heard a sound from outside the garage and rolled to his feet. He kicked his sleeping bag aside and had his shotgun aimed at the garage door by the time it opened.

Eric and Paulo came in. He relaxed.

"Rough night?" Paulo asked, eyeing the makeshift bed where Gil had spent the night after he'd realised the police were on to his flat.

"It's all rough from here on in," he said. "Did you bring that change of kit?" He'd rung them earlier, from a payphone miles away.

He checked it out, but they seemed to have brought everything he would need. "Right," he said. "Let's have that motor inside."

***

Helen stared at her hands. There was a cup of coffee on the table next to her, but she hadn't touched it. How could she, with a man lying critically injured in hospital, and it all her fault.

Oxford was sitting next to her. She didn't need to look at his face to know he was as miserable as she was. They were both in DI Scott's office, and Scott wasn't happy either.

He paced from one side of the room to the other. "When we ask for SO11 assistance," he said, looking at Oxford. "Under no circumstances do we ever leave their operators unprotected." His voice was quiet. He was good at that – handing out a quiet bollocking that left one feeling worse than any screaming match could.

Helen felt herself flush. He was right. The worst thing was Oxford taking most of the flak, when she was the senior officer on the obbo – should have been, anyway.

"Guv," she said, "It wasn't his fault. I put him on the spot for a favour."

Scott rounded on her. "And that makes a difference? He

shouldn't have let you." He paused and pulled a sour face, like a head teacher disappointed with a favourite pupil. "One of you should have had the sense to come and ask for extra cover."

"It was my operation," Helen insisted. "My responsibility." It was bad enough as it was. She wasn't having a good friend taking the rap for it.

"Don't make this personal, Helen," Scott warned. He rubbed the bridge of his nose. "All right – that's all for now." He turned to Oxford. "You go back to work, Alan. Let me know the minute you hear about tonight's job." Oxford got up to go. So did Helen, but Scott turned to her. "Helen, stay a minute."

Oxford shot her a sympathetic glance, then left. Helen sat back down.

"What's going on?" Charlie asked. Helen stared at him, wondering just how much she should tell him. He wasn't a man to be unreasonable – he was always on his team's side when he could be – but she hated having to admit to personal problems. "This isn't you," he persisted. "Why weren't you there?"

Helen licked her lips. "David sprang this late duty on me," she said. "I had to stay with the kids."

She'd hoped he'd leave it at that, but she was disappointed.

Charlie pursed his lips. "Why didn't you say something?" he asked. "I could have arranged cover."

Helen hesitated. "There's a history to this," she said at last. "Anyway... it turns out he'd lied." She looked up at Charlie. There was no going back now, no pretending everything was fine. It made it all more real, somehow, to be telling someone about it. "David went drinking instead. When we came in we had a steaming row." She paused. She wasn't about to tell Scott that David had thumped her. "He doesn't want me out on late obbo with Alan." She grinned sourly. "Thinks he's giving me one."

"I see," Scott said. His tone was carefully neutral.

Helen picked her coffee up and stared at it. A thin scum had formed on the surface, and she thought better of drinking it. "How do you think I feel, Guv?" She couldn't look at him. "Knowing that SO11 man is lying there in hospital because my husband can't deal with my career." She looked up at Scott.

"You're going to have to sort it, Helen," he said.

Helen sighed. "Don't worry, Guv," she answered. "It's sorted." That was one word for it, anyway. "It won't happen again – I've left him."

Scott's eyes widened. "Left him?" he repeated. "What about the kids?"

What about them? They'd thought it was an adventure at first – getting up in the middle of the night, cramming things in bags. Until they realised Daddy wasn't coming too. Janey had burst into tears then, and that had started Andrew off... Helen thought there might be a lot of that to deal with. "They're with me," she said. "We're staying with a friend until we can get fixed up." She tried to smile, but didn't quite manage it. *I'm not going to do the emotional little woman act on him. I'm not,* she told herself fiercely. She swallowed hard.

Scott nodded. He sat down. "Take some time off," he said. "Get your head together – square things with the kids."

Helen had already considered that. "No Guv," she said firmly. "I think it's best the kids stick to their routine – the nursery, the child minder. Same goes for me. This Rogers investigation is important." At least it involved something other than the memory of staring at David after he'd slapped her and wondering why she didn't hit him back. She'd taken out men armed with knives and guns before – it wasn't like she was scared of him.

Scott cut into her thoughts. "All right," he said. "But if there are any more problems I want to know about them, okay?"

Helen nodded. She stood up and walked to the door, but before she went through it, she turned and said quietly, "Thanks, Guv."

***

Gil stirred his scrambled eggs with the plastic fork from the fast food place. The eggs were cold and congealing, and tasted like they'd started out in a waste processing plant rather than a chicken. He'd already given up on the American-style sausage.

He stared around the lock-up garage. He was fairly sure this place was still safe – there was nothing to suggest that Eric and Paulo had been wearing a tail when they arrived. They sat on crates near him, also eating disgusting fast-food breakfasts.

Their Audi was sitting at the back, under a tarpaulin just in case anyone took a casual look through the window.

Gil dabbed his mouth with his serviette, then picked up his coffee. "They can't have been there long," he said.

They'd been round and round this conversation already, but he needed to be sure the others were with him a hundred and ten percent. Nothing less would do.

"Yeah," Paulo said, "But now they know we're at it."

The coffee, even heavily sugared, was bitter. Gil grimaced at the taste. "Yes," he said patiently, "But if they'd had us from the previous jobs we'd be banged up by now." He tried the coffee again. If anything it was worse than before. "Nothing's changed. They've still got to catch us on the pavement." He stared at Paulo. At Eric, who refused to meet his eyes. "After tonight they won't get the chance," he finished.

"Tonight?" The word exploded out of Eric. "You don't still want to go through with it? What if they're waiting for us – with shooters?"

Gil glared at him. The man was becoming a liability. "What's the matter, Eric?" he sneered. "You never used to wimp out of a good fire-fight." Suddenly he wasn't just trying to put a bit of backbone into the man – he was furious with him. He looked away, to Paulo, before he said something that would really start a fight. "Besides, we're still the only ones who know the target, right?" He looked back at Eric. "We'll be clear before they know what hit them."

Eric looked at Paulo. "All right," he said after a long pause. "Go for it."

***

The car park behind the McDonalds at Canary Wharf was half-full of cars, but there were no people around.

Perfect, Sonja thought. She swung the Volvo she was driving into a bay near some bollards that closed the car park off from a side street. Gil had sent Sonja a stolen driving licence through the post. She'd used it to hire the Volvo.

She got out and looked round, doing her best to seem casual. There was still no-one in sight. She went round to the back of the car and opened the boot. As she took her shopping bag out, she slipped the car keys into the exhaust pipe.

Then she went into McDonalds and had a cup of tea. And went home on the tube.

***

The target was a white square painted onto the cut-out silhouette of a man. There were three bullet holes in it, all slightly left of centre.

A shot rang out. Another hole appeared in the target, again slightly left of where they should have been. And again. And again.

Grace lowered her Smith and Wesson. She glanced at Ted Donachie, and he reeled in the target on its overhead wire while she took off her ear defenders. Then he did the same.

He tapped the target. "It's a good group," he conceded in his Scottish burr. "But you're still doing it."

"Doing what?" Grace asked. Apart from pulling to the left, which she already knew.

"Flinching," he said. Grace pulled a face. No-one had ever accused her of being a coward. "You're anticipating the fall of the hammer," he explained.

Grace wasn't having that. "Rubbish," she snapped. "You're saying I'm scared of it?"

Donachie looked straight at her. She'd never thought about it before, but he had nice eyes – eyes that had seen a lot of pain, she thought. Something must have put that haunted look in them. She'd heard some of the others say that his wife played around behind his back, and that he refused to do anything about it, or even admit it was going on. She wondered if that were all it was.

She didn't think he'd wind her up – not like the other blokes on the team would.

"Aren't you? Just a little bit?" He tapped the target again. "No-one would blame you after what happened."

Grace stared at him. He knows, she thought. Maybe he was right. Maybe he'd been there himself. For sure he didn't seem to be blaming her.

She took a deep breath. "It's like the spots you see when you look at a light bulb. I look at my eye and there he is again." She could see Worsley now, that look of surprise on his face – not pain, just surprise – and tumbling slowly backwards into the water. "Lying there, in the water."

She couldn't meet Donachie's gaze, so she stared at the target with its six bullet holes that accused her of incompetence.

"Do you wish it had been you instead?" Donachie's voice was gentle.

"No," Grace snapped. She regretted it immediately. "Look, I'm not sorry for what happened. I'm just angry he made me do it." It was true. She'd been through it all with the counsellor – she'd thought she was over it, but now she found she was boiling with anger again. "Left me no choice," she said, and realised she was talking as much to Worsley as to Donachie.

"You tell the psych that?" Donachie asked.

Grace laughed, a short soft sound without humour in it. "She said the image would fade with time, but not to try and blot out the memory." She stared sadly at the target. "I guess it's like everything else – it just becomes part of what you are." The trouble was, she thought, she didn't want it.

She felt Donachie's hand on her shoulder, and turned towards him. To her surprise, she found she was smiling.

"Like they say – what doesn't kill you makes you stronger," Donachie said. Grace nodded. "Let's try again," Donachie went on. He pointed at the next target. "Over here."

They moved over to it, and Donachie handed Grace his pistol. The chamber was out. She looked at it. Each cartridge had a small dent in the bottom.

"Using reloads, huh?" she said. That meant the cartridges had been used once and then refilled.

"Anything to save money," Donachie said. He grinned.

Grace closed the gun. She put her ear defenders back on and turned to the target. She raised the gun in the approved two handed style. Her shoulders tensed as she aimed. Her finger squeezed the trigger. Her hand jerked to the left as the hammer fell.

It made a distinct click, but there was no discharge. No bang. Grace stared at her hand.

She'd never noticed before, what with concentrating on the

target. She felt her face grow hot.

Donachie grinned at her. She pulled her ear defenders off, and only then realised that he had left his off.

"See?" he said. "Anticipating. I put spent cartridges in the magazine." Grace stared at him, not sure whether she should be angry or not. He's helping you, she told herself firmly, and found that a small smile was spreading slowly across her face. "Try again," he said.

This time, she left her own ear defenders off. She turned to the target. Aimed. Fired. She realised she'd been less tense, and her hand didn't seem to have moved so much this time. Tried again. This time, she was totally relaxed and her hand was rock solid.

"See?" Donachie said.

"Okay," Grace agreed. She grinned at Donachie.

He stepped back. "This time try to relax," he said from behind her. "Don't think about it. Look past the weapon, focus on the target and –"

Grace squeezed the trigger. There was a deafening bang. Grace gasped in surprise. "What was that?" she demanded.

She turned to Donachie and registered the fact that he was wearing his ear defenders. "That was a ball," he said. He glanced at the target. Grace followed his gaze. The shot had hit the centre of the white square. "Nice shot," he said.

"Oh yeah," Grace said. She was pleased with the result, if not the method. "If that was the ball, what was the dummy?" she demanded. She saw Donachie take a breath to answer, and worked it out just ahead of time. "Don't say it," she said. "Just don't!"

Donachie shrugged, all innocence, and suddenly they were both laughing.

***

Charlie walked across the squad room to Bingo's desk. Ash and Oxford were working at their desks, listening to the tapes from Rogers' flat through headphones. Charlie grinned. If he knew Ash, she'd make sure they analysed every word, every syllable, every pause for breath. And then come up with the goods.

He arrived at Bingo's desk and leant against it. "Did you get the details on the money boxes?" he asked.

Bingo looked surprised. "What, after last night?" He scowled. "There's no way they'll go to work now."

Typical Bingo, Charlie thought – making an assumption that would mean as little work as possible for him. "The tape said they go tonight, so that's the basis we work on," he said in a voice that dared Bingo to disagree. "Now, what did you get?"

Bingo handed him a sheet of paper. "Four companies all doing cash machine refills in our area. Total of thirty-six drops, any one of which might be the target." His tone said he thought even trying to second guess Rogers was a waste of time.

**

The only thing to do now was to make the best of the situation, Helen thought. Bring Rogers in before he did any more harm; make sure they had enough evidence to get a conviction – and that it was good enough to make the verdict stick.

She sat at her desk listening to the tapes from Rogers' flat. If she had to, she'd go through every foot of it, but before it came to that she'd decided to check the times marked in the Occurrence Book.

She pressed the fast forward button, noting as she did so that Bingo was having yet another heated exchange with Scott. She couldn't hear what they were saying through her headphones, but then again she hardly needed to – it was bound to be about something Scott wanted doing that Bingo couldn't be bothered with.

She glanced at the display panel, and seeing that she'd arrived at the right place, stopped the machine and pressed play. Rogers' voice came over the headphones.

"We're not cancelling it," Rogers said. He seemed to be soothing someone. "Just bringing it forward to tomorrow night."

"Tomorrow night?" That was Swift speaking.

"Sooner it's done the sooner we're away."

That was all for the moment. Helen pushed fast forward again. She rubbed at her eyes. They were stinging with tiredness. She stopped the tape, then pressed play again.

"Does Sonja know about it yet?" That was Swift again.

Thank you Paulo Swift, Helen thought. At least that confirmed that the wife was involved.

Rogers' voice came on. "I sent her out to pick up the second motor on that nicked driving licence."

"Nice one, Sonja," Swift said.

That seemed to be the last comment of any interest on that tape. Helen ejected the tape and snapped the next one in. She wound forward to the first marked position, then played the tape.

This time, Sonja was speaking. "It's Sheena," she said. "I can't sleep. I'm worried sick. There's something going on –"

"What do you mean?" Rogers cut in.

"She's coming in all hours. Acting strange," Sonja said. She was close to tears.

Helen tapped her notepad with the tip of her biro. She glanced up, and noticed Scott going into his office, with Bingo following him.

That girl was the key to the plot. She was sure of it now. She changed tapes and found the next log entry that mentioned Sheena.

"Sonja?" Rogers said in her earphones. He sounded concerned. Almost tender.

Yeah, Helen thought. And I'll bet Adolf Hitler was fond of his old mum, too.

"It's getting worse, Gil," Sonja said. "I thought you said you'd speak to her?"

There was a pause. "I know love," Rogers said. "I just haven't had time."

Helen frowned. Something about that wasn't right. She replayed the tape. It wasn't anything they'd said, but... she glanced at the Occurrences Book. That conversation had taken place on October twenty-fifth at nine in the evening. Nothing odd about it. She frowned again, and then, remembering ferreted around on her desk until she found a file of surveillance photographs. She pulled them out, sorted through them. Found the ones showing Sheena meeting her dad outside school. At quarter to four – on October twenty-fifth.

"You liar," she whispered at Rogers' picture. But she

couldn't quite see what it amounted to. She made a note of the discrepancy, ejected the tape and started to put the next one in. As she looked for the next mention of Sheena, her eye lit on a log entry under the last one she'd seen: twenty-one thirty hours. Subject's female companion departs target premises. Tenor of conversation: intimate.

So he'd had a woman back there. It seemed out of character. A trained covert operations man compromising his base for a quick tumble. Even as she thought it, Helen knew.

She knew.

She jammed the tape back in and wound it on.

"Chop chop," Rogers' voice said. "Don't want to be late back. And don't forget what I said – no more worrying Mum."

It could be innocent. They might have spent the evening playing Monopoly.

But by the time she'd finished listening to the tape, she was sure they hadn't. Helen was shaking with anger as she made her way over to Scott's office. She got there just as he and Bingo were coming out of it.

"I want some of ours and some of SO19 at each of those four prime sites we picked out –"

"I think I've got something, Guv," Helen interrupted. She pretended not to see Bingo's scowl.

"What is it?" Scott asked.

"Last night Sonja Rogers made a phone call to her husband, worried sick about Sheena. Apparently he'd promised to speak to the girl, only he told Sonja he hadn't had the time."

Scott frowned. "So what?"

"So, according to surveillance pictures, he picked her up from school that same day."

Bingo made a disparaging face. Well, they all knew what Bingo I've-been-married-twice-wanna-be-number-three Tate thought about family values, Helen thought.

"Why would he lie?" Scott asked.

Once Helen told him, all three of them knew they had what they needed.

***

Alan glanced at Ash. Her face was drawn, and her eyes were

dark with fatigue. But she looked triumphant. Not happy – how could she be, when she'd just left her husband and she felt responsible for John being injured.

"There," Ash said. She pointed down the road to the school gates. A hard-faced, sandy haired woman was coming towards them. She had a girl – a small, plain, blonde girl – by the arm, and she was hurrying her along. Poor little kid, Alan thought.

Ash nodded to Oxford. They got out.

The woman stopped when she saw them. There was panic in her eyes. In the next second, Alan thought she might make a break for it. Then she almost visibly forced herself to relax.

Ash spoke. "Sonja Rogers, I'm DS Ash. This is DC Oxford." Sonja looked away as her worst fears were confirmed. "Flying Squad," Ash finished.

Sonja pursed her thin, badly made-up mouth. "What do you want?" she demanded.

"Would you come with us, please," Ash said. It wasn't a question. "We'd like to ask you a few questions."

Sonja shot a desperate look at Sheena. The girl looked devastated and embarrassed both at the same time. "Am I under arrest?" Sonja asked.

"Yes," Ash said quietly. Alan knew that would be more for the girl's sake than the mother's. "You do not have to say anything," Ash said, and then continued to tell Sonja her rights. "But it may harm your defence if you do not mention when questioned something which you later rely on in court. Anything you do say may be given in evidence." Sonja stared at her, almost seeming bored – like a woman who'd heard it all before, Alan thought.

But then she looked at Sheena, and for a moment Alan thought she might argue after all. She must, however, have thought better of it. "What about my little girl?" she asked.

"That's all right," Alan said, feeling suddenly as sorry for the woman as he already did for her daughter. "She can come too."

He stood to one side. Sonja headed towards his car. After throwing a desperate look at one of her friends, so did Sheena.

***

Sonja fiddled with the handle of her teacup. The interview

room was bare and cold – just a table and a couple of chairs. The motor of a twin cassette deck whined.

Nothing, she thought. Whatever they've got on Gil or his damn squaddie mates, they've got nothing on me.

The woman copper who'd brought her in spoke. Ash, that was what she'd said her name was. "We believe your husband is responsible for a number of armed robberies on security vans," she said. She was a pinch-faced little bit of nothing, and she had a Belfast accent. In her years of worrying about what Gil was doing while he was posted out there, Sonja had grown to hate that accent. But she didn't let that show. It would be weak, and everything now depended on her being strong. "We believe you also know something about these robberies. Do you still say you don't want a solicitor present."

The logic was simple. Sonja explained it again. "I don't need a solicitor. I haven't done anything –" Nothing they could pin on her, Sonja thought. "What's more, I haven't the faintest idea where my husband might be." She grinned ruefully. "Wish I did – he owes me five months child support."

"Really?" the constable, Oxford, said. "How come the Child Support Agency has no record of it?"

They'd thought of that when they dreamed up the plan. Sonja didn't miss a beat. "It was an informal arrangement." She smiled slyly. "Come to think of it, maybe I should give them a call."

Ash didn't seem impressed. "Mrs Rogers, maybe I should point out that we've been watching you for quite some time." She paused. Sonja stared back at her without blinking. They were just trying to scare her into giving something away, that was all. But the copper went on, "We've got recorded telephone conversations showing contact between you and your husband as recently as yesterday evening." You bastards, Sonja thought. Prying into people's lives. Ruining their privacy. She felt her expression change and knew they must have noticed. "Do you still say you know nothing about these robberies?"

Oh she was a bitch, all right, that Irish copper. She seemed to be enjoying it.

"No comment," Sonja said. Let them make something of that if they could.

"Mrs Rogers, do you know your husband has already shot and injured two security guards?"

She hadn't known. Gil hadn't said. He hated to worry her. But two men injured? That was bad. "No comment," she said even more firmly. The sound of her voice reassured her. He wasn't a violent man, her Gil, even though he'd been in the army. Yes, he carried a weapon, but as he'd told her, that was so no-one got any funny ideas. It actually reduced the chances of violence. And anyway, all they wanted was what was due them: the secure future they should have had if the army hadn't kicked him out just for doing his duty to his country.

Ash exchanged a look with the constable. She pushed her hair out of her face. "Very well," she said. "There's something I want you to listen to." Oxford put a portable cassette machine on the table. He slipped a cassette in. "You'd better prepare yourself. It's not very pleasant," Ash said. She leaned over and pressed the play button.

Sonja watched the spindles begin to turn. She didn't know what they were going to make her listen to, but she was quite certain it was just a trick.

***

Preparation was half the art of war. That Chinese general, Sun Tzu, might not have said it in his book about war, but he should have.

Gil sat in the lock-up garage. Sunlight filtered in through the grimy windows and shone dully on the metal of the Browning semi-automatic pistol he had stripped down for cleaning.

Across from him, a beam of light from a mechanic's lamp that hung from a hook on the wall was trained on the engine of the Shogun. Eric and Paulo worked on the car, tuning it to within an inch of its life. After all, their lives might depend on it.

Gil picked up his can of WD40 and gave it a good shake. He pulled off a strip of cotton wadding and sprayed lubricant on it, then threaded it onto a cleaning rod.

He grinned to himself as he shoved the rod into the barrel. Soon, he thought at the gun. Soon, my lovely.

***

Sonja stared at the tape deck. The spindles turned. Whatever they make you listen to, they've made it up. She told herself that, but she felt her hands tighten round her tea cup and knew that they were getting to her.

The tape hissed.

"Dad?" Sheena's voice said.

It's a fake, Sonja thought. A rotten fake. But she couldn't see how it could be. Not really. Not in real life.

"What is it?" That was Gil's voice. He sounded tender. Sonja strove to remember the last time she'd heard him sound like that. It must have been years back.

"Dad, I'm scared." That was Sheena again. Jesus – had Gil told her about the jobs? What else would scare – Her daughter's voice cut her thought off. "What if I get pregnant?"

It took a second for the words to register. Sonja felt herself grow cold. Christ, she thought. Dear Christ. She felt as if the solid ground had dropped away from beneath her feet.

She stared around the room. Ash looked at her. The expression on her face – was that pity or contempt? Sonja didn't have time to think about it, or even what her poor little girl had been forced to go through. The tape was relentless.

"Don't talk stupid," Gill said. "I look after things, don't I?"

Look after things, Sonja thought numbly. I suppose he had. She wondered, suddenly, how long it had been going on. If he'd done it to her in their bed – the bed he slept with Sonja in.

She felt like weeping. But Ash was looking at her with that expression Sonja couldn't stand, and she'd be damned to hell before she'd cry in front of the bitch.

And still the tape wound on.

"But if I did?" Sheena said. She sounded terrified. "What about Mum? She'd hate me." Oh no, love, Sonja thought. And then she thought, that's how he controlled her – how he made her do it. She felt the first stirrings of anger. Of strength? "I couldn't face her," Sheena said.

My poor daughter, Sonja thought. My poor, poor little girl.

On the tape, Gil said, "Get dressed. I'll give you money for a cab." Then it hit Sonja – all those times Sheena had been late home, all her tired, fretful sulks, all Sonja's worries about boys and whether she was doing drugs. All Gil's fault. And she'd confided in him.

Ash leaned over and turned the tape off. "I'm sorry you had to hear that." She actually sounded as if she meant it.

Well, Sonja didn't want her pity or her regret. And then it came to her – they'd done this so she would betray Gil. Faked the tape – yes, that was it, faked the tape – so she would give him up out of anger.

Well she just wasn't that stupid. "It's not true," she screamed. She slammed her hand down on the table so hard her cup rattled in its saucer. "It's a fake." She stared at Ash with all the contempt she could find. "You're sick, you are!"

Ash stared at her silently. A long, quiet moment passed. "No, Sonja," she said. "We obtained legal authority to bug his phone and his flat." She paused and licked her lips. "The truth is, your husband has been sexually abusing your daughter." She stopped again. Sonja wanted to scream a denial, to tell the bloody woman to stop making things up. But she couldn't do it. Not with that cold grey stare on her, challenging her to believe. "What you have to decide," Ash said, "Is which one of them you most want to protect."

Sonja felt her mouth work as she tried to swallow. Her heart was thundering and she heard the blood rushing in her ears. Her bottom lip began to tremble and her eyes burned.

"Well?" Ash asked softly.

He was her husband. He loved her. Sonja knew it, knew it as well as she knew her own name. She remembered what it was like to hold him, to be held. His hands on her body, his mouth on her lips... and then, sickeningly, she thought of him doing that with Sheena.

Ash quickly laid photographs in front of her. Reluctantly, she looked at them. They showed Gil meeting Sheena from school. Gil touching her arm. Offering her a bear – a Pooh bear.

She knew it was true then. He'd given Sheena a bear just like that when she was six years old.

"These are pictures of your husband picking your daughter up after school," Ash said.

Sonja stared at them. How old was she, she thought. How old was she when you started to touch her, you pervert?

193

"Look at the date and time on the back," Ash commanded.

Sonja did as she was told. It had been taken yesterday afternoon. And she'd phoned him in the evening, and he'd said –

"He told you he hadn't seen her, didn't he," Ash said. That Irish accent was really beginning to get on Sonja's nerves. "Would you like to see some more pictures?"

"No!" Sonja screamed. No she didn't want to believe it, no she didn't know how to deny it, no she couldn't stand it. Not her husband. Her baby...

"Perhaps you'd rather listen to the tape again?" Ash was implacable.

Sonja shook her head. She felt like there was nothing left inside her, nothing at all. They'd won, she realised.

She didn't care if they'd set this up, if they'd only told her so that she would betray Gil. She wanted him dead. She wanted him put where he couldn't get to Sheena. She wanted him castrated.

"All right," she said. She felt the tears burning down her cheeks. "All right."

"I have to remind you, Sonja, that you are still under caution." The bloody copper was all business now, oh yes. Sonja stared straight ahead, looking at the minute imperfections in the plaster on the wall, trying to make sense of them. Trying to make sense of anything.

"Tell us about this job tonight," Ash said quietly.

"The city," Sonja said. Her voice was tight with anger. "Security van. I placed the change-over vehicle in a burger bar half a mile away." She stopped. The anger in her was a white hot blaze. She could scarcely think about him without wanting to lash out. "If you try and take him, he'll make a fight of it."

"Hopefully it won't come to that," Ash said soothingly.

She didn't understand, Sonja thought. She stared up at the policewoman. "I want him to fight," she snarled. "I want you to shoot the bastard." Though even that was too clean, too quick. If she could have made him suffer through the years as he'd made Sheena suffer, she would have done it. Oh Sheena love, she thought. "Now," she said, "can I see my daughter?"

***

194

Sheena took the can of drink from the policewoman who had said to call her Grace. Her mother had gone off with the other policewoman, the one who had come to the school. Now Sheena was sitting in the hallway. She'd found a seat with her back to the room where Mum was. She didn't want to think about what was going on, and it was easier if she didn't have to look at the door, so she sat and looked at the posters about how to deal with people who knocked at your door, and how to get help if you were the victim of a crime.

They all thought she didn't understand what was going on, but she did – Dad was up to something, and whatever it was was against the law.

Sheena sipped her drink. She wondered if they were trying to get Mum to tell on Dad, and if they'd start on her next. Maybe that was what this drink was – a bribe.

But she'd had another thought in the car. Suppose they knew about her and Dad? Suppose they told Mum. They were the police, after all. They knew just about everything about everyone. It was their job.

She didn't want to think about it. She wouldn't think about it.

Grace started asking her stupid questions about school, like what her favourite subject was. They always asked that, adults did. How should she know what her favourite subject was? Hometime, she thought. That was a good one. She wished she could go home now.

She heard the door of the interview room open. She wouldn't look.

"Sheena?" Mum sounded as if she'd been crying.

She knew. The bastard police had told her. Sheena didn't turn round. She couldn't.

"Sheena, love..." Mum said again.

Sheena realised she was crying, tears pouring down her face. She turned. Her mother was standing in the doorway of the interview room. She looked very small, and her mascara was smeared all over the place.

Before she knew what she was doing, Sheena found herself clinging to her mother. "Oh Mum," she sobbed. "Oh Mum, Mum." She couldn't stop crying. "He said not to tell. He said-"

"Shh," Mum said. "Shh now. It's all right. It's all right."

And the strange thing was, Sheena felt better than she had in years.

CHAPTER 23

The tension in Oxford's Granada was almost palpable. Helen glanced at him. He was grim faced, and she knew that he felt as she did – that this case had become personal, now they knew what Rogers had done to his daughter.

There were a couple of SO19 officers in the back seat, both carrying MP5 rifles. Like her, they were wearing flak jackets, and were holding their uniform chequered baseball caps on their laps.

They were parked up on a slip road near the Eastern end of the Limehouse Link, ready to cut Rogers off as he tried to pick up his changeover vehicle – the Volvo Sonja had left for him in the car park at Canary Wharf. Neon streetlights in the tunnel up ahead cast a fluorescent glare across the end of the road, but here they were in twilight.

"From OP," said a voice from the radio. "I've got eyeball on the vehicle – a silver Shogun. Subjects making their run... now." There was a pause. "Going for the money box. All units standby."

This was it. Helen felt her mouth go dry. It wasn't fear, just tension. The cold weight of her Smith and Wesson in its holster was a comfort.

***

Gil stepped out of the alley just as the security guard came out of the bank. There was a scream of burning rubber. The Shogun hurtled into view and swung round in front of the money van, trapping it.

Gil grabbed the guard and yanked him over to the front of the truck. He jammed the sawn-off shotgun up by the man's ear.

"Open the chute and throw the cash out," he yelled to the driver, "Or I'll blow his head off."

The chute opened. The money cassettes were pushed out. Paulo grabbed them and shoved them in the back of the Shogun, while Gil held on to the guard. He looked round nervously. They were okay, they were okay – but his gut said otherwise and he trusted his gut. He rammed the barrel hard into the guard's face.

"Come on," he snarled at the driver. "Hurry it up or I blow his head off."

It was taking too long. It was taking too fucking long, and Gil's gut clenched when he thought about it.

**

Charlie watched the raid go down from Donachie's Sierra. Bingo and Harris were in the back. Even from where he sat, Charlie could see the glint of the weapons.

He ached to go in, but it would have been the guards' death warrant.

He got on the radio. "From six-three. Remember, no intervention here. That's no intervention unless shots are fired."

**

Gil wrenched the guard's arm up behind his back while Paulo chucked the last few cassettes into the Shogun and got in himself. When he was done, Gil shoved the man away from him, but he kept the shotgun trained on him.

"Down on your face," he said.

The man dropped to his knees with his hands behind his head, then lay right down. Gil backed away from him towards the car. He kept the shotgun on him as long as he could, then jumped in the back seat.

"You done yet?" Eric sounded as weedy as ever.

"Kick it," Gil snarled. "Go!"

He slammed the door. Eric gunned the engine and they were away.

**

Charlie leaned forward to listen to the radio.

"From OP," the disembodied voice said. "They're running. Subjects still with the silver Shogun. Heading... east along Commercial Road."

Next to Scott, Donachie started the engine.

Charlie spoke into the radio. "From six-three. Eyeball car move in. Let's keep them in view."

The Sierra moved smoothly out. Charlie suddenly caught sight of Harris in the wing mirror. She was tense, eager even.

Well, it made a change from Bingo, who was sitting next to her trying to look bored and not quite making it.

***

The Shogun barrelled down the Limehouse Link. The overhead lights flashed by, glaring off the grimy walls.

"What did I tell you?" Rogers shouted. The adrenaline was still screaming through his body. "Made in the shade!" He punched the air for sheer joy. "Whoa!" he yelled.

Paulo grinned. He cheered as well, and for a moment the car was full of laughter. Then he stopped. Turned to look back.

"Gil," he said urgently. "I think there something coming up behind." He stared, intent on the road behind. "I think it's a gunship".

Gil looked back. The car behind was closing on them fast. He grinned. He felt like he'd been made for this moment. The blood sang in his ears. He reached for the shotgun, turned round and braced himself between the front and rear seats. Then he released the catch on the door. It swung open.

***

Charlie's Sierra closed on the Shogun. He willed Donachie to get the last possible drop of speed out of the car. They were closing, closing.

The rear offside door of the Shogun opened. Rogers leaned out. Something in his hand glinted silver. Light flashed. A shot cracked out. Lead shot spattered the windscreen.

"He's firing," Charlie yelled unnecessarily. "Drop back!" If he had anything beefier than a sawn-off in there, they could be in trouble.

A second shot cracked out. The windscreen shattered. Charlie punched the glass out with his gloved hand. Donachie did the same. Air rushed in and punched at them like a heavyweight's fist. Charlie's eyes watered.

The Shogun came to the tunnel exit. It slewed round to the right cutting across the road.

Ash would need to get in position, Charlie thought. He picked up the radio.

***

Their turn soon, Ash thought. She peered into the gathering

199

gloom ahead.

Scott's voice crackled over the radio. "Suspects still heading east. Seven-two, hold all further traffic and get into position – ."

Oxford had the car in motion almost before Scott had finished speaking. He held the wheel with one hand, and with the other pulled on his chequered baseball cap.

Ash leaned forward and spoke into the radio, pulling on her own cap as she spoke. "Seven-two, understood."

The squad car raced into a tunnel. Behind them was open road. But ahead of them – in the direction Rogers was coming from – there was a sharp bend.

Oxford swung the car across the on-coming traffic. The officers from the other vehicle got out and directed a couple of on-coming civilian cars into the slip road, then blocked it with their vehicle. Ash got out of the car. The other officers followed her.

She smiled tightly at Oxford. "Ready?" she asked.

"Ready," he said. They pulled their weapons out and waited.

***

The superior man knows when to make a tactical retreat.

Gil put the shotgun down on the floor of the car. They were almost there – almost out of the damn tunnel. They'd get to the Volvo all right. Just a bit of luck, that was all they needed. He pulled the Browning from its holster and cocked it. It felt good.

The dirty white walls of the tunnel rolled past. Eric slowed fractionally as he swung the Shogun into a sharp bend.

"What about the cassettes?" Paulo asked. He had his own Browning in his hand.

"Just grab what you can and run," Gil said. He put his hand out to steady himself as the car leaned into the bend.

"Police!" Poulson screamed.

The car lurched. The open door flapped shut, then bounced open. Tyres squealed as the back of the Shogun slewed round and spun to a halt. Gil slammed into the back of the seat. He smelled burning rubber and the coppery scent of fear.

He grunted, but grabbed the money cassettes and was on his feet in the same moment.

"Come on!" he yelled.

***

The doors of the Shogun opened. Helen raised her weapon. In her peripheral vision, she saw Oxford and the other officers do the same.

Three men leaped out of the car. Three weapons – semi-automatics, Helen noted reflexively.

"Come on!" the first one out screamed.

Rogers, Helen thought, identifying him from his photograph. The one behind him was Swift. Poulson had got of the driver's door.

"Armed police? Stay where you are!" one of the SO19 officers shouted.

"Drop your weapons," another added.

Helen kept her weapon trained on Rogers. Those semi-automatics were powerful enough to drop a man with one bullet – but all three had their weapons pointing to the ground.

They were realists then. Not suicidal. She remembered Sonja saying Rogers would make a fight of it. It seemed she was wrong.

Helen almost regretted that.

Poulson and Swift threw their guns to the ground.

"Don't shoot," Swift shouted. "I'm unarmed? Unarmed." He stretched his hands out in front of him.

Rogers hesitated. For a second Helen thought he might yet go for it.

"Put it down, Gil," Helen said. He didn't move. Not a muscle. But his face said he was thinking about it. "Do it now," Helen shouted. "This is your last chance."

An odd expression – wistful, almost – passed across Rogers face. He dropped the semi-automatic.

"On the floor – kneel down," Helen said. Rogers dropped to his knees. So did the other two. "Lie down," Helen commanded.

They did so. Helen and Oxford moved in to deal with him, leaving the others to the SO19 officers. Helen kept her gun trained on Rogers, while Oxford pulled his arms behind his back and cuffed him.

"Up we get," he said, starting to haul Rogers to his feet.

Helen put her hand on Oxford's arm. "No, Alan," she said. She couldn't keep the contempt out of her voice. Didn't want to. "Leave him there. It suits him."

Rogers looked up at her. "What's your problem, bitch?"

Helen glared down at him. "I'll tell you," she said, thinking of Sheena, so certain her mother would hate her for what she had done to him. "For better or worse I've got this compulsion to go to work on rubbish like you."

She turned away, unable to bear the sight of him.

"Steady on," he said. "Haven't you heard of the Geneva Convention? Even prisoners are entitled to some dignity –"

Helen paused. Dignity? What dignity was there for a small girl, raped since she was little more than an infant and taught to enjoy it? What dignity in that wrecked life?

She turned back to Gil. "I've spoken to your daughter, Mr Rogers," she said. "I think I know what you deserve."

He looked up at her – no guilt there, no compassion. He didn't even seem to understand what he'd done.

Helen walked away from him, over to Scott who was congratulating the team.

Just for a second, she wished Rogers had made a fight of it – because then, she could have shot him back.

And when you shoot, you shoot to kill.

PART FOUR
WILD CARD

CHAPTER 24

The Glendower Casino was located in the basement of a discreet but substantial Georgian building. In the darkness of the small hours, only the lights shining from behind the shutters at its upstairs windows indicated that it was still in use.

A silver Cosway with a single occupant purred past its door.

In the police surveillance van parked around the corner from the Casino, a Flying Squad officer noted the Cosway in his monitor. He turned from the screen and started in on the sandwiches he'd brought with him from home.

The other officer on duty turned to see what he was doing.

Neither of them noticed the Cosworth appear on the second monitor, the one that showed the rear of the Casino.

***

Charlie Scott stared at his watch. Four in the morning, and nothing had happened. But their intelligence had been good. He was quite sure the raid was going to go down. He'd committed a lot of resources to this operation – officers undercover, the surveillance van, and marksmen on the roof covering both entrances to the Casino.

Ash was sitting next to him in the driver's seat of the Volvo. He glanced at her. She looked about as bored as he felt – and he was sure that Donachie, who was in the back, felt the same way.

He picked up the radio and contacted the surveillance van. "What are we looking at?" he asked.

"A long night and nothing to show for it," the officer said through a mouthful of food.

Charlie scowled and broke the connection.

***

Bingo was in his element. Or what he'd very much like to become his element.

The private room of the casino was all red velvet and polished mahogany. Brass fittings glinted in the subdued

207

lighting. And it had that intense quietness that meant big money was being staked.

Bingo licked his lips. It wasn't his cash he was staking, but the tension was getting to him all the same. He stared at his hands, thinking about it. There were five other men at the table, all equally focused – but then, they stood to lose their own money.

The dealer was a dark haired woman dressed in the casino's uniform of a red skirt and white blouse. She took a pack of cards from the shoe and began to unseal it.

The pit boss watched her every move. She was an older woman, blonde haired and ice cool, with a red slash of lipstick. She was sitting on a high stool so she could see everything that went on. Her red skirt was a discreet length, but it was slit just enough to reveal legs that seemed to go on and on forever.

Nice, Bingo thought. He forced his attention back to the dealer, who was ready to start the next hand.

"Okay, gentlemen," she said. "I'll set the stake at twenty thousand pounds." She started to deal. The cards swished as she skimmed them face down on the baize. Bingo felt his pulse hammer at his temples. He itched to pick up his cards. She was nearly done – they all had two cards each and she'd started to deal the third. She fumbled. The card flipped out of her hand and landed face up. It had been intended for the man next to Bingo. He breathed in sharply.

"Sorry," the dealer said. Her cheeks flamed.

Behind her, Bingo saw the pit boss scowl impatiently.

***

Ted leaned forward to talk to Scott and Ash. He felt like he'd been waiting in the car all his life, rather than just all night.

Well, it wasn't like there was anyone waiting up for him at home. Mary was off out somewhere, seeing friends. He reached into his pocket for some Rennies, but he'd finished them long before.

"So who knows we're in?" Ash asked.

"Head office," Charlie said, "And Doug Watson – he's the head of security." Ted saw his face in the rear view mirror. He wasn't a happy man. "The game's invitation only – strictly cash. I still say it's going to go."

Ted made a derisive noise. "Tenner says we draw a blank,"

he said.

Scott shook his head. He was always up for a bet, and now was no exception. He got his wallet from his pocket and pulled out a tenner, which he placed on the dashboard.

"You're on," Scott said. It was an open secret that he'd been well pissed off that Bingo got to go and play the punter in tonight's undercover instead of him.

Easy money, Ted reckoned. He reached into his jacket pocket for his money. Nothing. Tried the back pocket of his jeans. Still nothing.

After several minutes of frantic searching he still hadn't found it. Ash glanced at Scott. They were both grinning.

"Bingo," Ted said at last. "I'll kill him."

***

Bingo pushed a bundle of notes across the table. It was more cash than he'd ever seen in one place, at least outside of a haul, and it broke his heart to let it go. Only three of them were still in. A one in three chance of winning. Even if he did have to give the money back.

The man to his right skimmed his bet across the baize as casually as if it were Monopoly money. His face was set like stone.

"The stake is sixty thousand pounds," the dealer said. She seemed quite recovered from her earlier gaffe. "Are we all finished?"

Bingo exchanged glances with the other players. No-one spoke. Eventually, the man on the end nodded to the dealer. He turned over his cards. Bingo winced. The man had an ace, ten and three. Bingo forced himself not to show his disappointment. He flipped his cards over – his highest card was a jack. The last man showed his hand. Pair of sixes and an ace. The smallest flicker of a smile played across his mouth and was gone.

The dealer turned her own cards over to show a pair of queens and a joker. "Pair royal with wild card wins," she said. She raked the pool in.

"I'm out," Bingo murmured. He left his cards on the table and wandered away. He left the private room and went out into the main gaming area.

There were several tables in play – blackjack and roulette as well as poker. He made his way towards the bar at the far side

209

of the room. At one point he brushed past Oxford who, dressed in a black suit and bow tie – and minus his usual gold jewellery – was every inch the security man.

Bingo arrived at the bar. Harris, playing the part of high-class barmaid to perfection, asked him what he wanted to drink. He ordered a Scotch and soda, and resisted the temptation to chat her up. The aggro he'd get later just wouldn't be worth it.

He sipped the drink, then took it with him as he went to look at some of the other games. The atmosphere here was less intense. A few people were actually smiling. Once, he heard someone stifle a chuckle.

He still had some money of his own. Well, he admitted to himself, technically it was Donachie's money. But what Donachie didn't know wouldn't hurt him. He went over to the cashier and exchanged the note for chips.

Then he headed for the roulette table. Several men were playing, and a couple of women.

Bingo waited for the next game, then laid his bet. As he did so, he noticed Oxford, who was still mingling with the crowd. Bingo noticed him catch someone's eye. He turned. There was a burly man standing next to him, also dressed in a dark suit and bow-tie. Security man for sure, Bingo thought, and only then realised that it was Doug Watson, the head of security. They hadn't met, just in case they gave the game away.

The wheel spun. Bingo lost his money. As he placed his next bet, a slick looking guy in a sharp suit and an expensive tan came over. Granger, the manager, Bingo decided. For all its attempted exclusivity, the Glendower Casino was part of a group and owned, at root, by a multinational corporation.

Granger took Watson to one side. "What's going on?" he said in a voice loud enough for Bingo to hear it easily. Watson looked at him blankly. Granger nodded in Oxford's direction. "Get rid of him," he said.

"He's only just started," Watson protested.

"You can't trust them," Granger said flatly. Watson shrugged and walked away.

Charmed I'm sure, Bingo thought.

Granger turned and smiled at him. Bingo smiled back.

"Do I detect a slight hint of racism in your company policy?" he asked mildly.

Granger looked at him suspiciously. "Who are you?"

Bingo let his smile widen into a grin. "Equal Opportunities, Mr Granger. We've been keeping an eye on you for quite some time now." He watched Granger's face fall, then turned and left.

As he went past Oxford, he risked giving him a quick wink.

***

Grace hadn't served behind a bar since she was a student. They'd only been undercover a week, and she'd already remembered why she hated it.

She half filled a pint glass with bitter, and while it settled went and mixed a double vodka and orange for the punter she was serving. As she pushed the glass up on to the optic, Val came round behind the bar. She got a glass and served herself a gin and tonic, then leaned back against the shelves. Grace finished serving her customer and joined her.

"I can't see Sam lasting – not the way she's going," Val said. She sounded well fed up.

Grace grinned. "That bad, huh?"

"Useless," Val said. She sipped her drink. Her lipstick left a crimson stain on the rim of the glass. "And do you know – I just heard her asking Granger if she could skive off early." Grace looked at her sympathetically. "She said she's got a headache," Val said. "Lazy cow."

Granger came over. Val nodded to him shortly and walked off. That's one unhappy lady, Grace thought. She turned to see what Granger wanted.

"Someone's just thrown up in the men's room," he said. He smiled at her ingratiatingly. "Clean it up, there's a good girl."

"You're not serious?" Grace said. Pulling pints was one thing. Mopping vomit quite another.

Granger's smile died on his lips. "You know where the mop is," he said. He turned away.

Grace glared at him, thinking of a few other things she could do with a mop. But there was no way out. She went out into the lobby and got the mop and bucket, then headed into the men's room.

Apart from the foul smelling mess in the corner, the place

211

was spotless – all Italian marble and gleaming chrome. Grace sighed and filled the bucket.

While she was cleaning up, Bingo came in. He leaned on the partition between two of the cubicles, and watched her.

"You will go for these glamorous jobs," he said.

Grace gave him a filthy look, then realised it was the friendliest of wind-ups, and let her face soften into a smile. Bingo grinned back at her and put his earpiece in, so he could listen into his concealed radio as well as talk.

That was easy, Grace thought. Nice, even. Since she'd got friendly with Ted Donachie, she'd found it a bit easier to get on with the other blokes. Not easy. Just easier.

"Looks like we're going to be leaving empty handed, Guv," Bingo said into the radio.

"Tell him about Sam," Grace prompted. She expected Bingo to complain that she was trying to do his job – his sergeant's job – for him. But he just nodded and said, "Yeah, and there's a new girl in, looking very nervous." He grinned and mouthed 'thanks' at Grace.

She kept mopping, but she suddenly felt pleased with herself.

***

Donachie sat back in his seat. The talk of gambling had led to the idea of playing poker. He was holding a pair of sevens, and a pair of twos, and the only question in his mind was whether the next card he got dealt would fill his full house or leave him with the two pairs.

However, play had been suspended because Bingo had radioed in. From what he'd just said, it looked to Ted as if his bet with Scott was quite safe.

Not that Scott seemed to see it that way. "Okay," he said into the radio. "Let's see it through."

Ted leaned forward. "How much of my money have you lost?" he demanded.

"Sorry, Ted," Bingo's voice said. "I didn't quite hear that."

"I said, you're dead," Ted answered.

Ash and Scott both turned round to grin at him. He smiled back, and smiled some more when he got his third seven in the next deal.

CHAPTER 25

It was time. Tommy Raymond walked away from the roulette game he'd been playing, and headed for the door at the back that led to the private room. Danny and Kelvin followed him.

As he went through the door, he heard the dealer say, "The stake is fifty-five thousand pounds, gentlemen. Any advance?" Music to my ears, Tommy thought.

Kelvin shut the door quietly behind them. The dealer looked up. She was older than the one he'd seen earlier: equally dark, but much cooler.

"I'm sorry, gentlemen," she said. "This is a private game."

The pit boss stared down at them from her high stool. She was all icy beauty, and she never said a word.

Tommy pulled his Browning semi-automatic from its holster under his jacket. The anodised metal gleamed dully as he aimed it at the dealer. "Get on the floor, now," he said.

They weren't stupid, those women. Neither were the high rolling punters around the table. They lay down exactly where they were told, and they never made a sound.

***

Bingo stared at Harris while he talked to Scott. She'd actually seemed quite friendly for a moment. Could it be that old GBH, the ice-maiden herself, was finally melting? He made a mental note to do some finding out about that later.

Meanwhile, he was still on the line to Scott. "I'm going to stay off the air for a while," he said. "I'm going back in there."

"Okay, Bingo," Scott said.

Bingo broke the connection, pulled his earpiece out and put it in his inside jacket pocket.

Grace leaned on her mop and glared at him as he went out the door. He turned and winked at her, but she just scowled.

Ice maiden? He thought. More like a whole bleeding glacier.

213

The screens of the monitors cast a pallor across the inside of the surveillance van. Now both officers were fully alert. They watched the screens intently.

A silver Cosworth passed slowly across the monitor showing the front entrance to the casino.

"Second time around," the officer who had seen it earlier said.

He was about to radio DI Scott, when his colleague said, "Hang about."

He paused, and turned to look at the monitors. The Cosworth was now driving slowly past the rear of the casino.

***

Scott had lost three hands in a row. He was usually a good poker player, and better than that, lucky. But not tonight. He sat twisted round in the passenger seat and stared at Ash over his hand.

She smiled at him. "If we were playing strip poker you'd be down to your knickers by now," she said.

"Not your lucky day, is it," Donachie added.

Scott sighed. He glanced at his hand – rubbish, with a six as high card – and folded. If this got out, his reputation was really going to suffer.

The radio spared him further embarrassment.

"Silver Cosworth, Guv," said the voice of one of the officers in the surveillance van. "Second time around. One male driver."

"Okay," Scott said. Even as he spoke, the others were getting ready for action, cards forgotten. "This could be our pick-up."

***

Tommy stood by the door, gun at the ready. The dealer, pit boss and players had been handcuffed to their chairs and gagged with gaffer tape.

Danny and Kelvin shovelled money into black plastic bags.

Six players. Stakes hitting what – fifty, sixty thousand a time? Tommy grinned.

Never give a sucker an even break. And gamblers were all suckers.

***

God, Bingo thought as he crossed the main gambling room.

If being on duty were always like this, he'd happily work till he was ninety. One of the women – not a gambler, but with one – caught his eye. Diamonds flashed at her throat and ears. He smiled at her. She smiled back, then turned and put her hand on the arm of the much older man she was standing next to. He put his arm round her, touched her protectively in the small of the back.

Damn, Bingo thought. If he weren't on duty –

He pulled open the door to the private room and stepped through. Someone grabbed his shoulder and yanked him sideways. He stumbled. Saw a flash of metal out of the corner of his eye.

Something slammed into the back of his head. Pain lanced through him and he fell forward. Everything turned to grey mist in front of him as the floor came up to meet him. He heard himself moan, and felt something else hard grind into the small of his back, but it was all so far away.

He shook his head. He saw a dark shadow off to the side. His vision blurred and returned, and he realised it was the barrel of a gun.

Ought to make a fight of it, he thought. But the gunbarrel was so close he could almost smell the cleaning oil, and he thought better of it.

The pain in his back was unrelenting. The best he could do was to look up. Two men were raking stake money into a black plastic bag.

Oh shit, he thought, and lay quiet.

The pressure on his back eased. The two men by the card table moved towards the door, guns at the ready. They disappeared behind him. He counted to ten, slowly. Heard the door open. As he turned, it was just closing.

***

Grace swilled the water away down the sink. The stink of vomit, heavily disguised by industrial strength disinfectant wafted up at her. She wrinkled her nose, and thankful she was finished, headed for the door.

She opened it. As she did so, a man came out of the door to the private gambling room. She saw the gun in his hand. He'd seen her. He stepped forward. Raised the gun. She froze.

What to do? She wondered. Nothing – nothing she could do.

Bingo stumbled out into the corridor. He looked dazed – Christ, hadn't he seen the gunman? Grace felt her eyes widen, hoped the villain would think it was because of him. He kept looking at her. Go away, Bingo, she thought.

He pulled out his radio. "In here with guns," he said, and the gunman turned. "Go, go, go," Bingo shouted.

The gun coughed. There was a flash of light. Bingo grunted and fell forward, a huge crimson stain spreading across his shirt.

Someone at the end of the corridor yelled, "Come on."

The gunman pelted down the corridor. Sam stepped out at that moment, and he grabbed her. He pulled her in towards him, and jammed the Browning up under her ear. Grace hesitated for a second. To hell with the stupid woman. She dashed over to Bingo. He was breathing, but Jesus... that blood. And his face was a terrible pale colour. She turned. The gunman was dragging Sam down the corridor.

Grace ignored them. She bent down and spoke into Bingo's radio.

***

"Bingo's been shot," Harris panic-stricken voice yelled over Scott's car radio,.

"Christ," Donachie whispered from the back seat.

Charlie picked up the radio. "Attack!" he called. "Attack!"

***

Tommy ran into the stairwell, dragging the dealer with him. He took the stairs two at a time, forcing her to keep up with him. She stumbled. He yanked her upright. Rounded into the second flight. Kelvin and Danny were just ahead of him.

They came to the street exit. He pushed the woman at Kelvin and punched the number into the combination lock. The door swung open.

***

Ash brought the Volvo screaming to a halt outside the rear entrance to the casino. Other squad cars, and an SO19 van arrived seconds later. Officers poured out of them and started taking up positions around the door.

The silver Cosworth barrelled round the corner. It lurched to a halt just as the casino door crashed open.

A man came out, shoving a young woman in front of him. He had her arm twisted up behind her back, and a handgun shoved against her ribs. He hesitated. Two other men, both younger, came out after him. They clearly hadn't expected a welcoming party.

"Put the gun down," shouted one of the SO19 sergeants.

The gunman didn't comply.

"Now!" shouted another officer. "Get down on the ground, now!"

The gunman moved towards the Cosworth. Someone screamed orders at him – to drop the gun, to get on the floor. He ignored them, kept moving, using the woman as a shield.

"I'll shoot her," he yelled.

"Put the gun down," shouted the first SO19 officer.

The gunman swung his weapon round and fired into the crowd of officers. The round ricocheted off the van. There was a confusion of shouted orders and officers moving around.

Instantly, one of the other men made a break for the car. He threw himself, and the money, through the rear door. The gunman shoved the woman in.

Instantly, one of the SO19 snipers fired on him. He took the bullet full in the chest. The impact blew him backwards. He spun across the pavement and slammed into the wall of the casino.

The third gunman dropped his weapon and put his hands in the air.

The Cosworth took off, with its passenger door flapping open. It sideswiped a squad car that had its own door open. There was a squeal of tearing metal as both cars lost their doors.

The incident was over in a matter of seconds.

"Go!" Charlie yelled to Donachie, who leapt out of the car and raced towards the casino. Charlie and Ash then took off after the Cosworth, sirens wailing. Another squad car followed.

Come on, you can do it, Charlie thought to himself, and didn't know whether he meant Ash catching the villains or Bingo surviving the shooting.

CHAPTER 26

Oxford was with Bingo when Ted got there. He'd already called an ambulance.

"Christ," Ted muttered as he looked at the bloody mess on the front of Bingo's shirt. He couldn't see how the man was still breathing.

Harris was sitting near Bingo, with a blanket draped over her shoulders. She was ashen. Oxford was crouched besides Bingo.

"Get outside and wait for the ambulance," Oxford said. Ted still stared. "Show them where to come," he said. When Ted didn't move, he snapped, "Now!"

That got to him. He ran back towards the door. He heard the sirens howling as he raced up the stairs.

The ambulance was just arriving as he got outside. Its rear door opened and two paramedics jumped out. One of them glanced around, and took in the sight of so many police units.

"Is everything safe?" he asked.

"Yes," Donachie snapped.

The paramedic ran to the gunman's body. He bent over it.

"Inside," Donachie said.

The paramedic stood up, apparently satisfied that the man was dead. He trotted alongside Donachie to the casino doors carrying his bag of emergency equipment. His colleague followed them.

"How many patients do we have here?" he asked. "I can call a second crew–"

"Just the one," Donachie said. "Now hurry."

He led the paramedic to the corridor where Bingo was lying.

"Okay," the paramedic said. "Now, what happened?"

Harris got up when she saw them coming, and went over to Bingo. Oxford was still crouching next to him, but he stood up when they arrived. For a second it almost looked to Ted as if he were standing guard over Bingo. "He's been shot," Oxford said. "He's in a bad way."

The paramedic moved in. "If I could just –"

Harris moved round. "Is he dead?" she said. Her voice was little more than a whisper.

"Just get out of the way, like the man says," Donachie snapped.

The paramedic turned to his colleague. "He's lost a lot of blood. I'll pack this wound." He put his case on the ground and knelt by it. As he opened it, he said, "You get the cot and we'll get him to A&E." His colleague nodded and raced off.

The paramedic turned to Bingo. He pulled an mask attached to a small gas cylinder out of his case.

Oh Jesus, Ted thought. Just let him be okay... he was a waste of space some of the time and a lazy so and so at best, but a good copper – a good thief taker – for all that. And a good mate... Ted gnawed the knuckle of his thumb. A good mate. He'd never been a praying man, but he supposed now was a good time to start. His stomach hurt. He wished he had some Rennies, and then felt both like laughing and crying when he realised what an ironical thought that was.

The paramedic had put the mask over Bingo's mouth and nose, and he was murmuring to him while he worked on the wound.

Ted looked at Harris. She was shivering, near tears. She hadn't seen him. He looked away, knowing she would have hated him to see her like that.

***

Danny twisted round to look at the girl. She was clinging to the back of the seat, while the air pressure tried to force her out of the ragged hole where the door had been.

Behind them, sirens wailed, but the cop cars couldn't make up any distance on them.

Nick, the driver, floored the accelerator. The Cosworth leaped forward.

"Let me out," the girl screamed over the rush of air. "Let me out!"

"Shut it," Danny yelled.

***

Ted trotted along beside the stretcher as the paramedics rushed Bingo towards the ambulance.

The doors stood open. They came to a halt.

"I'll put a Gelofusine up inside," the paramedic said to his colleague. "You call through to air control and tell them what to expect."

They manhandled the stretcher up, and Ted got in after them. As the doors closed, he saw the bodybag being zipped up over the gunman.

Someone must have loved him, he thought. He couldn't bring himself to care.

The ambulance sped away. Ted perched at the cab end of the ambulance, wanting to do something – anything – but not knowing what. The paramedics stayed close to Bingo.

One of them said quietly, "BPs dropping fast."

Ted got up to see what he could do to help.

"Let's get this line up quick," the other paramedic said. He had a plastic bag filled with some clear fluid. He turned.

"I'm trying to replace some fluid to bring his blood pressure up," he said. Ted nodded. "Will you –"

Ted realised he was in the way and tried to get out of the way. "Is he okay?"

The paramedic was all professional patience. "If you could give me some room here–"

Bingo sighed. His eyes fluttered shut. Immediately, several pieces of equipment beeped.

"What's happening?" Ted demanded.

The paramedics were working over him, each one knowing what to do without asking the other or getting in the way. The one that had been speaking to Ted turned and said over his shoulder, "He's stopped breathing." Fuck, Ted thought. Oh fuck no. "I'm going to have to put a tube down." Ted must have looked terrified, because the paramedic went on, "Don't worry, it's under control... stand clear please."

Yeah, sure, Ted thought. But he went back to his seat at the front and sat there, staring at his hands and wishing he knew how to pray.

***

They weren't getting any closer to the getaway car. Charlie glanced at Ash. Her face was a mask of determination, pale in the moonlight. She was going as fast as she could – far faster than was legal or safe.

They approached the underpass at the Strand. Ahead of them, something white moved against the early morning half-light.

A second later, it was obvious that it was a woman standing in the road and waving her arms. Sam. Ash braked hard, and the Volvo's tyres screamed as it skidded to a halt. It stopped inches from the woman.

There was a terrific jolt as the car behind failed to stop in time. Charlie slammed forward and came up against his safety belt. Beside him, Ash was winded.

He looked out the windscreen. Sam was crying, but he wasn't bothered about her. The Cosworth was nowhere in sight.

"Shit!" he said, and slammed his hand against the dashboard.

***

The ambulance came to a halt outside the A&E department of St Mary's Hospital, Paddington. The doors opened and the paramedics handed Bingo out of the ambulance. They were immediately surrounded by doctors and nurses.

Ted got out after them, but no-one paid him any attention.

They had put Bingo directly onto a trolley, and as soon as his drip was transferred they ran with him into the hospital.

Ted trotted along beside them. Every so often, he got a glimpse of Bingo's face. It was ashen, with a bluish tinge round the mouth and nose.

They ran through a waiting room, down a corridor, round a corner. Someone yelled something, but it was so much gibberish to Ted. More corridor, and then a set of double doors. The medical staff pushed the trolley through. Ted made to follow. One of the doctors turned. He shook his head slightly and closed the doors in Ted's face.

CHAPTER 27

Charlie walked down the stairs from the squad room to the ground floor of the station. He was on his way to the canteen, where they had put the casino staff and customers. DCI Uttley was with him, and the conversation wasn't a particularly pleasant one.

Before they got to the bottom, a senior SO19 officer came up to meet them. "I need a word," he said to Charlie.

"Join the queue," Charlie said sourly.

He and Uttley went on down stairs, leaving the SO19 officer scowling at their backs.

"So how much are we looking at," Uttley asked quietly.

Scott sighed. "Over three hundred grand on the loose."

They reached the ground floor, and went through into the custody area. Ash was standing by the desk with the custody sergeant.

The lad they'd nicked at the casino was emptying his pockets out, and the sergeant was listing his belongings.

"I want him printed and photographed now," Scott said. He didn't have the energy for pleasantries, not even for Ash.

He and Uttley carried on their way. The station was busy with a change of shift, and a lot of the local plod were going in and out of the locker rooms.

"Do we know who we're dealing with?" Uttley asked.

"Not yet," Charlie admitted. "I've sent fingerprints of the one we took out over to the Yard to see if we can get an ID." They turned into the corridor that led to the canteen. "The casino has security coded doors, so we're looking for someone on the inside."

"Grace hasn't come up with anyone?"

It was a reasonable question. Charlie only wished he had a

better answer. "No," he said. "That's why I'm keeping her in there."

They went into the canteen. Oxford was standing a little way off from the others – Charlie had already decided to pull him out. Harris was sitting with the staff, while the customers had gathered in a separate group. In their classy clothes they looked completely out of place in the canteen, which was done out in best regulation formica and vinyl.

Charlie took up a position where he could talk to both groups. "Okay," he said. "We're going to start taking your statements."

Oxford wandered over to Charlie, carrying a cup of tea. He'd taken his bow-tie off and loosened his collar. They moved a little way off from the others.

"What about the security tapes and staff records?" Charlie asked quietly.

"On their way over, Guv."

"I want you and Helen to go through them, see what you can turn up." After the success Ash had on the Rogers case, Scott half expected her to perform miracles with that kind of work.

Oxford nodded. Behind him, the casino manager, Granger, stood up. "How long are we going to have to sit around like this?"

Uttley cut in before Charlie could answer. "Until we're satisfied – so I'd make myself comfortable if I were you."

Charlie turned round. He glared at Granger, and mentally put him last on the interview list. Then he turned to Harris. "If you'll come with me?"

She looked warily at Val. "You all right?" she asked.

That was good, Charlie thought. Harris was beginning to shape up nicely. "When you're ready," he said. He had to treat her exactly like the others – and that meant acting pissed off with her.

He led her out into the corridor and then into an interview room. He closed the door and she sat down.

"How is he?" Grace asked immediately.

Christ, Charlie thought. It hadn't occurred to him that she would have been sitting out there fretting about Bingo with no way to find anything out.

"They're operating on him now," he said.

Harris scowled. Her hands were clenched into fists. "I just feel so useless, Guv – just being stuck out there with that lot."

Charlie nodded sympathetically. But a job was a job. "Well, I need you to stay with them." He walked over to the door, assuming that was the end of the matter.

"What!" Harris said. She looked thoroughly browned off.

"We need the insider," he said. She didn't seem impressed. "Someone's going to have to carry the can for this, and right now the ammo's pointing in my direction," he went on, "So don't go all moody on me, because believe me right now I don't need it." He opened the door. "I'll get Alan to take your statement."

He found Oxford in the squad room, going through the records with Ash. The place was alive with officers. Charlie threaded his way between the desks towards Oxford, but before he could get there Ash called him over. He went to her desk, and Oxford joined them.

"Guv?" she said. "Samantha Ryan – the girl who flagged us down..."

Charlie nodded. How could he forget? "What about her?"

"Well, according to her staff record her last job was at a building society in Balham."

"So?" Charlie said, trying not to sound impatient. With Ash it was always worth the wait.

Oxford chipped in. "She was only there a week. It got raided."

Thank God, Charlie thought. At last it was coming together. "Where is she now?" he asked.

"St Mary's – they're treating her for shock," Ash said.

Well, with any luck she'd have a bigger shock coming. "Is Ted still over there?" he asked.

"Should be," Oxford said.

"Right," Charlie said. "Get him to have a word with her."

At least now he had something, however slim, to take to Uttley.

***

Accident and Emergency was full of nurses and doctors and porters, all of them striding purposefully about. Ted stopped a porter to ask after Sam, and got told to talk to a nurse. He looked for one, but they all seemed so busy... he gave up and took to wandering round the ward pulling back the curtains round the beds – here, an old man finding it difficult to breathe, there a six year old girl with a gash in her leg the length of his hand – until he found Sam. She was lying back in bed with her eyes closed.

"Sam?" he said. She didn't respond. "Sam?" he said louder.

A nurse appeared out of nowhere. "She's sedated," she said. "We're keeping her under observation."

Ted nodded. The nurse produced a specimen jar. There was a small lump of grey metal at the bottom of it. "Souvenir for your friend," she said. "Lucky it didn't go right through him."

Ted held the jar up and peered at the bullet. "How is he?" He couldn't be dead. She was much too cheerful for that.

"Stable," she said. Ted smiled. "He'll have to stay here for a while," she added warningly. "Who's his next of kin?"

Ted thought about it. He really didn't know. "Don't know," he said at last.

"Wife?"

"Two," Ted said. He allowed himself a small grin. "Both divorced." And about a million assorted girlfriends, he added to himself.

"Children?"

"None that he knows of," Ted said, and thought, or that he's admitting to.

"What about other relatives?"

Ted thought about that. "There's his mother," he said, though where he dredged that piece of information up from he couldn't have said. "She's still alive. Don't know where she lives, though – the Midlands, somewhere, maybe." The nurse scowled in frustration. "He hasn't got anyone," Ted said quietly. It suddenly seemed a terrible, lonely thing.

The nurse noted the information down.

"Can I see him?" Ted asked.

The nurse told him where Bingo was. He found the ward eventually and made his way along it. Most of the beds were full. A lot of the men were either sitting up in bed or they were actually up and about in their dressing gowns. Almost every bed

225

had flowers or cards beside it, or little gifts of Lucozade or fruit.

Bingo's bed was right at the end. Ted went and stood beside him. He was in a hospital gown, and his bedside cabinet was bare of flowers and cards.

Ted stared at him. To be that alone. To have nothing and no-one. He thought of his wife, Mary, out every night with what she was pleased to call friends, no matter how it hurt him. He wondered if she realised that this – this loneliness – was where she was heading. Or would have been, if he hadn't loved her so desperately that he'd forgive her anything.

He reached out and touched Bingo's hand, knowing the man couldn't feel it. It seemed little enough, but it was all he could do for the moment.

***

Charlie walked carefully up to the holding cells because he was carrying two full cups of tea. He got the duty officer to let him in to Kelvin's cell. The room was tiny, with walls the colour of grime and a floor pockmarked with cigarette burns. It smelled of old clothes and despair.

Kelvin seemed very young, sitting there wearing the boiler suit he'd been given when they took away his own clothes. He didn't even look up when Charlie came in. A cigarette hung from his fingers, and the ashtray was full of stubs.

"Thought you might like one of these," Charlie said, holding out one of the cups. Kelvin still didn't look up. Charlie put the cup down at his feet. "You okay?"

Still no response. Charlie lounged against the wall and sipped his tea.

After a bit he tried again. "Do you want to see a doctor?"

Kelvin shook his head. It wasn't much, but at least it was a response.

"Okay," Charlie said. He spoke quietly. He was prepared to put aside his personal feelings if that would get him the right result. "Listen, I'm going to have to do a formal interview with you soon. That means another officer, duty solicitor, everything being taped." He paused. Sipped his tea. "Maybe it will be easier for you if you tell me what it's all about now, eh?" Come on, he thought at the bloke. Cough. "Just you and me. No tape recorder. No recriminations." He paused for another sip of tea.

226

When he spoke again, his voice was even quieter. "Your mates won't have to know anything about it."

It didn't work. Kelvin just sat there staring at the floor as if it were the most interesting thing he'd ever seen.

"What about a name?" Charlie cajoled. "You've got to have a name."

Still nothing. He might as well have been made of wood.

Charlie sighed heavily. He walked to the door and opened it, but before he left he turned back to Kelvin. "Okay – if that's the way you want it," he said. "But I think you're making a big mistake."

He went into the corridor and closed the door behind him. As he walked away he heard the sound of Kelvin crying.

***

Charlie found DCI Uttley in the squad room, and walked back to his office with him. He was grim faced, and Charlie knew he was probably under pressure from his own superiors.

"What have you got for me?" Uttley asked.

Charlie stared straight ahead. "Nothing yet," he admitted.

"What about that bloke downstairs," Uttley asked. "Is he likely?"

"He'll roll like a car ferry," Charlie said. "But not yet."

"Bloody hell," Uttley exploded. "I've got a press conference – I need something." He paused. Thought. "What about Tate?"

"Good," Charlie said. "He's out of surgery."

Uttley seemed happier. "Right. How do I look?"

Charlie looked him up and down. "Fine," he said, uncertain what was required. "Nice suit." He frowned. "I'd have a look at your hair, though." He turned and left.

"What's wrong with my hair?" Uttley demanded.

Charlie grinned.

***

By the time the Guv came in, they were all gathered round the video machine waiting for him.

Ted leaned against a desk as Ash put the cassette in. He was still feeling a bit melancholy after seeing Bingo at the hospital. Poor bastard. Well, with a bit of luck, the rest of the gang would be known villains, they could go and pick them up and that would be that.

Scott found himself somewhere to stand, but before Ash played the tape she held up a photo. It was the dead man. "SO11 have ID'd him as Tommy Raymond. Previous for TDA, burglary, theft." She paused, giving them time to think about whether they'd seen him, or had a snout who might know him. "Jumped bail six years ago, up for a Post Office job. Probably ended up in Spain."

"So why come back?" Scott asked.

"Maybe he needed the cash," Donachie said. "You know – one last job to set himself up for life."

No-one had any better ideas. Ash pressed the play button. The security tape showed the gang coming out of the casino with Sam as a hostage, but the tape was snowy and blurred. What you get for re-using tape, Donachie thought. Cheap so-and-sos.

"Anybody?" Scott asked.

There were a few muttered nos and lots of shaken heads.

"I reckon she must be the insider, though, Guv," Oxford said.

Scott turned to him. "Why? Because of that building society job?"

Oxford nodded. "And because Grace said she just stood there, like she was waiting to be grabbed."

Scott turned to Ted. "Sam's still under sedation," he said. "She won't be talking till tonight."

Scott sighed. "Okay." He returned his attention to Oxford. "Let's get some stills taken from the obs tapes. Fax them over to SO11 and we'll see what else they can come up with."

***

It was good to be out of the station, Grace thought as she sat in the cab that was taking her home, even if she did still have to pretend to be a barmaid. Val sat next to her. She seemed to be taking things pretty hard – she was still pale, and though she'd got her colour back, she kept playing with the end of her hair.

"I didn't know the police put people on the inside," she said. It wasn't the first time she had said it, but she still sounded bewildered. "The one who was shot, he was a copper." She paused. Turned her ring round. "They must have known about it."

228

"Yeah," Grace agreed. "I suppose they must." She looked out the window at the shops they were passing, to stop herself staring too closely at Val.

"So they could have stopped it, couldn't they?" She paused. "I mean, they didn't have to shoot him, did they?"

Grace wondered whether she meant Bingo or the gunman. "Shoot who?" she said.

"That bloke," Val said. "Outside."

"Oh. Right," Grace said. She wondered how to get Val talking about herself – and how to make her slip up, if she were going to. "What sort of things did they ask you?"

Val pulled an I-don't-know face. "Same sort as you, probably. Had I seen these blokes before?" She looked disgusted. "I mean, how am I supposed to know if I've seen them before? We get so many faces in and out of that place."

Grace nodded. "Yeah, that's what I said."

Val looked affronted. "Well, it's easy for you – you've only been there a week. What did they expect?"

That gave Grace her opening. "So how long have you been there, then?"

"Eight years." Seven and a half too long, by her expression.

Grace grinned. "What about Sam though – first day and all that happens."

Val shot her a wry smile. "I wouldn't worry too much about Sam."

Just bitching? Grace wondered – or something else. She didn't have time to probe any deeper, because the cab pulled up outside a swish looking block of flats.

Val opened the door. As she got out, Grace said, "Don't fancy putting the kettle on, do you?" She wanted to get to the bottom of that last remark.

Val turned. She was outside now, and fumbling in her shoulder bag. "Some other time, yeah?" She glanced up at the flats. "All I want to do right now is go to bed." She turned to the driver to pay him.

"See you tonight, then?" Grace said.

Val turned and left. Grace took the cab on home. Maybe Val had a point.

CHAPTER 28

Early morning mist swirled across the Thames, chased by the stiff breeze. Ted shoved his hands in the pockets of his donkey jacket as he led Oxford along the riverside walkway by a low wall. Beyond that wall, there was a churchyard – ranks on ranks of forgotten headstones and crosses and stone angels. Ted thought about Bingo lying alone and lonely in his hospital bed. This time his shiver had nothing to do with the cold.

The man they had come to meet was up ahead, leaning on the wall and looking across the river. He was Jack Villiers, an acquaintance of a friend of one of Ted's snouts, and this meeting had taken a lot of doing to set up, especially so quickly. Ted knew that Oxford had been a bit funny about snouts since his drug-dealer informant had been topped, so he hoped he wasn't going to blow it. But Oxford was steady. He'd be okay.

Villiers turned towards them. He was a heavy set man, with a complexion ravaged by fags and booze and probably a few other things.

"What's all this about?" he demanded of Ted.

"A mate of ours got shot this morning," Oxford cut in. "Know anything about it?"

"He's polite," Villiers said, voice dripping sarcasm. "What happened to the sledgehammer wake up call? Squad gone soft?"

Ted couldn't be arsed with it. "When did you last see Tommy Raymond?"

Villiers considered. "Tommy? Must be years ago." Perhaps he really was working it out when he paused. "Must've been in... eighty four?"

Oxford sighed theatrically. "Oh, please –"

"What?" Villiers snapped. "He jumped bail and I did ten years." He sounded bitter. "Funny enough, he never even sent me a postcard."

It sounded like it might just be right, Ted thought. The

bitterness certainly was. But that might just be the reason Villiers hadn't been along on this latest little joy ride.

"And you've not seen him since you got out?" Ted asked.

"Seen him? He went to Spain," Villiers protested. "There's a twelve stretch waiting for him if he comes back. He knows that." He took a tin of tobacco out of his pocket and started rolling up.

"I saw him this morning," Ted said, watching Villiers reaction intently.

"Where?" Villiers seemed genuine enough.

Ted didn't even try to soften it. "Lying dead outside the Glendower Casino with an SO19 bullet in him."

Villiers fumbled his roll-up. The paper fluttered away and was lost on the breeze. He'd gone visibly paler.

"We want to know who he was working with," Ted said.

He expected protestations of innocence, but he didn't get them. "I can't believe it," Villiers said. "He had it all set up so sweet out there. He wouldn't come back." He gave up on the rollie and stuffed the tin back in his pocket. "It can't be Tommy."

"It is," Oxford said flatly. "Want to see a picture?"

But Villiers wasn't listening. He was off in some other place, in the past. "I got two years for a burglary. Nineteen seventy five. When I came out, I had nothing. Tommy gave me two grand to get straight." He paused, thinking about it. His jaw worked. "It was a lot of money, then."

Christ, Ted thought. This Tommy Raymond might have more people sorry to see him gone than Bingo would. It was a chilling thought. "Jack, no-one cares," he said coldly. "Now – who was he with?"

Villier's attention snapped back. Suddenly he was all business. "Mind if I ask an ethical question?" Ted raised his eyebrows at him. "What's in it for me?"

Ted reached into his inside jacket pocket, and pulled out a flat envelope. Jack reached for it. Ted pulled it back out of harm's way.

"He sometimes worked with Gary Lane," Villiers said, grudgingly.

Oxford shot Ted a disparaging look. "His parole's five years off – we checked," he said dryly.

Villiers eyed the envelope. Ted made to put it back in his pocket.

"Gary had a son," Villiers said quickly. "If Tommy'd come back to do a job, he'd only use people he trusted."

Ted glanced at Oxford. In his own mind, he was sure that was all they'd get. Oxford agreed, apparently, because he nodded.

Ted handed over the envelope. "So much honour," he said. "So many thieves."

Villiers didn't so much as crack a smile. The envelope disappeared into his jacket. Then he turned and left, treading carefully between the ranks of the dead.

***

Charlie marched Kelvin from his cell to an interview room. The lad seemed even younger than before, and he had a nervous tic under his right eye.

Ash walked ahead of them, with Phil Bishop, the duty solicitor.

"Hey, Phil," she said, just loud enough so Charlie could hear her too, though she probably didn't mean him to. "Do you do divorce work?"

So she really was that serious about it, Charlie thought. He wasn't surprised – he'd rarely known anyone as committed to her work as Helen Ash. Or his work, either, come to think of it.

"Sorry, Helen," Bishop said. "I'm strictly criminal." He took a business card from his wallet. "But maybe you should have a word with her."

Ash looked at the card. "Partner?" she asked.

"Wife," Bishop said.

They reached the interview room. Ash opened the door. Bishop went in. Kelvin shot Ash a terrified look as he followed him.

Charlie touched Ash on the arm to stop her going in. "That's a big decision you're making," he said.

"No choice," she said. Her face was pinched and there were dark patches under her eyes.

Before Charlie could say anything else, Oxford appeared at the top of the corridor. He waved some papers. "Guv!" he called, and hurried over.

"What have you got," Charlie asked.

"This just came through from SO11." He jerked his head at the interview room. "Our man with no name is Kelvin Jenkins." He handed over the documents. "One of the two we're missing is Danny Lane – known associate of Tommy Raymond."

Charlie felt some of the tension drain out of him. Finally he could go to Uttley with something – and now he had a real lever to use against the kid. "Address?" he asked.

That was where his luck ran out. Oxford shook his head.

"And the driver?"

"Nothing," Oxford said apologetically.

Scott shrugged. "Good job. Keep on it."

He turned and went into the interview room. Ash followed him.

Kelvin was sitting at the table, with his hands knotted in front of him. He kept glancing at the big twin-deck cassette recorder that took up the end of the desk. Bishop sat off to the side, clipboard and pen at the ready.

Ash sat down and took out the case notes. She skimmed them while Charlie switched the tape recorder on.

"Interviewing Kelvin Jenkins –" Charlie said, watching Kelvin for his reaction: he jerked back like he'd been hit when he heard his name. Charlie carried on as if nothing had happened, "– in the presence of his solicitor, Mr Philip Bishop," Interview being conducted by DI Scott and DS Ash." He glanced at his watch. "Time is eight fifteen am."

Ash took over. "Okay, Kelvin – we know who you are and we know about Tommy Raymond and Danny Lane." Kelvin bit his lip. He was breathing hard. His hands writhed together on the table. "Tell me who the driver is," Ash persisted. Kelvin wouldn't look at her. "You're small time, Kelvin," Ash said gently. "Three months inside and nothing to come home to. You were desperate. We understand." She actually managed to say it as if she meant it. "But unless you help us out, three months will seem like a holiday."

Kelvin glanced up at her. "I'm not a grass," Kelvin muttered and looked away immediately.

"You still think you're going to get your share of the cash?" Ash asked gently.

"I'm not a grass," Kelvin muttered. This time he wouldn't even glance at her.

"Kelvin, we know Tommy has done this before, but not you or Danny." She paused. "If we can sort this mess out now, it'll save you both a lot of trouble, believe me." Kelvin didn't answer, but his shoulders drooped fractionally. "Danny is your friend, isn't he?"

Kelvin nodded.

"Then help him out," Ash said. "Tell us where he is." Kelvin looked up at her. His eyes were red-rimmed and they stared out of a stark white face. She went for it. "You'll be saving yourself a lot of time inside."

"Fourteen Sandfield Estate," Kelvin muttered. He put his head in his hands and began to sob.

***

The squad lined up in front of Uttley's desk. The weapons cabinet was open. Uttley handed each officer a weapon – a Smith and Wesson .38 – and, separately, ammunition. The officers signed the weapons register and left the office immediately.

***

There were small gardens at the back of the row of council houses, partitioned off by wooden fences. Ash glanced back at Oxford and the two other officers she had in her team. They were ready to go – weapons drawn, up for anything. She counted along the row of houses till she came to the seventh one, which had to be Number Fourteen.

She approached it quietly, using the wall for cover, and clicked open the garden gate.

***

Danny sat at the rickety table, counting the money. It was mostly stacked neatly in piles, and the empty black plastic bag lay at his feet. He stared at the cash, wondering if he could possibly have miscounted.

Nick came through the door.

234

"Have you got any idea how much money we've come away with?" Danny asked.

"Quarter of a million, that's what Tommy said," Nick answered.

Danny grinned. "Yeah. Well, Tommy got his sums wrong. We've got well over three hundred grand here." What the hell were you supposed to do with that kind of money? He supposed he'd figure it out.

Nick sat down hard on the other chair.

Danny looked at him. They scarcely knew each other.

"Who do you think set us up, Nick?" he asked. "Someone must have – there's no way the police could have got there so quick."

"Weren't me, Dan," Nick said, all defensive. "I need the money – you know that."

"Someone did," Danny said. He knew it in his gut. "I don't think it was Tommy – not with that bullet he took. And I know it wasn't me."

"Kelvin," Nick said immediately. "He must have been mouthing off."

"Kelvin's a mate," Danny said. "I know him better than I know you."

Nick got up. "You're losing it, mate." He backed away. "Just give me my share and I'm out of here."

Danny explained it. "Nick – Tommy just shot a copper and we stole over three hundred grand. When the police come looking for us, they'll be more than a little cross." Nick glanced at the door. "I don't think it's a good time for you to go anywhere."

Reluctantly, Nick sat back down.

***

Helen moved into the garden. The team split up and they moved towards the back door, still using what cover there was.

***

Charlie approached the front of Number Fourteen. Donachie was right behind him, and then the rest of the team. When he got to the front door, he paused.

"In position, Guv," Ash said over the radio.

Scott looked at his team. They were ready. "Okay," he said;

235

and then, into the radio, "Attack, attack!"

Donachie booted the door open and they burst into the house. Charlie heard the back door crashing open.

"Armed police," Ash shouted from the rear of the house.

Nothing happened. Charlie gave the word for the team to search the house. A few minutes later, they reported back: the place was deserted.

They trooped out to the squad cars. Charlie, Ash and Donachie went to one and threw their gear in the back.

Charlie pinched his nose. He was too tired even to think about the disaster this operation was turning into.

"What now, Guv?" Ash asked before they got in.

It was a question he hadn't much wanted to hear. He palmed his eyes and came to a decision. "Look, we're all knackered," he said. "Let's just go home, get some sleep and see what we can turn up later."

That was a popular idea. The others nodded. Ash found a piece of paper in her pocket and scribbled on it quickly. She handed it to Charlie.

"My new number," she explained.

Charlie nodded. She might have let her marital problems screw things up that once, when the SO11 man got shot during the Rogers case, but by God she hadn't let it intrude since.

"Kids okay?" he asked.

"Yeah," she said. "My mother's with them." She smiled thinly and got in the car. Just because she was coping didn't mean she was having an easy time of it. He resolved to bear that in mind.

***

Danny watched the cop cars move out. He was standing outside a row of lock-up garages on the estate, half hidden by the open door. He was ready to dodge back inside if any of the filth so much as glanced in his direction, but none of them did.

When they'd gone, he went back inside the lock-up. Nick was still sitting at the table.

"It's all right, they're going," Danny said.

"Do you still think it was me stitched us up?" Nick demanded.

"No," Danny said. He considered the possibilities, then said again, "No." He thought about the cops. "They were well tooled up," he said. He was a bit in awe of the fact that something he'd done could have rated that much hardware, but he didn't want Nick to know that.

"What are we going to do?" Nick demanded.

Danny eyed the piles of cash sitting on the beaten up formica table top. "I don't know," he snapped. "What the hell happened? Tommy had it all worked out."

"Yeah, well I had plans of my own," Nick said. His voice dripped venom.

"We all had plans, mate. Villa in the sun – tell me about it."

Nick pulled a sour face. "Kelvin must be spilling his guts."

Danny slammed his hand down on the table. Some of his carefully arranged piles started to slide together. "Kelvin's not like that," he insisted.

"So tell me what the cops were doing round here? Sightseeing?" Nick said. His face was flushed and it looked like he might just be up for a fight.

Danny looked at him in disgust. He could see it all now – they lay into each other, one of the neighbours calls the local cops to the disturbance, and wham – Mr Plod is the latest local hero on the Sandfield Estate. "You really want to go out there and say hello?" He let Nick think about that. "No chance. We stay put."

Nick stared at the floor. "This is a nightmare," he muttered.

Danny couldn't resist it. "No mate – you wake up from nightmares."

CHAPTER 29

Bingo's flat was the pits – unmade bed, unwashed dishes, papers all over the floor.

Ted ignored all that, though he thought it might be a nice idea to come back later and have a clean up before Bingo was discharged. His current idea was to find Bingo's pyjamas and take them in for him – he'd hated to see him lying there wearing that hospital gown.

He went into the bedroom and rummaged through the clothes in the chest of drawers, but found nothing. He twitched aside the duvet. A condom packet fell out, but no pyjamas.

The doorbell rang. Ted hurried down to answer it. Harris stood there. He stared at her in surprise, but she didn't seem surprised to see him.

"You look about as rough as I feel," she said.

"Thanks," Donachie said dryly.

He stepped aside and she walked in. He closed the door behind her.

"How did you know I was here," he asked.

"Your car's outside."

"Yeah," Ted said, "But–"

"Your wife told me."

Gawd, Ted thought. He wondered what Mary would have made of that. She had a long list of male friends, but it was strictly a one-way street – she didn't like it if he got too friendly with other women.

He sighed and followed Harris upstairs. She stopped just inside the door and surveyed the mess. "What are you doing?" she asked.

"Looking for pyjamas." He hoped she didn't think he'd caused all this mayhem.

"Maybe he doesn't wear any," Harris said as if it were a deduction worthy of Sherlock Holmes.

Ted grinned. "Well done, Detective."

He sat down on the edge of the bed.

"So what's been happening?" Harris asked. Officially, she was still undercover.

"We raided an address of one of the guys we didn't pick up."

Harris looked thoroughly pissed off. Ted knew she'd hated playing the pretty girl barmaid all week. "Wish I'd been there," she said.

"Waste of time," Ted said. Harris glared at him. "The place was empty," he explained.

Harris sat down next to him. "What about Bingo?"

"He's on a ward," Ted said. He didn't tell her how miserable seeing him alone like that had made him. He didn't want to bring her down any further than she was already.

But Harris was staring off into space. "One minute he was pointing a gun at me, and–"

"It's over, Grace," Ted said. It wasn't that he didn't want to help, but he was just too tired to play the counsellor again.

"I froze," she said as if she hadn't heard him. "I couldn't do anything." She stared at her hands, which were long fingered and pale. "I could have stopped it."

Ted repressed a sigh and gave in to her obvious need. "And he'd have shot you instead of Bingo."

It didn't help. "I couldn't do anything then, and I can't do anything now." Her eyes glistened with tears. Ted reckoned if he saw her cry, she'd never forgive him for it. "I just keep getting pushed out of the way..." she turned to look at him. She was very pretty, even upset. "Even you, at the casino..." her voice trailed off.

He hadn't thought of it like that. He'd been too frantic. "I know," he said, wanting to make it better for her and not knowing how. "I'm sorry."

Her shoulders slumped as if his pity were too much for her to bear. "It was all my fault," she said, as if that were somehow why she kept getting shunted aside.

Ted touched her hair. He meant to brush it out of her eyes, make her look at him, beg her for a smile. But the second he touched her, something else happened. She looked up at him. He cupped her cheek with his hand. She covered it with her own. And then, without really intending to, he was moving towards her. He kissed her gently on the lips.

Christ, he thought. What am I doing? Mary? How long was it since Mary had made him feel like this?

And then Grace was kissing him back, and her arms were round him, hands running over his back and down, and Mary vanished from his thoughts.

***

Grace looked at Ted, who standing by the window. Blue smoke wreathed the air around him. Grace stood up. She was mostly dressed – what they had done had been quick and fierce. She pulled her pants up, and her jeans, and zipped them, then stepped into her shoes.

Then she turned and started to shake the duvet out. It seemed like the least she could do. Ted turned to watch her. She stopped, embarrassed. He looked at her and tried a smile.

She smiled back. She wondered what he wanted. And what she wanted, too. "I don't know," she said.

I've screwed up, she thought – it'll be all over the squad room. And with Ted too – who'd been a friend. Only fool would lose a friend for a moment of passion. Especially when that friend was well and truly married.

"Me neither," Ted said, breaking into her thoughts.

She stared at him a moment longer, then went back to tidying the bed.

***

Bingo sat up in bed. It was the first time he'd been allowed to. He was bored out of his skull and the change in position didn't do a lot to help.

After he'd been sitting for a while, Ted Donachie turned up. He handed Bingo a carrier bag. Bingo frowned and looked inside. He pulled out a pair of pyjamas in a lurid maroon paisley pattern.

"You don't like them," Donachie said. He seemed tense about something, and it brought out his Scottish accent.

"They're fine," Bingo said.

"They're awful," Donachie contradicted.

He was right. But Bingo was touched that he'd even thought

to visit, never mind go shopping on his behalf. "Ted, I–"

"Sorry," Donachie said.

Bingo grinned. "It's a pair of pyjamas, Ted – not life or death." Donachie didn't seem convinced. "I'll die if someone sees me wearing them, but –"

He realised what he said. There was a long, dreadful silence.

Donachie slicked his hair back. "How are you feeling?" he asked eventually.

Bingo considered a snappy reply, but dismissed it. Look where his last effort had got him. "You see people get shot, you never think how bad it really is," he said at last. Suddenly he was back in that time of agony, when he'd seemed to be floating just above himself and everything he could see was swirling red and grey. "Christ it hurt. I remember thinking, maybe if I just go to sleep for a while..."

"I thought you were dead," Donachie said sombrely.

"Me too," Bingo said. It might have been funny if it hadn't been true. "All I could feel was this bloody pain... and then I heard you. I thought, if he tells me to hang in there any more, I'll die just to shut him up."

That did raise a smile from Donachie. "Maybe next time."

"They told me you were here all morning," Bingo said. He'd been surprised – he hadn't thought anyone on the team would have bothered.

"I didn't know who to get in touch with..." Donachie's voice trailed off. He stared straight at Bingo. I don't know either, Bingo thought. My mum, I suppose, only it would probably have killed her.

He decided he had to change the subject, and since he was the patient he reckoned he got to choose. "Have you seen these nurses?" he asked. "I reckon if I play my cards right I could be in for a nice long bed bath tomorrow morning."

Donachie shook his head in mock despair. "You're obsessed."

"You're jealous."

"You're right." They both laughed, earning themselves a pleased look from a pretty blonde nurse who happened to be passing by.

***

Ted left Bingo in better spirits than he'd found him, which was all he'd wanted.

He went back down to the observation ward to see if Sam Ryan was up and about yet.

She wasn't there. The bed had been stripped back to the plastic mattress cover. He found the nurse he'd spoken to the day before..

"Where is she?" he asked after he explained.

"She discharged herself just now," the nurse said.

Ted cursed and ran. He pushed through the crowded corridor towards the exit. He'd almost given up when he saw her in the distance.

"Sam!" he shouted. She turned. Clocked him.

And started to run.

Ted tried to go after her, but there were too many people. By the time he got to the end of the corridor, he'd lost her.

He was out of breath. He put his hand out to the wall for support. "Shit," he said.

***

Just when Charlie thought nothing else could possibly go wrong, something did. Donachie radioed in. He listened, then cut the connection.

He was in the squad room with Ash and Oxford.

"Samantha Ryan's just done a runner from the hospital," he said.

"I thought Ted said she was sedated," Ash said. She seemed resigned to this latest complication already.

"Yeah," Charlie said, "Well, she's wide awake now. You've got an address for her, haven't you."

Oxford checked his computer file and nodded.

"Okay, Helen," Charlie said, "You and Oxford get over there and see what's going on."

They got up and left, and Charlie went to see Kelvin. That young man still had some explaining to do.

He was still in a state. He'd obviously been crying, and the cell was thick with cigarette smoke. The floor was littered with used tissues, and there was a half full box on the bunk. Charlie decided to give the softly softly approach one last try.

242

"That address you gave us? You're mates weren't there." He stood looking down at Kelvin, who was perched on the edge of his bunk.

Kelvin looked hopeful. "So I didn't really grass them up then, did I?"

Charlie considered. "No." He pushed the tissues with his toe. "Is that what all this is about?"

Kelvin nodded, shakily. "I don't want to go back inside." He took another tissue from the box, but he didn't use it, just balled it up in his fist.

Charlie went and sat down next to Kelvin. "Scared you?" he asked. He meant both prison and Kelvin's absent friends.

"Yeah," Kelvin said. "I didn't want to get in trouble again, but they said– "

"– it would be easy," Scott finished for him. Kelvin nodded. "I bet it was Tommy Raymond who said that." Kelvin suddenly looked wary, as if he'd just remembered it was a copper he was talking to. Damn, Charlie thought, but he went on, "Did he ever mention someone called Samantha Ryan?"

"I can't," Kelvin blurted. He looked away, wild eyed. "I can't tell you anything." He clutched his bit of tissue. "I'm going down for this, aren't I? – Whatever happens?" So he had that much nous, Charlie thought. It made his job harder. "What's my life going to be worth inside when people find out I grassed on my mates."

Not a lot, Charlie thought. But he said, "Kelvin, listen to me: you may believe in honour among thieves, but no-one else does." He paused. Kelvin swallowed. "Everyone gives it up sooner or later." He moved closer, made his voice confidential. "This is just you and me – who's to know?"

"No, honest," Kelvin said. He sounded desperate now. "They didn't tell me anything. Not even Danny knew who the insider was."

Charlie looked at him. Maybe he was telling the truth. He tried a different tack. "The driver – what was his name?"

Kelvin thought about it. "Nick," he said at last. He began to tear the tissue into tiny pieces.

"Nick what?"

"I don't know." Kelvin looked at him with misery-filled eyes. "I swear. I never got a chance to meet him, did I?"

That didn't ring true at all. "Didn't he drive you to the casino?"

Kelvin shook his head. He seemed surprised by the question.

"So how'd you get there, then?" Charlie asked.

"On the bus," Kelvin said, as if it were the most usual thing in the world for armed robbers to travel by public transport.

It was so ridiculous it had to be true.

Kelvin was crying openly now. To his own surprise, Charlie found himself putting a fatherly arm round his shoulder.

***

Helen parked the car outside Sam Ryan's flat. By the look of the place – a rundown Victorian terrace – it was rented.

She and Oxford got out.

"David never got over me being in the squad," she said. They'd talked of little else on the way over. "I really think he's trying to wreck my career."

Oxford looked at her. "You don't need to convince me. I think you're doing the right thing."

He led the way up the steps to the door. Helen looked at the bells until she found Sam's name. She was on the ground floor.

"You know he thinks we're having an affair?" Helen said.

Oxford nodded sourly. He turned away and peered through the side pane of the bay window. "I think we're in business," he said.

Helen punched the bell. A few moments later Sam came to the door. Helen introduced herself and Oxford, and after insisting on checking their identification, Sam let them in.

Her flat was tiny – a bedsit with a galley kitchen off it. She had a half-full suitcase open on her bed, with more clothes piled around it and the drawers of her dressing table open. She continued to pack as she talked. If she were the insider, she was a damn cool customer.

"Why did you run away from him?" Helen asked.

"I didn't know he was one of your lot, did I?" Sam snapped. Her accent was very similar to Helen's. She folded a green jumper and laid it in the case. "I thought he was one those nutters from this morning."

Helen stared at her. If she were lying, she deserved an Oscar. "You mean you don't know who they are?" she demanded.

"Of course I bloody don't," Sam said. She looked properly offended.

"So where are you going now?" Oxford asked, from his position near the door.

"I'm getting out of London. Everywhere I go here, someone turns up and sticks a gun in my face." She rummaged in the dressing table for something. "Well, I've had enough," she said. She gave up on the dressing table and turned to face them. "I'm going home."

"And where's that?" Helen asked, more out of curiosity than a need to know. She was convinced now that Sam was telling the truth.

"Belfast," she said, and stared blankly at Helen when she exchanged a smile with Oxford.

CHAPTER 30

Grace hated the idea of staying undercover, but if she had to she was going to make the best of it.

She headed down Park Lane, then turned off to get to the casino. Val was ahead of her on the street. She raced to catch up.

"You managed to get some sleep?" she asked.

"Yeah," Val said. "I feel fine now." She looked it, too, Grace thought – calm and rested, not strung out the way she had earlier.

They got to the door. Doug, the head of security, was standing in front of it.

"What's going on," Grace asked.

"We're not opening," he said.

"I'm not surprised, after what's happened," Val blurted out. "I mean they didn't have to kill that bloke like that. Bloody Flying Squad."

"That was down to SO19," Grace said automatically. She realised what she'd said the second it was out of her mouth.

"They're the ones with the rifles," Doug explained. Grace realised he was covering for her – if he knew that, anyone might know the term.

"Did you know the police were in here?" Val asked Doug.

"I'm head of security," Doug said, with just a hint of pomposity. "Of course I knew."

"Was Sam another undercover copper?" Val demanded.

Now why is she taking an interest, Grace wondered. And it was damned strange the way she kept going on about Tommy Raymond, with never a word about poor old Bingo.

"I can't tell you," Doug said in his best jobsworth voice.

Val scowled. "Oh," she said. "Well, is it all right if I get some things from my locker?"

Even Doug couldn't find a reason to object to that. "Sure," he said. Grace smiled at him.

***

Val hurried into the casino. The coppers were still doing their stuff – they were all over the place with bits of equipment and video recorders and little plastic bags for putting things in.

She headed toward the locker room, but then took a left into the office. It was empty.

She turned the computer on. Come on, come on, she thought. It loaded and she clicked on the staff records programme. It wanted a password, but that was okay – she'd once volunteered to cover the office, and she'd found out everything she needed to know then. Passwords, the lot.

In her opinion, the damn casino were only getting what they deserved. Not that it had been her idea.

The programme came on. She keyed in Sam's name. The address came up, just as it should.

She was about to switch off when another thought occurred to her. SO19, she heard Grace say again. She keyed in Grace Harris. The computer thought about it for a moment. Then a message came up on the screen: File not found.

Stinking murdering undercover cop, she thought.

***

Charlie sat in the squad room with Ash and Oxford, who was sitting at a computer terminal. He nursed a cup of lukewarm coffee.

"You believe her?" he asked.

"Sam?" Ash said. "Yes. She's not the insider." Oxford nodded his agreement.

Charlie looked at his staff list. There weren't very many prospects on it. "So who have we got? Jude?"

Oxford typed something into the computer. The rattle of the keyboard was loud in the silence.

After a second or so he shook his head. "Married. Two kids."

It wasn't definitive, but it moved her right down the list.

"Anyone else," Charlie asked.

Oxford thought about it. "Val?" he suggested. His keyboard

247

rattled again. "Here we go – not married. In the past eighteen months she's had four holidays."

Charlie thought about it. She was definitely in the frame. "Credit cards," he said. "Get on to the companies. Let's see where she's been."

Oxford reached for the phone. Just then, Donachie came in. He looked surprisingly cheerful.

"How is Bingo?" Ash asked.

"Busy eyeing the nurses," Donachie said.

Ash smiled. So did Charlie. Bingo might be a pain in the arse, but he'd have missed him if the worst had happened.

"Thank God for that," Ash said.

Oxford started to speak into his phone.

***

Val walked through the main gaming room, where the coppers were still hard at it. She even managed to smile at one of them.

She went through the private room and out the back way. Only then did she break into a run. She took the stairs two at a time and punched the code into the lock, trying to look casual in case anyone saw her...

***

Charlie looked up as Oxford came into the squad room from Communications. He had a fax in his hand.

"According to her credit card statements she's been on four holidays." He grinned triumphantly. "To Spain."

Ash and Donachie smiled.

"That's it," Charlie said. "That's where she must have met Tommy Raymond." He pulled a disgusted face. "Tells him where she works – punters who play the big cash games – and all of a sudden Tommy's in love."

"What about Grace?" Donachie asked.

***

Grace sat in her car, talking on the radio to Scott. She had a good view of the back entrance where she knew Val usually parked her car.

"Val's the insider," Scott said.

Grace scowled. Then she grinned. She'd wanted a chance to

rove herself, and here it was.

Val came out of the building and walked quickly to her car.

"She's leaving," Grace said. "What do you want me to do?"

She thought, if he tells me to sit tight I'll scream. But he said, "Stay with her. Let us know where she goes."

Val pulled out. Before Grace could react, her car had disappeared round the corner.

I'm not going to screw this up, Grace thought. I'm not. She pulled out herself, and was relieved to see Val when she turned the corner.

Val led her through the West End. The traffic was pretty heavy, and once or twice Grace thought she'd lost her. But at least that meant she didn't realise she was being followed.

Eventually, Val turned into a council estate. She pulled up in front of a row of lock-up garages.

Grace swerved off, and found a spot where she could watch without being seen. As she picked up her radio to call in her position, Val got out of the car and headed towards one of the lock-ups.

Grace made her call. Then she had an idea. She got out of the car.

* * *

The lock-up stank of oil and hot metal. The big silver getaway car sat in the corner, and there were a few tools littered round. Val screwed her nose up as she went in. With Tommy gone, she expected to have to argue for her money.

But Danny surprised her. He handed her a holdall. "Tommy's share's in there as well," he said. "We thought that's what he'd want."

What Tommy would want, Val thought.

"Thanks," she said vacantly.

She looked in the bag. It really was full of cash. So that's it then, she thought. She turned to go, knowing she had to move fast now, when she spotted a gun on the table.

"What are you going to do?" Nick asked.

She smiled. You had to be brave. "Go to Spain, like we planned. Run the bar." Suddenly she couldn't do it, couldn't handle all that bravery. "I wish I could claim his body, bury him, give him a proper funeral. I don't know what's going to happen to him."

"You get out of it while you can," Danny said. "Go and run the bar – it's what Tommy would have wanted."

Val felt tears prick her eyes. She nodded. She noticed the gun again. "You still need that thing?" she asked. She had no real idea what she was going to do with it.

"Take it," Danny said. "You'd be doing me a favour, love."

Val picked up the gun. It was surprisingly heavy.

***

Grace finished letting down Val's tyres. Something was wrong. She turned. Val was standing behind her, with a gun pointed directly at her.

In the distance, police sirens began to wail.

"Your car," Val said. "Move."

Grace did as she was told. Val made her open the passenger door, but didn't get in. Instead she walked with Grace round to the driver's seat and pushed her inside. Val edged round the car, never letting the gun waver from Grace. I should do something, Grace thought. Now. While the windscreen was between them. But the damn gun was a Browning semi-automatic, and it would have fired through the glass with ease. Now, Grace thought as Val moved round the open door. But she still couldn't move. Val got in the passenger seat.

"Move out," she said. She waved the gun at Grace, who realised that this was surely the first time Val had handled a weapon. The thought didn't reassure her at all.

She pulled away, and they drove out onto the High Road. There was little traffic around.

After she'd driven for a few minutes, Grace said, "So which one was your boyfriend, Val?" Val said nothing, but she visibly flinched. "Must have been the one that got himself shot, right?"

Val gestured with the gun. "Shut it."

"Okay, okay," Grace said mildly. "Just tell me where I'm going."

"I said shut it," Val screamed. She was far closer to the edge than she'd seemed.

That made it the perfect time to go for the only plan she'd

been able to come up with.

Grace floored the accelerator and mounted the kerb. She yanked the steering wheel and the passenger side of the car scraped the wall. The metal screeched in protest, and the bumper and wing mirror tore off and flew across the bonnet. Grace pulled the car back on the road to avoid an on-coming pedestrian.

"Do that again and I'll kill you," Val screamed.

***

Charlie and the team were outside the lock-up Grace had directed them to. A clutch of SO19 men, carbines at the ready, stood waiting to back them up.

"Attack! Attack!" Charlie shouted.

Donachie rammed the door open. It burst inward and Oxford and Donachie rushed in.

"Armed police!" Oxford shouted.

The two men inside threw their hands in the air.

"On the floor," Donachie yelled.

The men complied and were cuffed within moments. Donachie poked one of them in the ribs with his toe. "Where's Grace?" he demanded.

***

Grace put her foot down, forcing the car to serve just for the hell of it.

"What are you doing?" Val demanded. She was wild-eyed now.

"Well, wherever we're going, Val, I'd just like to get there," Grace said. Val glanced at the clock. The were doing nearly seventy.

There were roadworks ahead. Grace narrowly avoided them, making sure the passenger side slammed along the barrier. Warning lights and a Men At Work sign jounced across the road.

"Stop it," Val screamed.

"What?" Harris shouted. She jammed her foot even harder on the accelerator.

"I said stop it!"

"You want me to stop?" Grace asked as the car went ever faster.

251

"Yes!" Val screamed.

Grace floored the brake. The car skidded across the road and rammed a lamp post. The force of it threw them both forward. Grace slammed into her airbag.

Val smashed into the windscreen. The glass shattered, and blood ran down it.

Grace sat where she was for a second. Her heart was racing and she couldn't seem to breathe. Panic attack, she thought. She forced herself to take some deep breaths.

Blood ran down the windscreen. But Val was alive – Grace could see her chest moving, though her breathing was shallow.

Grace fumbled at the radio. Her hands were shaking and her fingers wouldn't move the way she wanted them to. But in the end she managed.

The door was buckled. She cursed softly as she forced it open. When it gave, she clambered out awkwardly. Her whole body ached. She wiped the sweat from her face. Then she had a sudden thought, and reached back into the car to get Val's gun.

She sat by the side of the road to wait.

The squad arrived more or less at the same time as the ambulance. Someone draped a blanket round her shoulders. She stared up at him. It was Ted. He held out an evidence bag, and she dropped the gun into it.

He smiled. "What a mess," he said.

Grace looked at the carnage, and then at him. She knew he meant more than the wreck. "Yes," she said, "But it's nothing that can't be cleared up."

He smiled at her sadly. And walked away.